PRAI

Cate of the Lost Colony

"Lisa Klein has given us an unforgettable heroine torn between two exciting, dangerous worlds and two very different men. . . . A fast-moving story that is hard to put down, this book pulls the readers into the head and heart of a historical but very modern woman."

—Karen Harper, *New York Times* bestselling
author of *The Queen's Governess*

★ "This robust, convincing portrait of the Elizabethan world with complex, rounded characters wraps an intriguingly plausible solution to the 'lost colony' mystery inside a compelling love story of subtle thematic depth."

—*Kirkus Reviews*, starred review

"Klein deftly balances the romantic appeal with the grueling reality of survival, the lives of original inhabitants, and factual background of English colonization."

—*Booklist*

"Fans of Klein's distinct breed of historical fiction and romance will enjoy reading about her newest heroine. . . . Klein's knack for breathing new life into old stories has made her a fan favorite. . . . And they will not be disappointed with Cate."

—*VOYA*

BOOKS BY LISA KLEIN

Ophelia
Two Girls of Gettysburg
Lady Macbeth's Daughter
Cate of the Lost Colony

Cate
of the Lost Colony

Lisa Klein

BLOOMSBURY

NEW YORK BERLIN LONDON SYDNEY

For Carolyn French

First published in the United States of America in October 2010
by Bloomsbury Books for Young Readers
Paperback edition published in February 2012
www.bloomsburyteens.com

For information about permission to reproduce selections from this book, write to
Permissions, Bloomsbury BFYR, 175 Fifth Avenue, New York, New York 10010

The Library of Congress has cataloged the hardcover edition as follows:
Klein, Lisa M.
Cate of the Lost Colony / by Lisa Klein.—1st U.S. ed.
p.   cm.
Summary: When her dalliance with Sir Walter Ralegh is discovered by Queen Elizabeth in 1587,
lady-in-waiting Catherine Archer is banished to the struggling colony of Roanoke, where she
and the other English settlers must rely on a Croatoan Indian for their survival. Includes author's note
on the mystery surrounding the Lost Colony.
Includes bibliographical references (p.   ).
ISBN 978-1-59990-507-5 (hardcover)
1. Roanoke Colony—Juvenile fiction. 2. Roanoke Island (N.C.)—History—16th century—Juvenile
fiction. [1. Roanoke Colony—Fiction. 2. Roanoke Island (N.C.)—History—16th
century—Fiction. 3. Raleigh, Walter, Sir, 1552?–1618—Fiction. 4. Elizabeth, I, Queen
of England 1533–1603—Fiction. 5. Great Britain—History—Elizabeth, 1558–1603—
Fiction. 6. Lumbee Indians—Fiction. 7. Indians of North America—North Carolina—
Fiction. 8. Orphans—Fiction.] I. Title.
PZ7.K678342Cat 2010   [Fic]—dc22   2010008299

ISBN 978-1-59990-739-0 (paperback)

Book design by Nicole Gastonguay
Typeset by Westchester Book Composition
Printed in the U.S.A. by Quad/Graphics, Fairfield, Pennsylvania
2 4 6 8 10 9 7 5 3 1

All papers used by Bloomsbury Publishing, Inc., are natural, recyclable products
made from wood grown in well- managed forests. The manufacturing processes
conform to the environmental regulations of the country of origin.

Cast of Characters

Italicized names denote fictional characters; all others are historical figures.

IN ENGLAND

Lady Catherine Archer

Queen Elizabeth I

Lady Mary Standish, lady-in-waiting to the queen

Dick Tarleton, the queen's fool

Frances and *Emme*, maids of honor

Anne and *Veronica*, ladies-in-waiting to the queen

Sir Walter Ralegh

Carew Ralegh, Ralegh's brother

Robert Dudley, Earl of Leicester, adviser to the queen

Sir Francis Walsingham, the queen's spymaster

Earl of Shrewsbury, Queen Mary's jailer

Lord Burghley, adviser to the queen

Humfrey Gilbert, Ralegh's half-brother

Anthony Babington, plotted to assassinate the queen

Mary Stuart, Queen of Scots

The Earl of Essex, Robert Dudley's stepson

IN ENGLAND AND ROANOKE

Arthur Barlowe and Philip Amadas, captains of 1584 voyage

Thomas Harriot, scholar; goes to Roanoke 1585

Simon Fernandes, pilot 1584, 1585, and 1587; an assistant to Gov. White

John White, painter; goes to Roanoke 1585 and as governor 1587

Ralph Lane, acting governor 1585

Sir Francis Drake, captain; rescues colonists 1586

Thomas Graham, courtier; later a soldier at Roanoke 1587

Abraham Cooke, captain of the *Hopewell* 1590

COLONISTS ON ROANOKE ISLAND

Eleanor Dare, John White's daughter

Ananias Dare, Eleanor's husband, an assistant to Gov. White

Virginia Dare, daughter of Ananias and Eleanor

Darby Glavin, an Irishman

George Howe, an assistant to Gov. White

Georgie Howe, son of George Howe

Joan Mannering, Georgie Howe's aunt

Ambrose Vickers, a carpenter

Betty Vickers, Ambrose's wife

Edmund Vickers, son of Ambrose and Betty

Thomas Harris, Betty Vickers's brother

Jane Pierce, a single woman

Roger Bailey, an assistant to Gov. White

Christopher Cooper, an assistant to Gov. White

Alice Chapman, a midwife

John Chapman, Alice's husband, an armorer

James Hind, a soldier

Griffen Jones, a Welsh farmer

Edward Spicer, ship's master; later, a captain

NATIVES OF VIRGINIA, OR OSSOMOCOMUCK

Manteo, a Croatoan Indian

Wanchese, a Roanoke Indian

Wingina, a Roanoke chief

Sobaki, Wanchese's wife

Weyawinga, chief of the Croatoans

Tameoc, a Croatoan warrior

Mika and *Takiwa*, Tameoc's kinswomen

Part I

Chapter 1

The Queen's Maid

At a young age I learned how quickly one's fortunes can change, a truth that never betrayed me. One day I was the beloved daughter of a Hampshire gentleman who had been chosen to serve the queen. The next, he was killed fighting in the Netherlands, and I was an orphan. My mother was already dead and my old nurse was almost blind, so I was taken to live with my aunt and uncle. They had three daughters of their own, none of whom desired another sister. Nor did my aunt want me, especially when it was discovered I had no inheritance, for my father had spent it all to win the queen's regard. At the tender age of fourteen I was at the bottom of the goddess Fortune's wheel, poor and loved by no one. Not two months later, that fickle wheel had turned again, carrying me to the top.

The messenger stood by, waiting as I read the letter. Fresh tears sprang to my eyes at the first lines, but I blinked them away and read hastily to the end. The page trembled and I had to steady my hands on the back of a chair.

"Read it to me, now," commanded my aunt.

So I did, my voice halting with amazement.

13 October 1583

To the Lady Catherine Archer

Though misfortune has befallen you, be assured your Father in heaven has not forgotten you, nor has your loving queen, who is mother to all her people. I understand your grief, for at a young age I also lost my father.

For his sacrifice on the field of battle, Sir Thomas Archer will be remembered as a most true and faithful subject. I am told that he loosed from his bow a keen arrow in you, his only offspring. Your attendance upon me at Whitehall I would consider a due and honorable extension of your father's service. With all confidence that you will prove a young woman worthy of a place among my ladies, I remain your loving queen,

Elizabeth R

My aunt reached out to pluck the letter from me, but I held it fast to my bosom. The queen of England had penned this message and folded it with her own fingers! My aunt would not take it from me. I had little enough that was my own.

"The queen requires me to attend her!" I said, my voice rising with excitement. To be granted such a prize was like being invited into the firmament to shine next to the sun.

My aunt lifted her eyebrows in disbelief. Or was it relief? I knew she was thinking of her own daughters, who needed food, clothing, and dowries, while her husband did nothing but gamble and drink.

"It is an honor she does not merit," she said in rebuke to the messenger. "It will not take long to pack her things. Go, Catherine."

I floated from the room on a cloud, wondering if the queen was as beautiful as everyone said. Was her bed covered with cloth of gold? Did she eat from plates made of crystal? Were her shoes set with jewels? I would see these glories for myself, living in a palace and waiting on the queen daily.

My cousins, clustered in the hallway, sniffed and made sour faces.

"Uncle always did think he was better than us," said the eldest.

I wanted to remind them that my father had died in the queen's service, while theirs was little more than a drunkard. But I said nothing and only stuck out my tongue as I passed.

The queen had sent a litter for me, a covered chair atop a brown palfrey. A small chest with my few belongings was secured behind. We set out before dawn the next day. I felt like a grand lady riding so high, but I was a little afraid of falling off. The messenger on his horse seemed to be smiling at me, whether in pity or friendliness, I could not tell.

All the way to London I thought about my father. I had sat dry-eyed through his funeral, unable to believe he was dead. His visits home had been rare, for he lived at court as a gentleman of the queen's privy chamber. He even spent Christmases there. I never questioned why he chose the queen over his family. It was just the way things were. After all, who would not desire to be in the queen's presence? I had never been out of Hampshire County and I shivered with the anticipation of arriving in the greatest city in the kingdom and meeting the queen. As we passed through the villages and the golden fields and woods of russet-leaved trees, I wished my father could see me riding in the litter. I longed for him to hug me. He would smell of civet and his beard would tickle my face as he kissed me. But alas, he was dead. I would not see him at court or anywhere ever again.

A dull pain pressed behind my ribs and rose into my throat.

This was more than missing him. This was grief at last, and I let it out in quiet weeping as raindrops spattered on the canopy overhead.

Why had my father gone to the Netherlands? He had written in a letter, "It is a great honor to be chosen to escort the French prince from London to Flushing. Thankfully Her Majesty, after much indecision, has declined to marry him. Rejoice, daughter, for England need no longer fear submission to a Frenchman, one who is, moreover, a papist." Though I did not understand everything he wrote, I was proud of my father. I expected him to return once the prince was delivered overseas. He did not write that he would stay in the Netherlands and take up arms. Perhaps he did not want me to worry. My uncle explained that Elizabeth was supporting the Dutch Protestants who were trying to drive Spain out of the Netherlands. I only knew that Spain was wicked for wanting to rule England and to force its Catholic religion on the people of Britain.

So while I had imagined my father on the deck of the queen's flagship, wearing a cloak with fur-lined sleeves, he had been fighting in a field in the Netherlands, knee-deep in mud and blood. I thought of him riding into battle, proudly wearing the queen's livery. Did he call my mother's name when he died, or Elizabeth's?

He came home in a coffin, and we buried him in the churchyard beside my mother.

I drifted in and out of sleep as night fell. The smell of damp horseflesh filled my nostrils and I remembered standing in the midst of a cheering crowd in the rain when I was about six. Bells pealed from the cathedral tower and fiery squibs shot into the sky. The queen was passing through Winchester with my father in attendance. I watched for him, but all the men looked the same in their velvet doublets and feathered hats. I was close to tears because I could not find him.

Then I saw the woman on a white palfrey with blue trappings. Her white gown was embroidered with gold, and a crown sat atop her long golden hair. With one hand she held the reins while extending her other arm to the onlookers. I could not take my eyes off her brightness, which even the rain did not dim.

"Long live the queen!"

"God bless Your Grace!"

Forgetting my father, I ran forward to touch the queen. Trying to reach the hem of her skirt, I grazed the horse's fetlock and smelled its wet flesh. Then my mother pulled me back.

"Mama, she is more beautiful than anyone in the world!"

I felt my mother's arms stiffen around me.

Father did not visit us that day. When I asked my mother why, she only said through tight lips, "He serves a most demanding mistress."

Had I really seen the queen pass and touched her horse? If I had, why couldn't I recall her face? I wondered if it had all been a dream. I could no longer ask my mother. The plague had taken her five years ago. But she really died of loneliness long before that.

It was late at night when we arrived at the queen's palace. A woman of middling height with a few wrinkles in her pleasant face greeted me, introducing herself as Lady Mary Standish. She wore a nightgown and a coif as if she had come from her bed. I followed her to the kitchen, where she gave me some cold meat, bread, and ale. As I was eating, a man dressed in motley skipped into the kitchen. He was short and sturdily built, with bright eyes and a nose pressed flat against his face, which gave him an odd look.

"Good e'en, Lady Mary, guardian of the maids and their maidenheads." He winked at me and plucked at his hair. I could not help staring at him.

"Dick Tarleton, why are you here so late? You had better not be dallying with the scullery maid," she scolded.

"Nay, never!" he said like an actor overplaying his role. "Our royal mistress was melancholy tonight and demanded a jest. But by Jove—or rather, by the suffering Job—my poor feet ache from so much cavorting. My calluses feel like barnacles on the bottom of a boat." He appealed to Lady Mary. "Oh rub my feet, kind lady, and I will repay the favor at your will."

"Go to, fool," said Lady Mary gently. "You have a wife at home."

"She will truss me like a turkey and baste me with my own juices," he complained. Then, cowering under his raised arms, he minced out of the room.

"Is the little man a lunatic?" I asked Lady Mary.

She burst out laughing, then, remembering the late hour, put her hand to her mouth. "No, he is the queen's clown and the only person who can say whatever he pleases without any consequences."

"Even lies and lewdness?" I asked, thinking of his jest about maids.

"Even lies and lewdness," she echoed. "He manages to turn it all into truth."

As she spoke, Lady Mary led me up three floors to the maids' dormitory. There several girls slept in beds crowded under the rafters like a flock of sheep curled in the lee of a cliff. It took me but a moment to fall asleep.

Awakening some time later to the murmur of voices, I pretended to be still asleep.

"I just peeked at her. She's a plain one," said someone with a high voice.

"No, just a little roughened from her journey," came Lady Mary's voice.

"She has no fashionable clothes," said the first voice again, with a note of pity.

Then a third voice said with disdain, "What do you expect of one bred in the country?"

"Emme and Frances, you shouldn't spy in her trunk," Lady Mary rebuked them.

I stirred under my blanket with shame.

"The queen will be disappointed in her," came Frances's voice again. "She expects us to be pretty."

"Enough!" said Lady Mary. "I will wake her now and dress her for the queen."

"I *am* awake," I said, sitting up and glaring at the three of them.

Lady Mary looked surprised. She was dressed now, her ample flesh restrained by a dark-colored bodice. Frances, sitting on her bed, raised her hands to her face. The other beds were empty. Emme stood regarding me with light brown eyes that were not unfriendly.

"I am Catherine Archer, daughter of the late Sir Thomas Archer of Winchester and as much a lady as either of you," I said, hoping they would not laugh at me. Instead they looked startled. I got up and stood in my shift while Lady Mary measured me for new clothes.

"Frances, lend her a bodice and skirt, for she is nearer your size."

Grumbling, Frances obeyed. The sleeves were too long and she pinned them up. She didn't apologize when she pricked me.

Emme combed my hair and plaited it. "Her Majesty is sure to

remark upon your hair," she said. "It is the blackest that I have ever seen, and falls almost to your waist!"

"Catherine, you are to kneel in the queen's presence and look down until bidden to rise," Lady Mary instructed me. "You will address her as 'Your Grace' but only after you are spoken to. The queen does not like a too-soft voice, nor a too-loud one."

I nodded. My leg began to bounce of its own accord, and I tried to still it.

"Is she very . . . beautiful?" I asked.

"She is the *queen*," replied Lady Mary solemnly.

"And what must I do to serve her?"

"As the least of the maids, you will empty her closestool and wash her underlinens," said Frances.

Lady Mary gave her a sharp look. "Catherine is not a chambermaid, but a maid of honor, like you." To me she said, "With Emme and Frances and three others, you will perform small tasks for the queen and wait on her at table."

At least I would not be alone. I would share the work with the other maids and eat and sleep with them. Perhaps in time they would become like sisters to me.

And then Lady Mary was leading me down a staircase to a long gallery with guards standing at either end, holding sharp halberds.

"This is the queen's privy gallery. She may still be in her bedchamber," said Lady Mary, opening the door.

I blushed to think of meeting the queen in her bed. Did she sleep in a shift like any woman, or in royal robes? I followed Lady Mary into the room, which was lit by a single small window and dominated by a huge bed with gold-embroidered curtains drawn back. The bed was empty. I trailed her into the adjoining room and gasped. It was a bathing chamber complete with a gleaming porcelain tub and pipes for water. Next was a room full of musical instruments. I tripped after Lady Mary through a library filled with more books than I had seen in all my life and into a privy chamber containing benches with richly embroidered cushions. In the next room the remains of a meal were still on the table. I heard voices coming through the door beyond.

"Aha," said Lady Mary, crossing the dining room, "she is in her dressing chamber."

I hesitated. "What if she is unclothed?" I whispered.

"Her Majesty's ladies are always about her," said Lady Mary in a matter-of-fact tone, and opened the door without even knocking.

I seemed to see more than a dozen ladies, until I realized several looking glasses were reflecting everyone in the room. In them I could also see my own astonished gaze. Finally I discerned the queen at the center of the circle of ladies. Her back was to me as she faced the mirror. One lady knelt to fasten her slippers. Another held out a selection of glimmering jewelry. A third tended to her skirts, while a fourth stood on a stool combing her curled hair.

"Your Majesty, I bring you Lady Catherine Archer as you requested," announced Lady Mary.

The ladies fell back and the queen turned to face me. I could not help staring. I noticed how slender she was, how wide and white her forehead, how bright her hair. Then I saw a dull lock against her cheek and realized with a start the bright, curled hair was false. The lady with the comb had not yet finished her task.

Lady Mary nudged me and I fairly crashed to the floor, bruising my knee. I could have died with shame at being so graceless.

"Get up, my dear," came the gentle voice. It was the queen speaking to me.

"I cannot, Your Majesty," I replied, for I was trembling all over. "Without your gracious help," I added.

Then the queen took my wrists and lifted me to my feet. Her hands were slim, her fingers long and tapered. I counted four rings on each hand.

"Do not fear to look upon me, child. Think of me as your mother now," she said. It was a command, though softly spoken.

I lifted up my eyes to meet hers. They were bright and pale. She smiled and it was like the sun beaming from behind a cloud. I no longer saw graying hair against her cheek. I saw the woman on horseback who had once ridden through Winchester, ageless and beautiful. Gratitude welled up in me and I knew I would love the queen, even worship her, as long as she ruled. I would do whatever she commanded me.

Whitehall Palace was a bustling, crowded place. Besides six maids and a dozen ladies-in-waiting, the queen employed more than fifty grooms, footmen, and handsome guards known as Gentlemen Pensioners. She kept jesters and dwarves for entertainment and an army of servants, cooks, and kitchen maids. Everyone had a duty. Mine was to help Emme and Frances care for the queen's clothing.

When I first entered the wardrobe, a room twice as large as the maids' dormitory, my eyes could not take in everything it contained. There were cupboards with separate drawers for bodices, stomachers, coifs, gloves, and hats. Dozens of pantofles, overshoes with thick cork soles, lined the shelves. I counted fifty-one bodices and eighty skirts on rows of hooks before I gave up, my head spinning. With envious fingers I touched the gowns made of heavy brocade, floral damask, and shiny sarcenet. I admired the velvets wrought with embroidery as varied and colorful as a summer garden.

Lady Veronica, mistress of the wardrobe, opened a thick ledger before me. "Every new item of dress must be recorded here, and the removal of every worn out or damaged piece noted," she said. "Anything out of fashion goes to the tailor to be remade, unless the queen decides to give it away."

"Give it away," I echoed in wonder. "To whom?"

Lady Veronica shrugged. "To one of her ladies. Whoever is her favorite at the time."

Frances looked up from the chemises she was folding and smiled. "Her Majesty gave me one of her petticoats at my last birthday. The hem was damaged, but I repaired it."

I glanced down at her skirt. Following the current fashion, it was open in front to show the underskirt.

"I'm not wearing it now," she said with a wave of her hand. "It is much too fine."

I wondered why Frances, who seemed so unpleasant, had received such a gift. But I said nothing, only watched Lady Veronica as she showed me how to pair the sleeves and undersleeves and store them with the matching partlets.

Caring for the wardrobe proved more demanding than I had expected. The queen often got ink on her sleeves, which required dabbing with urine, a distasteful task that usually fell to the laundress. But in a pinch we had to clean many a spot of grease and dirt from the queen's clothes, sprinkling fuller's earth mixed with alum upon the garment and brushing to remove the stain. Lady Veronica taught me how to wash lace by laying it flat on a board, covering it with fine cloth, applying soap, then sponging it with fresh water.

The queen was most particular about her ruffs. They had to be made of the softest cambric so as not to irritate the skin of her neck. No laundress could set the gathered frills to her satisfaction. So I set out to make this my skill, brushing starch into the folds, drying, dampening, dyeing, and starching again, then poking the hundreds of pleats into perfect folds. The first time it took me all afternoon, though with practice I could soon starch and set a ruff in two hours.

It took that long—two hours—to get the queen clothed in the morning, her hair dressed, her jewels pinned on, her face painted and powdered. Sometimes she would change her clothes at midday or in the evening, especially if there were guests at court. I became breathless from running back and forth from the wardrobe to the queen's chamber laden with skirts, farthingales, and accessories.

For one accustomed to rule, she was often undecided about what to wear. One day Emme and I fetched her blue damask gown, but as soon as it was fitted and tied—which took fifteen minutes—she demanded the green sarcenet instead.

"*Which* green sarcenet?" Emme said in dismay as we stood looking around the wardrobe. "There are three of them here."

I ran back to the queen's chamber. "Does Your Majesty prefer the one that is bright green like an emerald, pale green like the grass in spring, or deep green like the fir trees?"

"What I do *not* want is a poem!" she said, sounding petulant.

Not wanting to anger her further, I murmured an apology.

"I've changed my mind," she said. "I prefer the blue gown after all." She peered at me. "Blue, like the sky at midday. Go and fetch it!"

Was I mistaken, or was there a trace of a smile in her eyes? I bowed and scurried away, only to have her call me back.

"Catherine! Bring also the embroidered stomacher my Eyes do love to behold me in."

I wondered if this was a line from some poem. Was she now teasing me? I smiled, not daring to ask which of the many stomachers she meant. Surely Emme would know.

"*That her eyes do love to behold her in?*" Emme repeated. She frowned, then searched until she came up with a stomacher embroidered with flowers interspersed with eyes.

"What does this mean?" I asked, looking at the strange motif.

"By her 'Eyes' she means Robert Dudley, the Earl of Leicester. That is her nickname for him." She lowered her voice to a whisper. "He is her true love. She did not marry *Monsieur* Frenchman because she has been in love with Leicester, and he with her, since childhood. But he is married, so she will probably die a virgin."

I blushed at Emme's frank words. "Lord Leicester?" I said. "The one with the fat belly and the red face?"

Emme nodded, and I recalled seeing this lord popping in and out of the queen's privy chamber—a place more public than its name implied.

"You're a book of knowledge," I said. "I must read you further."

"Now is not the time. Go!" she said, thrusting the stomacher at me and following with the blue gown.

"Very good, my dear Catherine," said the queen when I handed over the embroidered stomacher.

"*I* do live to serve Your Grace," I said, hoping she heard my pun.

The queen smiled at me, and I noticed the wrinkles that spread from the corners of her eyes and her mouth. I did some figuring. Why, she was fifty years old! She could be my grandmother. I tried to imagine her kissing Lord Leicester but could not. I thought of the stomacher under her breasts, pressed against her belly, and wondered what secrets Leicester's eyes had seen. Such thoughts made me blush again, and I quickly looked down.

Outside the chamber, Emme turned to me. "I desire to please the queen so much she will give *me* a nickname," she said. "A pet name is like a jewel compared to Frances's old petticoat!"

Chapter 2

An Outing in London

It was to be my first outing in the queen's company, a barge ride on the Thames. I put on a new dark blue skirt and matching square-necked bodice I had sewn under the watchful eye of Lady Veronica, the most skillful needlewoman at court. I had even embroidered some ivy on the bodice, a tedious task that made my neck ache and my fingers bleed. I combed my hair so the waves fell loosely down my back. Emme placed on my head an open cap threaded with pearls.

"The queen likes her maids to wear these," she said.

I touched the cap with pleasure. It made me feel like royalty.

"If only Father could see me!" I murmured. "He would be proud."

"And your mother would be, too," said Emme. "There's not a woman in the kingdom who doesn't wish for her daughter to be one of Her Majesty's maids."

I doubted that. Again I recalled how lonely my mother had been with my father away, and how she had pulled me back when all I wanted to do was touch the queen.

We hurried through the galleries to a chamber over the queen's private jetty, where her entourage waited. I spotted Lord Leicester, the queen's "Eyes," looking out of sorts. Elizabeth was leaning on the arm of a younger man who had red hair but was otherwise handsome to behold.

Dick Tarleton plied his wit among the party. "What a ship of fools is gathered here. Look at Thomas Graham, the fool of fashion. Why, his doublet and hose are all slashed to ribbons. He dueled with a madman and lost!"

Graham's face turned as red as his hair, but when the queen laughed, he had no choice but to laugh as well.

Then the clown bowed to the queen, who wore the ruff it had taken me hours to set. It stuck straight out from beneath her chin, a full twelve inches all around.

"My mistress, you look delectable with your head upon that great platter." He licked his lips and pretended to tuck a napkin at his own neck.

The queen smacked his head with her fan. "Fool Dick, I do not like your wit today."

A hush fell over the company. We followed Elizabeth down the stairs to the water's edge, where the waves lapped against a barge with a covered cabin, glass windows, and gilded fittings. Oarsmen waited, standing firm despite the rocking of the barge and the rain that had begun to fall.

With a flick of her wrist, the queen indicated those whom she wished to board her barge with her. Graham was not among them, but the clown and Frances were. Emme sighed and boarded the second barge, which was like the first but with less ornament. I was too excited to feel slighted. Stepping aboard, I lost my balance and was pitched onto the seat beside Emme.

As the vessels floated away from the jetty, a peal of bells broke out from across the river.

"God's teeth!" said the burly Leicester, now in an even worse mood. "Can't Her Majesty go anywhere without Lambeth Church proclaiming it to the whole city?"

"Tush! Why are you so ill-humored, my lord?" said Lady Veronica, sitting beside him. She was a widow of about thirty and still well favored in her looks.

Other church bells joined the chorus.

"Now the Thames will be clogged with traffic all the way to London Bridge!" grumbled Leicester.

Lady Veronica, not one to be ignored, leaned against him so her bosom swelled over her bodice. She put her lips to his ear.

I looked away, embarrassed. "Is there something about the water that makes everyone so amorous?" I whispered to Emme.

"You see why some prefer *not* to be on the queen's barge," she whispered back.

Opposite Leicester and Lady Veronica, Thomas Graham sat beside Lady Anne, the queen's distant cousin and the prettiest of her ladies. Stroking her hair, he did not seem disappointed at being relegated to the second barge.

"I don't think we ought—," Anne began. She glanced at Leicester, whose eyes were now fixed on Veronica's bosom.

"He is blind to us," said Graham.

"The queen has more than one pair of eyes."

"Frances? That little puritan will never know," scoffed Graham.

Anne gave Emme and me a significant look. Emme shook her head, as if to say she would not tell.

"Come now, my lady. Don't be coy," Graham cooed. She relented and kissed him, inserting her fingertips in the slashes of his doublet.

"Is that how Frances earns her favor?" I whispered to Emme. "By spying on lovers?"

Emme nodded. "And not just that. Why, if you wear so much as a piece of Spanish lace, she'll report the fact to Sir Francis Walsingham."

"Who is Francis Walsingham?"

"He is the councilor who always wears the close black cap on his head—the queen's spymaster. He thinks every Spaniard is the devil himelf."

"Ah, the man with the eyes like black glass beads," I said with a shudder.

"Let's not speak of such grim matters today, Catherine," said Emme with a wave of her hand.

So I put my mind to watching the city glide by, new to me and full of wonders. Great houses peered over the stone walls that held back the river, walls broken at intervals by steps and streets ending at the river's edge, where women washed clothes and men cast their fishing nets. They shouted at the sight of the queen's barge.

Anne was now sitting on Graham's lap.

Swans bobbed on the waves near a green islet and boatmen rowed their wherries between the north and the south banks of the river. Several boats followed the queen's barge, from which the sound of a lute drifted back to us.

Emme pointed out the Inns of Court where men studied the law, the abbey of the Blackfriars, the spires of St. Paul's Cathedral, and the palaces where the queen's favorite noblemen lived. The barge bumped against a jetty and we clambered out beneath the London Bridge, a wide and noisy thoroughfare crowded with houses and shops. The current churned through its many arches, making it dangerous for the barges to pass, so we reboarded on the other side and resumed our journey. Soon I heard the cries of fishmongers and smelled their wares.

"Billingsgate," Emme informed me, wrinkling her nose.

We glided by a harbor crowded with all manner of vessels, from fishing wherries to tall-masted sea ships.

"By damn, that's Walter Ralegh's ship, the *Roebuck*!" exclaimed Thomas Graham, dumping Anne from his lap in order to peer out the window. "Laden with Spanish treasure, I'll be sworn. I'd give my eyeteeth for a share of that gold!"

"And I would not love you if you had such gaps in your grin," said Anne, frowning.

"Who is Walter Ralegh?" I asked Emme.

"Why, have you not seen him at court? He is unmistakable— tall and quite proud," she said.

I shook my head. There had been little opportunity to observe the gentlemen courtiers, let alone learn their names.

"The queen sent him to Ireland to put down the rebels, then to the Netherlands when she sent *Monsieur* Frenchman away. Now he profits from . . . shipping," Emme explained with raised eyebrows.

"I've heard his dream is to colonize the New World," said Graham. "I'd sail with him. What a feat that would be!"

"Every young man fancies himself an adventurer," grumbled Leicester.

"I do love to gaze on his finely turned legs," sighed Anne.

"But his sights are set only on the queen," said Veronica. "Just like my Lord Leicester's." And she tapped him with her fan, pouting.

"If this Walter Ralegh went to the Netherlands, he must have known my father," I said to Emme, and she touched my arm in sympathy.

The sound of a fanfare meant that the queen had reached her destination. A moment later our barge bumped into the wharf and we disembarked, climbing the steps to the street. As soon as I saw the high stone wall with its bastions and battlements and the tall keep with its four turrets, I knew we had arrived at the famed and feared Tower of London.

My father had told me many stories about the Tower, where the kings of England had once lived and where traitors were now kept. Elizabeth's mother, Anne Boleyn, had been beheaded here after being accused of adultery by her husband, King Henry. Yet look how Leicester and Veronica carried on! Did no one remember the past? Surely the queen could not forget. As a young girl, she had been imprisoned here by her sister, Queen Mary, a Catholic who feared that Elizabeth was plotting to overthrow her.

"But why would our mistress come here?" I wondered aloud. "The Tower must hold terrible memories for her."

Graham, in a giddy mood, replied, "Why, to visit the Royal Mint and hear how well each coin flatters her. Such praise may help to fill my flattened purse."

"Thomas, you are incorrigible," said Anne fondly. "But I think it is to see the *menagerie.*"

I nodded, having no idea what she meant.

As we neared the Tower I stared up at the forbidding wall with its narrow slits. From the squared battlements protruded tall spikes topped with what looked like bundles of blackened rags. I squinted in order to see better.

"Is this the *menagerie?*" I asked, imitating Anne's accent.

She burst out laughing. "Yes, it is a *menagerie*—of criminals and traitors! Thomas, do you hear how witty this new maid is?"

"They are heads, Catherine!" Emme hissed. "Some of them have been up there for years."

As I stared, the raglike bundles resolved themselves into skulls with torn flesh like strips of stiff leather. Their white teeth shone in grimaces. The breeze stirred remnants of hair. Blackbirds pecked at the eye sockets of one that looked more human than the rest. Probably he had been alive only days ago.

I hurried after Emme and Anne, who were passing under the portcullis. In the courtyard the queen laughed, her good spirits restored despite the drizzling rain. Indeed, everyone was merry except for the stern-faced yeoman guards in their scarlet and gold uniforms. I wondered how the queen could be so gay while standing in the very courtyard where her mother had met her death.

I followed Emme toward one of the inner towers, wondering again about the young Elizabeth. Where had she been confined? Had she been afraid? The sound of iron clanking against stone mingled with my thoughts. Surely she had not been chained in a dark dungeon? We entered the Tower. An overwhelming smell of animal waste made me put my hand to my mouth. I heard a screeching and saw colored feathers flash overhead. Then a wailing filled my ears, like that of an angry cat magnified a hundred-fold, and a roar sounded in reply, echoing inside the stone tower. What monstrous creatures were here? In the dimness I glimpsed the tawny hide of a beast straining against an iron collar, the fur around its face like a giant ruff, sharp teeth bared. Feeling my gorge rise with panic, I pushed my way out of the Tower and ran into the courtyard, gasping the damp air.

All the way back to Whitehall, everyone talked of the queen's *menagerie*. The roaring beast I had glimpsed was called a lion. The catlike wailing came from a leopard, one of four in an iron cage, Emme said. She described their spotted fur and their long, slim tails. Anne snarled, curving her fingertips at Graham, which only made him more amorous toward her.

"My favorite was the bear," Emme said. "It was a marvel, with white fur, as if the sun had bleached it!"

I wished that I had swallowed my fear and stayed so I could have seen that bear. While the others chattered about the animals, I watched the city through a veil of rain that fell into the roiling river.

As the barges passed the magnificent houses on the north bank of the river and neared Whitehall, the rain stopped. Feeble sunlight shone through the clouds, and the queen's barge made suddenly for the wharf.

"I'll wager our Bess has conceived a sudden desire to walk home, obliging us all to accompany her," Leicester grumbled.

"You know how she likes to be seen. Look at the crowd waiting for her!" said Veronica as we stepped ashore.

"Make way for Her Majesty!" demanded the warder. Gleeful shouts arose as the queen passed. A woman ran forward and, before anyone could stop her, pressed a folded paper into her hand, while others threw nosegays. Most of the flowers fell into the mire of the street.

"Another petticoat ruined," complained Anne, lifting her skirts just enough to clear the mucky street.

In front of her, Elizabeth paused before a puddle that gave off a peculiar stink.

At that moment a man stepped out of the crowd. He stood nearly a head taller than any of the queen's guard. His hair was brown and curled, his nose sharp, his mouth wide. A pointed beard graced his chin. He wore a vivid blue doublet that swelled out in front, ending in the shape of a peasecod. His brocade hose were short and wide, setting off lean and strong legs. A cloak was slung over one shoulder. From his left ear hung a gleaming pearl. I drew in my breath at the sight of such a splendid figure.

In one graceful motion, he swept the cloak from his shoulder, laid it on the ground before the queen, and bowed low. The rich cloak, with its fur-trimmed collar and bright gold braid, began to soak up the vile water. I watched, stunned to see such a fine garment ruined. What was the meaning of this extravagant gesture? Who was this generous, impulsive man?

With a smile, the queen gave him her hand, stepped on the cloak, and crossed the puddle without soiling her feet. Seeing the garment already sodden, the other ladies followed suit.

Meanwhile Elizabeth drew the young man close to her and spoke in his ear. When she let go of his hand and moved on, I could see his face shining like that of a lover. I, who had never looked with longing at any man, was seized with a sudden envy of my queen.

I walked around the puddle, avoiding the sorry cloak. Unable to restrain myself, I stared at the man as I passed, drinking in his features. His eyes flickered over me and he smiled—surely not at me, but at the memory of the queen's touch.

"Close your mouth, you look moonstruck," said Emme.

"Who was that?" I whispered.

"He is the queen's new favorite, I daresay," she replied.

"But what is his name?"

"Why, my dear Catherine, that is Walter Ralegh!"

Chapter 3

From the Papers of Walter Ralegh

November 1583
Brother Carew,

I flourish in Her Majesty's favor. She grants me the use of Durham House, once the bishop's palace. It is my reward for quelling the savages in Ireland—that forsaken bog!—and for transporting the foolish Monsieur to the Netherlands, where we lost many good men fighting the Spanish papists. God bless their sacrifice but keep me from the same, for I long for more than a soldier's brief glory.

You will remember that our kinsman Humfrey Gilbert obtained from Her Majesty a patent to explore North America. It has been five years since his first voyage, and a year since he perished in his second unsuccessful attempt. My dream now is to continue his efforts to find a northwest passage to China and the Indies. If the queen grants me the charter, I will unlock the treasure chest of the New World, and our family name will be exalted!

To that end I flatter Her Majesty as if she were a maid

half her age. I almost thought she would marry me the day I threw my cloak in her path. That garment cost me £80, for it was trimmed in fur and gilded braid.

Still, its ruin was a small sacrifice for such favor. May it ever flow my way, like the Thames to the sea.

Yours,

W. Ralegh

Poetic Musings

> *Like the Thames that flows into the sea,*
> *The current of grace proceeds from thee.*

Nay, this might offend Her Majesty, for the Thames is often vile and clouded. The sea is the greater body, thus:

> *To my sovereign Queen:*
> *As the river to the boundless sea,*
> *So flows my tribute unto thee.*

'Tis a good beginning of a poem.

13 December 1583

Brother,

Today she called me her "Warter," mocking my Devonshire accent while alluding to the verses I lately sent her.

Made bold, I asked, "Would you permit your 'Warter' to sail to North America and return laden with treasure for you? I will christen all the land in your name, and you shall see the size of your kingdom swell. That is the way to defeat Spain and her ambitions." This was delivered in my intimate voice that causes maids to tremble. I swear she did too, being of flesh and blood like any woman.

She did not consent, but neither did she deny me.

W.R.

14 January 1584

Brother Carew,

At the New Year I gave Her Majesty a diamond worth even more than that costly cloak. I must go bankrupt if she does not yield soon.

Then she summoned me to her music room, making me wait while she practiced on her virginal. Finally she held up the jewel.

"Where shall I wear it?" she asked, touching her bosom through her sheer partlet. Then, "Fix it here," she said, offering me her sleeve instead. But I, obeying my own impulse, took the stone and went to the window, where I etched this upon the pane:

"Fain would I climb, yet I fear to fall." I kissed the diamond and laid it in Her Majesty's palm, saying, "I pray you, be not so hard as this stone," and took my leave.

But she commanded me to stay. She went to the window and with the same diamond began to scratch on the pane. Was she obliterating my words? Then she beckoned me to read what she had written beneath: "If thy heart fail thee, climb not at all."

And then she said, "Do you know that water can wear away even the hardest stone?"

Brother, would you not take this for encouragement? I did, and thus I live in hope.

W.R.

Poetic Musings

I tire of waiting. Despair wrestles with my hopes. Did I presume too far? If boldness will not move her, I will try humility. Thus:

> *I only sue to serve*
> *A saint of such perfection,*
> *Whom all desire, but none deserve*
> *A place in your affection.*

> *Thus if my plaints do never prove*
> *The conquest of your beauty,*
> *It comes not from defect of love,*
> *But from excess of duty.*

How I despise this state of subjection—and to a woman! A man is meant to rule himself.

29 January 1584
Dear Carew,

The queen has given me the license to a wine farm that will soon yield me £700 per annum. I think she loves my little verses, whether on scraps of paper or in speech.

When the renovations are complete, Durham House will rival Whitehall in grandeur. You must visit. I am having four new suits of clothes made, and new armor as well, that my apparel may reflect my status. Many envy me my exalted place.

And I envy you, the genial ranger of the Devonshire forests. You are free from the anxious fear and striving that attends this court of care.

Your humble brother,
Walter

Memorandum

15 February 1584. Attended the queen in the great hall last evening. Laughed at Tarleton's antics. My eye kept wandering to one of the queen's maids. I have seen her before, but where? Not the loveliest of the lot, but with striking gray eyes and hair black as jet and long as night. And the whitest of teeth, bared prettily when she laughs.

Have learned her name: Catherine Archer, daughter of Sir Thomas. I knew him in the Netherlands: a valiant soldier who deserved a longer life.

I swear the girl reddened when she saw me looking. But she did not look away, like the falsely modest do. Her cheeks are tinged like the dawn, or like the skin of a fresh-plucked peach.

By the Virgin's paps, she has seized my fancy and now moves my pen to praise.

> *At the table spread with treats,*
> *One tasty sweet did tempt me.*
> *But on my plate was richer meat,*
> *That I did need to feed me.*

That is, my royal mistress, whose "richer meat" must nourish me. But I think I prefer the other maid's sweetness.

2 March 1584
My dear brother,

I write with great reluctance, driven by the precarious state of my affairs. The costs to renovate my house and to live in accordance with my high expectations will soon ruin me. Despite Her Majesty's favor, I have as yet no source of income adequate to cover my growing expenses. I am in dire need of

£4,500. *(I have had to employ forty men and forty horses besides improving the house for comfort, and the silver plates alone cost £1,200.) Therefore I beseech your assistance. A full accounting is attached. Whatever terms you set I will accept.*

> *Begging your indulgence, I remain your devoted brother,*
> *Walter R.*

Memorandum

18 March 1584. Today C. came to Durham House with the queen. While my mistress admired the new Flemish arras, the maid fixed her gray eyes on me, and from them Cupid hurled his little darts, the sharp needles sticking in my heart. Stirred up, my wit flowed, delighting my queen, though its true purpose was to make her handmaid smile.

> *Double words do double duty,*
> *Praising one and another's beauty.*
> *C. is moon while E. is sunlight;*
> *Daytime to the other's dark night.*

(Let me not err by sending this to Her Majesty.)

27 March 1584
Brother Carew,

> *Praise be to the glorious Elizabeth! At last she has granted me Humfrey's patent to "discover and occupy those remote and barbarous territories not yet possessed by any Christian prince." I may hold these lands forever, yielding to her one-fifth of all the gold or silver ore extracted. Such terms are reasonable—indeed liberal—affording scope for great personal gain.*

Two ships will sail on a reconnaissance voyage next month, captained by my young servants Barlowe and Amadas. The scholar Thomas Harriot is even now instructing them in the use of the newest tools of navigation.

As England still has few skilled pilots, I have engaged the Portuguese Simon Fernandes, with whom I sailed in '77. Some call him a scoundrel and a heretic, but I know him to be a shrewd man of business. Walsingham once kept him from hanging for piracy, so his loyalty to England is firm. He claims to know of a port at a favorable latitude for establishing a base from which to conduct raids on Spanish ships.

In America I shall be a veritable king, one rich as Croesus.

Your fortunate brother,

Walter

P.S. Unfortunately the voyages will not be financed from Her Majesty's treasury, forcing me to seek investors. As the success of my endeavors will make us both renowned, can you recruit from the Devonshire gentry ten investors at £200 each, or two earls worth £1,000?

Chapter 4

The Queen's Gifts

It was six months since I had arrived at Whitehall, and I had served the queen in loyal submission without so much as a ribbon or scrap of lace for a reward.

"I think she does not love me," I said to Emme one night as we sat in the great hall, watching Dick Tarleton entertain the court. Everyone had drunk too much and therefore howled with delight as the clown danced a jig, played his fife and drum, and jingled his tabor all at once. "What will become of me if I do not please her?"

"She does favor you," Emme insisted. "She takes you with her when she goes to Durham House." She prodded me with her elbow and pouted, pretending to be jealous. All the maids and ladies were of one mind, that Walter Ralegh was the queen's handsomest courtier.

I sighed. "That is because I am plain and silent, a foil for her wit. I cannot hold a candle to her brightness."

"No, you simply have not mastered the art of flattering conversation," Emme said. "You must learn to imitate Anne."

"I cannot flatter the queen's bright hair, knowing it is false," I said.

"Or her white skin, knowing that it is covered with lead powder," said Emme, giggling.

"I wish I could write a poem. Do you know that Walter Ralegh sometimes speaks to the queen in verse? Why, it sounds as if it came naturally to him, and it certainly pleases her."

"Perhaps his wit is on display for *you*, Catherine."

"Nonsense!" I said, blushing despite myself. I thought of the way my heart fluttered when I was in the same room with him and fairly leapt when I felt his eyes on me. "I wish for the *queen* to favor me, for my fortune depends on her."

"She sets a great store by those who are learned and pious in the true religion," said Emme.

Indeed the queen made a spectacle of going to church on Sunday, preceded by heralds and guards in blue and gold livery and accompanied by all her councilors. We, her maids and ladies, wore our soberest attire and pretended to pay attention to the sermon.

"You may borrow my *Book of Martyrs*, by Mr. Foxe, and read it where she is sure to notice you," Emme suggested.

So while the ladies gossiped and plied their needles, I read about the Christians persecuted in all ages, through the time of the late Queen Mary. It seemed the whole world was the battlefield of the evil papists and believers in the Protestant religion, which Elizabeth had restored in England. It sickened me to read of so many men and women suffering death at the stake, their flesh broiled in the fire until the fat dripped from their bones. I put the book away. Neither the queen nor anyone else had taken note of my study.

Or so I thought. One day while I waited upon Elizabeth at her table, she asked me why I no longer read the *Book of Martyrs*. I nearly spilled the soup I was serving her.

"Your Majesty, I did not think you noticed."

"Nothing escapes my eyes," she said evenly. "I approve of the good Mr. Foxe. Does he displease you?"

Under her gaze I could not craft a flattering reply, so I blurted out the simple truth. "Your Grace, I could no longer read of the torments the martyrs endured, praising God all the while. Were flames engulfing me, I would scream in agony."

To my surprise, the queen burst out laughing, and soup bubbled from her lips. I rushed to hand her a napkin. She dabbed her lips, then grew serious.

"To be weak and fearful will not serve you well in this world or fit you for the next," she said.

I did not know how to respond. Finally I said, "Your Grace, I fear nothing but your displeasure."

"Nothing at all?" she prompted me.

I shook my head.

"You were afraid of my animals," she said. "I saw you run from the Tower."

Surprised that she remembered the incident, I said, "I did not expect to see such large cats. But I am no longer frightened of them. I would go to the Tower again, just to see them." I was afraid I spoke with too much zeal.

The queen smiled. Powder had settled in the creases of her face.

"I do not blame you for being afraid," she said gently. "When my father first took me to the *menagerie*, I was terrified. I thought the lion would devour me. Now I relish all the cats, lithe savages that they are. But I still cannot bear their loud shrieks. Like someone being tortured. And God knows I hate the Tower."

Her face had darkened with displeasure, which dissipated again like smoke. A half smile formed on her lips.

"Catherine," she mused. "I shall call you my little 'Cat.'"

I cast down my eyes to conceal my delight. "At Your Majesty's pleasure," I murmured, feeling myself grow warm and full of her favor. The queen had given me a nickname!

That night, as soon as Frances was asleep, I recounted to Emme my conversation with the queen.

"*Cat*. Why, that is a play on your name. It is clever," she said, grasping my hand. "I'm happy for you."

"Yet I fear it is not a strong mark of favor," I said. "She called the cats 'lithe savages.' Did she mean to warn me?"

Emme was silent for a moment. "At least she didn't call you a mouse. No, it is far better to be the cat."

"But a cat is a sly creature. Does she think me deceitful? How will I know?" In the dark, my insecurities multiplied like shadows on the wall.

From the next bed came a sigh. "Perhaps she meant nothing at all. 'Cat' is simply easier to say than 'Catherine,'" said Frances.

"And you're a spy with ears the size of trenchers!" Emme hissed at her.

I laughed at the thought of large wooden eating bowls affixed to the side of Frances's head.

"I wasn't spying. You woke me up with your chatter," Frances said. "But if you want to know the queen's mind on anything, ask Walter Ralegh."

Frances's advice startled me. "But I've never even spoken to him!" I said.

"Perhaps you should," said Frances. "The queen's cats are bold creatures."

I decided Frances was taunting me. "No, this Cat is heedful,"

I said. "Now good night." I pulled the coverlet over my head and tried to sleep, but the queen's words kept coming back to me: *Nothing escapes my eye.*

I was less certain that her nickname was a gift. But I would be true to it: sly and wary, but fearless.

One April morning, Emme, Frances, and I were airing out the queen's wardrobe and sprinkling the clothes with scented powder to keep them from growing musty. My arms ached from lifting the heavy skirts to hang where they would catch the breeze from the open windows

"Cat! Frances!" came the queen's commanding voice. "You will accompany me to Durham House within the hour."

Flushed with exertion and excitement, I appealed to Emme. "Please help me get ready. I am hardly fit to be seen."

She set down the muddy pantofles she had been cleaning. "You must wear my yellow satin bodice. It makes your dark hair stand out," she said. She helped me dress, combed my curls, fitted my cap, and plaited some of my hair around it.

Frances had put on a dark blue gown over her best petticoat, her gift from the queen.

"Are you going to be a bold Cat today and speak to Master Ralegh?" she asked.

I glared at her. "Perhaps."

"This may be your chance," said Emme. "Listen well and observe the queen's disposition. If she invites you to speak, choose words brief and fitting, uttered in a moderate voice."

But I was full of doubts. "Tell me what I should say," I pleaded. "I know Ralegh wants to sail to North America, but I don't even know where that is."

Emme bit her lip. "You look too lovely. Perhaps you should

remain silent. Speak only if the queen is absent, or she may become jealous."

Looking in a glass, I saw that my bodice was too revealing. I arranged the lace-edged partlet to cover more of my breasts.

"Don't do that," Frances said, tugging my partlet downward again. "No one will bother to lay eyes on you if there is nothing to see."

Seeing how Frances relished my discomfort, I was determined not to show any. So I let the air chill my bosom as we walked the short way to Durham House. Frances and I held up the queen's train, while our own skirts were left to brush the dusty cobbles. I knew Frances was silently fretting about her treasured petticoat.

Walter Ralegh himself met us at the gate, attended by a dozen or more gentlemen. I thought him resplendent in a doublet of bright blue taffeta with wide, slashed sleeves, matching trunk hose, and a buff-colored jerkin. Gold buckles shone on his shoes. He led the way through halls and stairways hung with Flemish tapestries as richly hued as any in Whitehall Palace. The queen stopped often to admire them, which seemed to please Ralegh.

On the topmost floor of Durham House was the library, a room filled with books, maps, strange instruments, and a globe of the world. The windows were open, letting in the cries of hawkers in the streets and wherrymen on the river. As Elizabeth entered the library, three men waiting there dropped to their knees.

"Thomas Harriot at Your Majesty's service," said one of them to the floor. He had wispy hair and a beard to match and wore the long black robe of a scholar. The queen bade him rise.

"Thomas and I were at Oxford together," said Ralegh. "He is a scholar of languages, a conjurer of numbers, and an expert in navigation." Then he introduced the other two men, captains of the ships he would send to North America. One was dark and of small stature, while the other was tall with an honest gaze.

Frances and I seated ourselves on a bench by the door. The queen picked up a compass—the only instrument I recognized—and examined it, then addressed herself to the business of Harriot and the captains. I tried to follow the conversation, but it contained many unfamiliar words and phrases.

"Will Your Majesty consent to peer through my *radius astronomicus*, with which I view the stars?" asked Harriot, his voice rising with excitement.

"I should like nothing better," she said.

"It is in my chamber under the eaves," said Harriot.

"Then let us go there," she said, putting down the compass. "Come, gentlemen."

But Ralegh demurred. "Thomas's room is quite small. I crave Your Majesty's permission to wait here."

The queen nodded and left the library with Harriot and the captains. Ralegh bowed as she passed, and when he stood upright again he was smiling. Frances poked me. I opened my mouth but no words came out. There was so much I wanted to ask, I didn't know where to begin.

Frances stepped into the silence. "Master Ralegh, if you please, where is North America?"

He beckoned us to the table, on which a large map was spread, the corners held down with books. He pointed to England, then ran his finger across the map, leaning slightly into me as he did so, and rested it on North America.

He smelled of civet. Father always wore civet, too. A wave of longing surged in me, but I pushed it down and stared at the map. England, our island kingdom, was crowded with names of rivers and towns. But North America, inside her jagged coastline, was a blank, featureless expanse. Tiny ships marked the seas between the two lands.

Frances touched a ship, then measured the gap between England and North America with her spread fingers. "That's not so far to sail," she said.

I felt nervous laughter bubble up inside me. "Oh, silly Frances, the ships are not drawn to their true proportion," I said. "If they were, this one would be greater than all of London!"

I clapped my hand to my mouth, embarrassed at my outburst. Frances slunk back to her stool, sat down, and stared at a shelf of books. I felt guilty for shaming her and knew that I would undoubtedly pay for it.

Ralegh was too much of a gentleman to laugh at either of us. But I detected a note of humor in his voice when he said, "And you, Lady Catherine, would you like to travel on such a great ship as that?"

His deep voice reverberated within me. I kept my eyes fixed on the map, thinking how immense the world was, and how I longed to see more of it beyond London, even beyond England.

"Oh yes!" But where to, I could not say. "Tell me about your voyages, Master Ralegh."

"Twice I sailed for North America with my kinsman Sir Humfrey Gilbert. On last year's voyage we were unlucky. A contagion swept through my crew and I was forced to turn my ship back. Humfrey continued, but foul weather and mists kept him from making landfall, and on his return, a tempest in the Azores sank his vessel and drowned him."

"Why do you want to go back, if it is so dangerous?" I asked.

"The promise of riches!" He whispered near my ear, making the skin on my neck tingle. Then he laughed and drew back.

"While I was yet a student of the law, one Martin Frobisher sailed northwest in search of a passage to the Indies. He did not find it, but he returned with barrels of black stone said to contain great wealth. Then the refiners could not extract the gold. It is my belief that they stole the riches."

"Perhaps he was deceived and the rocks did not contain gold," I suggested.

Ralegh shook his head. "Others have returned with pieces of gold this size." He made a fist. "The Spanish strike their coins from gold hewed from mountains in the Americas. If they can do it, so can we." His eyes blazed with passion.

I felt a shiver of excitement. "But don't the Spanish rule the seas and capture any vessel that crosses their path?"

"My ships have outrun their galleons, boarded them, and brought home prizes," he boasted. "Her Majesty turns a blind eye to such lawbreaking, and so it flourishes. When Francis Drake returned from sailing around the world, he had nearly a million pounds of booty. Most of it he kept," he added.

I saw the hunger in his eyes at the thought of such wealth.

"What kind of people did the explorers find?" I asked, my coyness now driven away by curiosity.

"Frobisher brought back some natives called Eskimo. I saw one with these very eyes. In the harbor at Bristol he showed his skills, handling a boat made out of a single hollow tree and spearing ducks as they flew through the air."

"What did this . . . *Eskimo* . . . look like?" I asked, struggling with the unfamiliar word.

"His face was round with narrow black eyes. He wore a garment of skin and fur down to his feet."

My eyes followed the downward sweep of Ralegh's hands, noticing his well-turned legs in their fitted canions and stockings.

"What became of him?"

"He suffered an excess of phlegm in the blood, which gave his skin a sallow hue. He died, like the others."

"Perhaps he was overcome with grief at being taken from his land, then watching his fellows die," I said, hearing my voice catch. It was hard to quell that sadness for my father.

Ralegh seemed to read my thoughts. "Your father was a true and courageous servant of the queen," he said in a low voice. "I did enjoy his company, and I find his daughter even more engaging."

I blinked and a tear fell onto my sleeve. Ralegh handed me a handkerchief edged in lace. It carried his scent, manly but sweet. I thought of the cloak he had spread at the queen's feet.

"How attentive you are . . . to mop the waters that . . . hinder ladies." Even as I spoke, I knew that my attempt at wit had failed.

"I miss your meaning, Lady Catherine."

So I shook out the handkerchief, laid it on the book, and walked my fingers over it. Ralegh threw back his head and laughed. His mirth was like a gust of wind. I tightened my fingers around the handkerchief.

Then I felt his hand cover mine. His palm was hot. He separated my fingers with his own, then drew out the soft folds of cambric between them. I glanced up and his eyes, light brown in hue, held mine. A flush suffused my throat and rose to my face. I shifted my eyes to the pearl gleaming at his ear.

"I didn't mean to keep it," I said, releasing the handkerchief.

"But I mean for you to have it," he said. He began to feed it into my sleeve, beginning at my wrist. His fingers played against the skin of my forearm as the handkerchief disappeared. I was too startled to say a word.

Footsteps sounded in the hall. I turned and saw Frances standing midway between the bench and the table. Had she seen Ralegh give me the handkerchief? Then the door was flung open and the queen entered just as Walter dropped my arm and I folded my hands in front of me. I was sure my face was the color of vermilion. With my thumb I tucked the lace edges of the handkerchief out of sight.

"Is not Thomas's scope an amazing instrument?" asked Ralegh, clapping his hands together.

"Indeed," said the queen in a clipped voice. "Now I should like to discuss the greater purpose of this voyage."

Ralegh nodded but before he could speak, the queen went on.

"I am not so foolhardy as to send my subjects to colonize a land about which we are ignorant, lest we fare no better than the Spaniards. Their cruelty incites the Indians to murder any European who steps on their shores."

"I would not send men to their slaughter," said Ralegh in deep earnest. "Not for a mere puff of fame."

"Nor will I tolerate adventuring for the sake of gain," said the queen. "Our purpose must be to bring true religion to the pagan peoples and induce them to follow the laws and customs of England."

"I heartily agree, Your Grace," said Ralegh. "Thus the chief aim of this first voyage," he continued with silver-tongued eloquence, "and the best hope of our future success, will be to study this yet-unknown land, its flora and fauna, and most especially its human inhabitants, that we might learn their language and customs and begin our venture in mutual friendship."

I saw how Ralegh's words worked magic on the queen. Her severe look softened into one of admiration, even affection. She stepped closer, lifting her eyes to his.

"And how, my dear *Warter*, will you do that?"

In a tone of triumph, Ralegh announced, "I will return with a tribute for Your Majesty, a relic of that far realm—that is, a natural inhabitant of the New World. I will bring back an Indian!"

For the rest of the day I felt the handkerchief against my skin and reviewed in my mind the scene in the library. I had been drawn to Walter Ralegh like a piece of iron to a magnet. A curiosity I hardly knew I possessed had driven me to question him boldly. Like one starving for knowledge I had devoured his stories. I had even touched his hand! Was it wrong for me to let his fingers press my arm? I couldn't ask Frances, for as a Puritan she disapproved of everything pleasurable. I wondered again if she had seen Ralegh give me the handkerchief. Surely his back had hidden our hands from her view. But she must have seen the turmoil written on my face.

That night when I undressed I secreted the handkerchief in the pocket of my nightshift. After lying down I took it out, sniffed it, and felt the lace edging all around. In one corner my fingers encountered raised stitching. Was it an emblem or lettering, a message in the cloth? I slipped from my bed and went to the the window to examine the handkerchief in the moonlight.

Embroidered in the corner were the initials *E.R.*

Elizabeth Regina.

The handkerchief had been a gift from the queen to Ralegh!

When the queen sent for me the next day, I was certain that she knew I had the handkerchief. But Her Majesty only gave me a ruff to set and asked me which jewel best became her, a cluster of rubies or an amethyst brooch. I recommended the rubies and, filled with relief, turned to leave.

"Catherine," she said, using my full name. My heart skipped a beat as I turned to face her again.

"Yes, Your Grace?"

"Cats are averse to water, are they not?" She peered at me with her keen eyes.

"Yes, usually they are. But I once had a kitten who liked to wash herself in a bucket—" I broke off, realizing that the queen had pronounced "water" as "Warter." Was she teasing me or warning me about Ralegh? What did she know? That depended on what Frances had heard with those big ears of hers.

Feigning innocence I asked, "Why should your Cat be afraid of the water?"

"Because I should not like her to drown," Elizabeth replied mildly.

Chapter 5

From the Papers of Walter Ralegh

14 April 1584

To Capts. Philip Amadas and Arthur Barlowe,

Everything necessary for the provisioning and rigging of two ships is being assembled and sent to the warehouse at Southampton. (Per attached inventory.)

Please review and inform me of any omissions or further requirements prior to your departure.

Yours,

Master W. Ralegh

P.S. In answer to your earlier query, I will not be sailing. The sea does not agree with me.

24 April 1584

To Capt. Arthur Barlowe,

I am pleased to hear all is ready for embarkation. I hereby charge you with the following duties on this voyage.

1. Record the particulars of your journey, your observations of the natives and their customs, and the flora and fauna of the land. *Your descriptions must be positive, that those who read your account will be given to wonder, not to fear, and induced to support future expeditions.*

2. Bring back a savage, the very finest of his kind. Let no force be used. In your dealings with the Indians, do nothing to offend them, but treat them with humanity, so they will be inclined toward friendship with us.

3. Survey the land for an outpost suitable for launching raids that shall serve two purposes: harassing Spain and financing our ventures. Remember, the risk itself brings reward.

Finally, although you and Amadas share the captaincy of this venture, you are to defer to the pilot Fernandes on matters relating to navigation, in which he has the greatest experience.

With every expectation of your success, I bid you bon voyage and await your return in the fall.

W.R.

Memorandum

Debts owed: Tailor, £125 (new cloak, shoes, suit & hat w. feathers)

Hostler, £250 (for 5 horses)

Armorer, £73 (one suit, including etching)

Salaries, £1,737 (for 35 men)

Income: Estates in Devonshire and Oxford, £625

Due from cloth exports, £87

Wine farm (due from last harvest), £330

Net owed: £1,143

Write to Carew for more funds & report on Devonshire investors.

Cannot find that damned handkerchief my royal mistress gave me. What if she asks about it? She likes to see her gifts displayed. Where did I lose that thing?

3 May 1584. At the Boar's Head tonight, Dick Tarleton settled a dispute between two soldiers over a certain lady.

"You are a very peasecod, or should I say codpiece?" he said to one then reviled the other. "Your wit's as thick as mustard and your brain moldy from lack of use." When the combatants were shaken with laughter and consequently harmless, they dropped their fists and were made friends again.

How I admire that fool's wit!

Later a comely wench offered herself to me, promising delights that not long ago I would have seized. Yet I declined them, which caused my drinking companion to mock my manliness. Remembering Tarleton's jest, I called him a "green peasecod with no more wit than a mustard seed," and upon realizing I had muddled the jest I threw the alepot at his head and kicked over the table.

Alas, where has my wit fled? Has love done this to me? Can I still write a passing good verse?

To C.A.
O lady whom I in silence serve,
Know the depth of my desire.
Only you I aim to deserve,
That your grace might slake this scalding fire.

Send me a secret token
To show the depth of your desire.
Say your love is not bespoken,
And with your grace, O slake my scalding fire!

After twelve days of silent torment, a letter! How firm her hand, how well-chosen each word.

Dear Master Ralegh,

I do not deserve your gracious attention. Yet I crave to hear from your lips more tales of sea travelers. Can a lady desire to be a discoverer?

My wealth being slender, I have no token of value to send you, but I declare I am not bespoken to anyone, save my royal mistress on whom my fortune depends. Therefore burn this in your scalding fire, lest it fall into an unfriendly hand.

The queen meets with her Privy Council tomorrow afternoon. I will devise some pretext upon which to visit you.

I remain your humble
Catherine Archer

She speaks of craving and of my lips, then in the next phrase of desire, then finally my scalding fire. O beneath her polite discourse, do I detect profound passion? I will not sleep this night.

An Account of a Meeting

On the promised day, upon the hour of three, my valet brought C.A. to me in the garden.

"My mistress wishes to borrow your volume containing the Spanish captain's account of his voyages," she announced.

"Clever Cat!" I said and sent the valet to fetch the requested book.

Glancing about nervously, she said, "Rather, I feel like the bird about to become the cat's meal."

"There is no danger here," I assured her, leading her through the elegant knots of greenery, the tall hedges, and the fig trees brought from Sicily. She scarcely seemed to notice my statues newly arrived from France. Then I brought her to a bower where petals of the flowering pear drifted down with each puff of wind. I tried to take her hand but she held it back.

"This coyness, lady, seems a crime; for here is solitude and time." (In her presence my verses flow like wine.)

She blushed very prettily but was not deterred from her purpose. She related a quip of Her Majesty, light words that weighed heavily on her. "Do you think she meant to warn this 'Cat' away from you, her 'Warter'?"

"I would not drown you," I said, smiling.

"I don't fear you, but her. She is . . . in love with you." She hesitated, as if revealing a secret, then added, "Everyone knows this."

"The queen can be jealous," I agreed, "but I daresay she was only enjoying a bit of sport with you. Do not be afraid to match wits with her."

Thus reassured, she smiled. I took her hand and she did not resist.

"Now let us talk about you," I said.

She talked but I remember little of what she said, for I was conscious only of her pretty teeth and lips. Then I related my upbringing in Devonshire and made her laugh over my escapades at Oxford, where I never read a single book. Her eyes widened to hear of my soldiering in the Irish wars and how I despaired of subduing that barbarous land.

"Thus you are determined to succeed in this New World enterprise. I am certain you will," she said. Under her admiring gaze, I longed all the more for the fame and favor of which I dream.

My valet had not returned with the book (a wise fellow who knows his master's wishes), and my dear Catherine was beginning to be uneasy again. Then from her sleeve she produced a handkerchief, saying "You must have this back. I dare not keep it."

I was confused, for I could not remember giving her my handkerchief. I said, "You are unkind to return my token."

"It is the queen's token." She showed me the embroidered initials in the corner. "She meant it for you, not for me."

So that is what became of the handkerchief! I did not lose it after all. I remembered the delight it had given me to insert the cloth in Catherine's sleeve that day in my library. It would be ungentlemanly of me to reclaim it.

"What was the queen's to give to me, became mine to give to you," I said. "'Tis a traveling token of favor." And I would not take it back despite her protests.

Moved and flattered, with blood suffusing her pretty cheeks, the lady departed—without the book. I shall have to carry it to Whitehall myself. Clever Cat, indeed.

And damn me that I was so surprised by that silly handkerchief I lost my chance to kiss her.

To C.A.

Over the "C" is my newfound land,
My America, north and south,
I'd explore you with this hand
Claim you with my mouth.

O let me but sail my bark
Into your shimmering bays
There to anchor my heart
All my remaining days.

Chapter 6

Spies and Savages

I committed Walter Ralegh's poem to memory. In my dreams I let him explore me with his hands and lips and woke up blushing. I imagined standing beside him on the deck of a ship bound for the New World, where strange men lived who had no idea we were coming to dwell among them. But I told no one, not even Emme, of my fantasies.

Meanwhile my mistress had no time for jealousies or jests. There were fresh rumors that her Catholic enemies were plotting to put her cousin, Queen Mary of Scotland, on England's throne. Though Mary had been forced to abdicate her throne and had been held captive for seventeen years, she still had many allies, both in England and abroad. And Mary had one great enemy, Sir Francis Walsingham, who could see a Spanish plot in even the most innocent event.

One day I saw the spymaster, his cap pulled closely about his ears, enter the queen's privy chamber. With him was the Earl of Shrewsbury, who guarded Queen Mary at Sheffield Castle. While Emme kept watch in the hallway, I tiptoed to the door and listened at the keyhole. The queen was speaking. Her voice was sharp and urgent.

"We threw Mendoza out of the country, but his spies are everywhere." Mendoza was the Spanish ambassador, whom everyone knew to be a devious little man. "No doubt they hide among my cousin's servants, seeking the chance to free her."

I heard Walsingham reply, "You underestimate me, Your Grace. Many of Mendoza's spies are in fact *my* spies."

But the queen was not pacified. "Mary betrays me *and* she bleeds me dry. She keeps a household of fifty at my expense. I cannot trust a single one of her servants. Dismiss them all."

"But Your Majesty insisted that she be treated with the respect due a fellow monarch," Shrewsbury said.

"You coddle her," accused the queen. "Has she has turned your head, too? Bewitched you with her charms?"

Shrewsbury began to protest but Elizabeth interrupted him. "Read every letter that goes in or out, search every scrap of linen sent to the laundry, every barrel, box, and hogshead of wine that is delivered, even check her chamber pot."

"We already do, Your Majesty," said Walsingham. "Be assured that I shall ferret out any evil. It shall not harm you."

"Let no one harm her, either," said the queen in a dire tone. "But be warned, My Lord of Shrewsbury, if a rebellion occurs while she is in your care, then you have betrayed me as well!"

Emme and I hurried away before anyone should open the door and discover us. Back in our dormitory, I asked Emme why the queen so hated her cousin.

"Why, Queen Mary is younger than our Elizabeth and said to be very beautiful. She has been married twice already, and she has a son."

"While our queen has no one to succeed her," Frances put in, overhearing us with her big ears.

"So she is jealous of her cousin, and afraid of her, too," I said, finally understanding. "But what will she do if she finds proof of a plot?"

"Why, she will have Queen Mary's head cut off. That is the punishment for treason," said Frances with relish.

I shuddered. With the queen so jealous and fearful of betrayal, it would be unwise of me to meet her favorite courtier in secret. So I wrote to Ralegh that I could not see him, but he persisted in sending me letters and verses. I read them with pleasure, then tied them in the handkerchief embroidered with the queen's initials and hid the bundle in the bottom of my coffer, beneath a pair of shoes I had outgrown.

It would have been wiser to burn them.

In September, Walter Ralegh's ships returned and word sped through Whitehall that the captains had brought back not one, but two savages. They dwelt at Durham House, where Ralegh saw them daily. I wrote to him—an innocent letter, begging only for a description of them—but I received no reply. Nor had he sent so much as a scrap of poetry in a month's time. But how could I be jealous, when it was not another lady but two warriors who had captured his fancy?

Finally the day arrived when the savages were to be presented to Queen Elizabeth. Rumors abounded concerning their great stature, fierce aspect, and the sharpness of their teeth. But had they been more dangerous than a *menagerie* full of wild animals, nothing could have kept me from court that day.

For the occasion the queen wore a new gown of brown velvet and a green taffeta bodice. The matching skirt was embroidered in gold with leaves and birds. I believe she was almost as excited as I was, for she could barely hold still as Lady Veronica tucked pins into her ruff, her bodice, and her train to hold them in place.

"I would be appareled like the Earth herself, for her best creatures should not look more glorious, more natural than I do," she said, admiring herself in the glass. Three gold chains about her neck and a headdress of gold wire set with emeralds completed her costume. I had never seen her look more elegant—or more artificial.

Wanting to be noticed myself, I chose a bodice and skirt of pale rose silk with sleeves slashed and pinked after the fashion. I now had a small wardrobe of my own, thanks to my salary from the queen and a small allowance from my father's estate. I even had a small strand of pearls which I wore because I knew that Ralegh liked pearls. I longed to see him almost as much as I did the savages.

The banqueting house had not seen such ceremony since the days when the queen courted *Monsieur*. The ceiling was hung with foliage, where songbirds twittered, their melodious calls echoing in the cavernous hall. The October sunlight streamed in the multitude of windows and glittered on the gilded pillars as the queen made her entrance, heralded by trumpets and flanked by guards in red coats trimmed in black velvet. The spectators who filled the benches facing the center of the hall greeted the queen with cheers and applause. Her noblemen wore breastplates and swords, befitting the ceremonial occasion. Elizabeth mounted the dais, and Emme and I spread out her train as she sat upon a low-backed chair with her ladies arrayed around her.

I heard scarcely a word of the queen's speech, for my attention dwelt on Ralegh, on the glossy hair that curled over the engraved gorget around his neck, on his velvet suit and the matching cloak worn over one shoulder. I imagined the number of pins required to keep it from sliding off and envied the valet who helped him dress. He stepped forth to present the queen with an oyster shell filled with pearls and spoke in praise of her virtue and her godly empire. All these words only made everyone more restless for the true objects of wonder still to appear.

When Ralegh finished his speech, a fanfare sounded. Two creatures of the most striking appearance stepped into the hall and were met with exclamations of awe. Their black hair was closely cropped on one side but chest-length on the other and plaited with feathers. Their skin was the color and sheen of polished rosewood and their feet were bare. Indeed, their bodies were mostly naked, except for the animal skins covering their loins. Disapproving noises came from Frances, but I felt no shame to look on them as they approached the dais. *So this was the state of nature in which man dwelt without kings, laws, religion, and government.* The thought filled me with wonder and a strange longing.

As they drew nearer, I saw that one of the Indians had a nose like a hawk's beak and a proud look. He wore a woven cloak trimmed with colored beads. His taller companion, to my surprise, seemed no more than a youth, his face unlined. He wore furs draped over his shoulders. His chest bore raised markings, like blisters, and were painted with white and black streaks. I had never seen a man's chest before, and was surprised to glimpse dark buds there, like my own chest before my breasts began to grow.

Feeling heat rise to my face, I shifted my gaze to the young Indian's face and willed him to look back at me. "Emme, he is magnificent!" I murmured behind my hand. He held himself motionless, but his black eyes flitted from side to side. For a brief moment they met my own.

At a signal from Ralegh, the two Indians bowed stiffly to the queen, who held out her hand, which they touched with their own rather than kissed. They then allowed themselves to be led around the hall—like bears in an arena, I thought—while the spectators covered their eyes or stared in awe, pointed, and even cried out in amazement.

My gaze followed the noble figures as I wished for a longer glimpse of the tall one's face, that I might look into the dark glass of his eyes and see another world revealed there.

Chapter 7

From the Papers of Walter Ralegh

4 November 1584

My dear brother Carew,

    I have good news of the voyage. My captains brought home two fine natives, Manteo and Wanchese. Now fitted with taffeta shirts and hose, they look like Englishmen, if one ignores their nut brown skin and coarse black hair. The scholar Harriot spends long hours with them and grows fluent in their tongue, which is called Algonkian. In turn they prove remarkably adept at learning English, though they speak in a rough and halting manner still.

    Manteo is the younger and more agreeable of the two savages. He shares his knowledge of the useful commodities afforded by the land and the tribes and their manner of warfare. While Manteo is of an open and trusting disposition, Wanchese is reserved and suspicious. I think he was taken from his village without his consent—which was against my instructions. Manteo, however, promises to be a valuable guide and ally.

Tell the lords and gentlemen of Devonshire that those who become investors will be among the first and the few to meet my Indians, who love to tell of the abundance of that New World.

Your brother,

W. Ralegh

Capt. Arthur Barlowe to Walter Ralegh
23 November 1584

I submit some notes toward my report. I know you desire to circulate said report as soon as it is completed, in order to feed the curious and capitalize on the public's interest in the New World.

Arthur Barlowe's Discourse of the First Voyage to Roanoke Island

Our safe arrival was auspicious. The shore very sandy and yet full of grapes growing bountifully there and on the green soil of the hillsides, climbing toward tall stands of cedars. The air so sweetly scented, like a delicate flower garden, that it seemed we had entered into a new paradise. . . .

The Natives Show Their Friendship. *Wingina, the king of the Roanoke, and his goodly warriors entertained us and we traded with them to our great advantage. A copper kettle fetched fifty skins! The king's brother clapped a tin dish to his chest, making signs that it would defend him against his enemy's arrows. . . . They hold us and our ships and weapons in marvelous admiration. Wingina urged us to go against the chief Piemacum, assuring us of the great commodities in his town. But whether it was for the friendship he bore us or to take revenge on his enemy, we could not determine, nor did we wish to engage in their disputes.*

Of Their Way of Life. *Their boats are made from the trunk of a single tree, which they hollow by burning and scraping with shells. By such means they fashion shallow boats, called canoes, that carry twenty men.*

A savage fishing from his canoe filled his boat almost to sinking within half an hour. As well as the waters, the land is bountiful, providing fat bucks, conies, deer, and all manner of edible plants: melons, walnuts, pease, and fruits, and especially their white corn, which they are able to reap three times in a single season.

In short: a people most gentle, loving, and faithful, lacking guile and treason, and living after the manner of the golden age. The earth bringing forth abundance, without toil or labor. The winters short, but no shortage of meat. The rivers teeming with mussels yielding valuable pearls . . . etc.

I agree there is little benefit in publishing the difficulties of our journey and the waywardness of some of the savages.

Despite the perilous shallows around the island of the Roanoke, it is favorably located. From there you may launch raids upon the Spanish and interrupt their trading.

With every good hope for the colony's future, I remain your devoted servant,

Arthur Barlowe

P.S. Allow me also to suggest that our first object upon returning to the island must be the erection of a fort. (As a matter of prudence.)

Memorandum

15 December 1584. Wanchese has contracted smallpox and must be isolated, especially from Manteo. He grows fearful of the boils

on his flesh and babbles in his own tongue. Will not let the doctors near. Does he think we poisoned him? He is sure to become even more suspicious. If he recovers.

28 December 1584. An attempt to assassinate our beloved queen has failed, God be praised! A doctor in league with the Jesuits accosted Her Majesty as she walked in the garden at Richmond. But then he lost his courage and found himself unable to carry out the deed.

May fortune and grace preserve our queen, for while she lives, I prosper. Should she die—and with none to succeed her—papist minions of the Scottish queen stand ready to rise.

That would be the downfall of all my dreams.

Wanchese recovers, but his face will be badly scarred. He has lapsed into a sullen silence.

10 January 1585
Dear Carew,

Your brother's striving and seeking have been rewarded at last by the royal mistress of his heart and fortune, who has granted him the honor of knighthood.

Furthermore she has appointed me lord and governor of the land to be named VIRGINIA in her honor. Mine is the task of colonizing the coastal areas and all the interior, bringing the inhabitants under Her Majesty's sway. She grants the use of her own ship, the 180-ton Tiger, *and 2,400 lbs. of gunpowder for the next voyage.*

I wish she had compounded the honor with money. But her nod may induce many of her nobles to invest, as well as merchants. Indeed, who could could resist the prospect of plunder coupled with the profits from trade in timber, pine resin, furs, etc.?

To you only, Carew, I confess my high ambitions while I pledge to serve my sovereign mistress. May the sun shed her "golden" light on all our endeavors.

Your honored brother,
Sir Walter Ralegh

Memorandum

4 February 1585. Her Majesty visited today accompanied by ladies, among them C.A. She appears more womanly than when I last saw her. In fact, I deem her almost a beauty. How could I have forgotten her for almost three months?

The queen looked paler than usual, making the vermilion on her cheeks glow like fever spots. She fretted about an eclipse to occur on 9 April. "You must delay your voyage, for my astrologers predict disasters on that day."

Hiding my disdain of such predictions, I replied, "For your sake I will not sail, but remain here to serve you." (I had already decided to forgo the risk of a voyage until the certainty of reward should outweigh it.)

"My dear Warter, you know how thirsty I can be," she said, as coy as a maid thirty years younger. "It makes me glad to know you will stay."

"Let storms and tempest do their worst; water but quenches, ne'er drowns your thirst," I rhymed, to her delight.

Yet she whom I truly wished to please with my verse did not regard me, but was agog over Manteo. The ladies seemed amazed to behold him (and the silent Wanchese) clad like gentlemen. "Frances needn't have refused to come," Lady Anne remarked, hiding behind her fan as if she feared to look upon them. But my C.A. had no such qualms, listening with her moist lips parted as my Indian spoke in slow and measured English. I could see how she longed to question him and the effort it took to hold herself still.

The sight of her with such lively interest in her gray eyes renews my ardor. I will recapture that gaze and not neglect her for so long again.

Notations Toward a Second Voyage to
Roanoke Island, Virginia

The number of men to remain as colonists: 100, including engineers, masons, carpenters, brickmakers, a physician, and an apothecary. An alchemist to test the metals and a lapidary skilled in all minerals, as well as farmers and laborers.

Number of trained soldiers: 60

To survey and map the land, and to depict flora, fauna, and natives: Thomas Harriot, scholar, and John White, painter.

The fort to be in the shape of a pentangle with five bulwarks, fifty feet wide within, and containing an armory. Outside, ditches with walls, and twenty feet beyond them a palisade of sufficient height to deter attackers. The fort to be seated upon a rock, peninsula, or island.

Governance & Law

Chief pilot: Simon Fernandes

General commander: Sir Richard Grenville

Both will return to England, leaving: Lt. Colonel Ralph Lane as acting governor and military commander; Manteo and Wanchese as guides.

Offenses and punishments

Fighting in the fort or within a mile thereof—3 mos. imprisonment

Stealing any man's goods—loss of hand

Striking or misusing an Indian—20 blows

Violating a woman—death

Drawing a weapon upon a governor, councilor, or captain— death

Abandoning sentinel or sleeping on watch—death

9 April 1585. Despite auguries of doom, the *Tiger* and six other ships sailed from Plymouth under fair skies. I found myself seized with the lust for adventure and almost leapt on board the *Tiger*. Then I hesitated, recalling how ill I become at sea, and in a moment the gap between the wharf and the ship's deck grew too great to o'erleap. And so I stayed, as I promised Her Majesty I would.

Chapter 8

Manteo's Quest

I am called Manteo, which means "he snatches from another," like a hawk. It is a fitting name for the son of a *weroance*. But I am more like Cloud-runner, the youth who lay in the grass and stared at the clouds. Like Cloud-runner, I sometimes dream that I am in the land of the star people. Their lodge gleams like the inside of an oyster. Cloud-runner lived among the star people until he grew homesick, and when he returned home he forgot his sojourn there. As I forget the time my father was killed in battle when I was only a few winters old. My people remember their past through the stories we tell.

I was born on Croatoan, one of the islands that are joined like a necklace of shells. They keep the sea from breaking upon the mainland. My mother, Weyawinga, is the weroance of the island. I know my way around its rocky shoals. I know the land of Osso-mocomuck from the bay of Chesapeake to the Neuse River, which villages are ruled by friendly weroances, and where our foes live. I know when to plant *pagatour,* or maize. I know which roots and berries can be eaten, and which ones kill.

I grew up on stories of young men who left their villages on dream quests and returned with gifts to save their people. *Openauk*, the wild-growing potato. Flocks of *kaiauk*, who make the ground rich with their leavings. When the youths came back they were men. Everyone respected them.

I grew tall and my voice deepened. I went to the lodge, crossing the sound in a canoe, alone. Fear was like a hand gripping my guts. I might be eaten by a bear or killed by the Pomeioc. For weeks I ate almost nothing. I breathed in smoke that left me dazed. Waited for my vision of what to pursue. It would be greater than a gift of food or skill with a spear, for I was the son of a weroance and deserved more. My dream would fill me with *montoac*, the spirit power that would make me a hero, like in the ancient stories.

I did everything a young man is supposed to do. But no quest was revealed to me.

Heavy with despair I set out for home. Then in the forest I had my vision. Men with skin as pale as the mushrooms that grow beneath rotting leaves. Wearing plates of shining *wassador*. What did this dream signify? Twigs and leaves crackled under their feet. Strange sounds came from their mouths. As they drew near I could even smell them. This was no dream! The men were as real as I. When they saw me, they made signs with their hands. They were so glad to see me that I was not afraid of them.

One of the men spoke words I could understand. They were seeking the village of Secotan. I agreed to lead them there rather than return to my village and admit my failure. The white men were hungry and had no skill at hunting. So I shot several rabbits and wildfowl. They were amazed by my bow, such a simple weapon.

The English, for so they called themselves, showed me their weapon, a musket. It produced fire and a loud noise. They offered me ornaments made from the shining wassador and a strong drink that opened my mind. They made signs that more would be given to me if I would go to their land across the waves. The montoac I sought was being offered to me! Spirit power was in the wassador, the drink, the mighty weapons of the strangers. My thoughts leapt like a herd of deer. I would go with these men and bring their powerful things to my people. Returning to Croatoan, I told my mother that this was my quest. She was afraid for me, but did not forbid me to go.

The sea was wider than I thought possible, the English boat big enough to hold everyone in my village. I had a companion, for Wingina, the weroance of the Roanoke, sent one of his warriors to learn more about where the strangers had come from. Unlike me, Wanchese was not pleased to leave the land.

Ossomocomuck has no end to it. The white man's village, London, also had no end. But it was to my land as day is to night. So bright and busy I had to close my eyes. So loud my ears hurt. So foul smelling I held my nose. London was a market where all wares could be traded at once. Men put sledges on wheels and horses pulled them along paths where people gathered as thick as gulls on the seashore. At first Wanchese and I were kept from the people. We were taken to live in a lodge so tall I wondered how it could stay upright. I had no words for the wonders I saw there. Truly I was Cloud-runner in the land of the star people.

The Englishmen Raw-lee and Hare-yet treated me like a sage, one who is wiser even than a weroance. I basked in their attention like a snake in the sun. But I had to wear clothes. (All the men and women of London, shamed by their paleness, covered their flesh with bright clothing.) I was given a shirt so fine it felt like air brushing my skin. But I did not like the shoes. I wished for my feet to touch the earth again.

Hare-yet taught me their tongue and I taught him mine. But Wanchese was jealous of my favor.

"There is wisdom in silence, but the white man talks like a jay," he said. He refused to learn their tongue. This made the English suspect him.

Then a disease fell upon Wanchese. Boils covered his body and burst open. One of their healers cut open his leg to let out the evil, making him well again.

"Do not trust these men," Wanchese told me. *"They are trying to kill me, but my spirit is too strong."*

I said Raw-lee and Hare-yet were men of truth. Had they not given me many gifts, as they promised? And such pale faces, like a stream in which the fish can be seen, could not deceive. That was my belief. Moreover, they honored us by presenting us to their weroance with much ceremony. Kwin-lissa-bet ruled not only London, but every village in the land. Her warriors were said to be as numerous as the stars. I thought she must be more powerful than Wingina or any of the rulers of Ossomocomuck.

The lodge of this weroance was like the dwelling of Ahone and all the gods. The men wore plates of shiny wassador around their necks. The *kwin* covered herself in riches that glittered like the sun on the sea. My mind was full of the vision but without any words to describe it. Yet I saw in the pale faces of the people thoughts I could name. Thoughts they could not hide. Fear, wonder, shame to look upon me.

But there was among them one face that regarded me with simple interest. It was that of a young woman. Her hair was as dark as my own, her eyes like the sea just before night falls. I thought, *Without their clothing and ornaments, maybe these people are not so different from me.*

The English ships sailed again, laden with goods. Wanchese

and I were both glad to return home. Unlike Cloud-runner, I did not wish to live among the star people. I wanted to share with my own people the great gift I had discovered: the montoac that was in the Englishman's language, his knowledge, and his friendship. This would bring us respect and make our enemies fear us.

This would make me a hero.

Chapter 9

A Favor Denied

From the time I saw Manteo at court, resplendent in his native garb, my curiosity about the savages could not be satisfied. I borrowed a book from the queen's library, *Diverse Voyages to the Americas,* but it was full of conjecture and woodcuts of half-human monsters. It was nothing but feigned tales, while I sought a true history. Thus, when I went with the queen to Durham House and Sir Walter brought Manteo and Wanchese into the company, I was beside myself with excitement. When I heard Manteo speak in English, I marveled at the great and perceptive mind he had. He seemed no older than I, but he had almost mastered my language, while I could speak not a word of his. Thomas Harriot had learned his tongue, but he was known to be a genius.

Pausing often and prompted by the scholar Harriot, Manteo spoke about the riches that lay beneath the great hills inland and the pearls resting beneath the flowing rivers. It was a speech he had prepared for the queen. All the while, I desired to ask this Manteo a question about his home and to meet his eyes again. In the company of so many men, however, it was not proper for me to speak. And so I drew no attention to myself but sat in mingled awe and misery. Of course Manteo was more interesting than I could possibly be, so I understood why Ralegh had neglected to send me letters and verses. His was the task of building a new colony, and the Indians were a part of that great enterprise. The queen had even knighted him, and he was now Sir Walter Ralegh. She, not I, was the mistress of his heart and fortune. I had nothing to contribute.

Ralegh's ships—with his Indians aboard—sailed again for the New World. I decided not to pine for what I could not have, but, like a humble gardener, to till the soil closer to home. Emme was always encouraging me to befriend those who could make my lot as a queen's maid easier to bear. Soon enough, an opportunity presented itself; Anne begged me for a favor. When I asked what it was, she did not reply but took my arm and propelled me through the gates of Whitehall and into the streets clogged with carts and shouting vendors. Shortly we came to a house near Charing Cross.

Thomas Graham waited inside. His red hair stood up like a brush. He offered me a glass of ale and some sweets, which I accepted out of courtesy.

"Why have you brought me here?" I asked.

Graham took Anne's hand and she blushed, then stroked his face. I envied them their love for each other, and thought sadly of Sir Walter's letters hidden in my coffer.

"Dearest Catherine," began Anne. "You know how long Thomas has waited for the queen to recognize his virtues. Now his fortune is reduced to pennies, and unless he obtains a position at court, he shall have to leave London altogether." Her chin trembled. "And I shall never see him."

"What will you do to make a living?" I asked Graham.

"Soldiering," he said grimly.

"I don't know how I can help," I said with a shrug.

"Catherine, you are mild and never give offense," said Anne in her most flattering tone. "If you asked a favor of the queen, she would surely grant it."

"I doubt she regards me as highly as you think," I said. "What do you seek?"

"To be appointed a gentleman pensioner. I am handsome enough, don't you think?"

I nodded, for despite his fussy dress Graham was tall and well featured.

"Then you will give this petition to the queen for me?" He held out a sealed letter.

"You may have my black taffeta bodice and the yellow sarcenet skirt trimmed in black," Anne offered, her hands clasped in hope. "They are still in fashion."

"Why not petition the queen yourself?" I asked her.

"One does not ask a favor for oneself!" she said. "No, it must be a friend who pleads for us."

Would I ever understand the ways of the court? I considered Anne's request. I was flattered that she called me her friend. She was a sweet lady and Graham, well intentioned. Though I pitied their circumstance, still I hesitated. Then Graham set his purse on the table, and I heard the clink of coins.

"I do not want the last of your fortune," I said, pushing it away. "I will help you."

Graham seized my hand and kissed it. "Do this, and I will perform any deed for you. Next to my lady, you I will serve." His words tumbled out. "Sir Walter and I have been companions, and if you—if he—only ask and I will— The debt is all mine."

I frowned and withdrew my hand. Was it impossible to keep a secret at court?

"I don't know what you mean. Sir Walter is nothing to me, or I to him," I said, trying to sound cool, though my cheeks were hot.

Anne gave me the promised gown. It was more beautiful than any of my clothes and after a few alterations fit me perfectly. She became like a sister to me, holding my hand and whispering in my ear such things as, "Your hair is so pretty." "Her Majesty is ill-tempered today; wait until tomorrow." "Shall I teach you a ditty?"

One night as we lay in our beds, Emme asked, "Why do you let Lady Anne fawn over you?"

"You advised me to make new friends," I replied, and explained how I had agreed to help her and Graham.

"You have a true friend in me. Why do you need a false one as well?" she asked, turning away.

I had no reply to Emme's question. Seldom did she misjudge anyone, and I began to worry something would go amiss with my suit. I carried the petition everywhere, not wanting to miss an opportunity to give it to the queen. One evening she called for a warm posset, and I carried it to her bedchamber, my hands shaking so, I was afraid of spilling it. She sat in a chair wearing a velvet-trimmed nightgown, her feet in pantofles. She nodded for me to sit on a stool nearby while she drank.

"I am pleased to see Your Majesty is content," I said, testing her mood. She had not lately reviled her cousin, Queen Mary, so I hoped that crisis had passed.

"I am content," she said. "Were I a cat, I would purr." She smiled, showing the radiance that made us all love her. In the candlelight I could barely see the wrinkles bestriding her nose and forehead.

I smiled in return. "I am also content, merely to be in your company."

"I don't know why I should be happy." Elizabeth looked into her cup and swirled the contents as if they would reveal something. "I am no longer young like you. My kingdom has no heir but many enemies."

"More numerous still are your loyal subjects who long to serve you," I said, looking directly at her, my heart speeding up.

The queen regarded me for a moment. "You are direct and well spoken, not coy or fearful like most women. I would have you in my government. How is it that a woman can be a queen but not a councilor or an ambassador?"

I swelled with pride at the compliment. I imagined myself a diplomat in the New World, wearing a fur-lined cloak and discoursing with Manteo, perhaps even in his native language.

"To be such a councilor is a dream that only Your Majesty could fulfill," I said.

After a moment she said, "You have not asked me for anything since you came here. In that regard you are also unusual. But do not forget I am both mother and father to you now, as well as your sovereign." Her tone was tender and inviting.

I wanted to sit at her feet and share my dreams of being as free as a man to travel to new worlds and seek my fortune and happiness in love. But the petition was in my pocket and I wanted to be rid of it.

So I said, choosing my words with care, "I will ask something, not for myself, but on behalf of another. There is a worthy man who is in need of your grace."

I produced the letter and knelt, placing it on the queen's lap. I kept my head down, thinking I had spoken well.

She undid the seal and read the petition, then flung it aside.

"Thomas Graham—a worthy man? I'll let the rascal guard the villains in Fleet prison, but never my sovereign person." She sprang to her feet and stood over me. "Why would you, Catherine, take up the cause of this strutting turkey-cock?"

I fell back on my heels, too stunned to reply.

"It shows a defect in your judgment," said Elizabeth coldly.

"I am not perfect. Nor is Thomas Graham," I croaked, feeling the tears coming. "But he and Lady Anne are deeply in love!"

As soon as those words left my mouth I realized my error, one that would cost my new friends—and me—dearly.

The queen's frown deepened into a thundercloud. "None of my ladies may love without my consent! I decide *if* you will marry, and *whom*." She stamped her foot for emphasis. "Do not forget!"

I left the queen's chamber in tears and sought out Emme. Finding her at her prayers, I poured out the whole story. She looked at me aghast as her prayerbook slid to the floor.

"How was I to know she hated Graham so much?" I wailed. "Surely Anne could have warned me."

Emme took me by the shoulders. "Don't you see? The matter has little to do with Graham. Elizabeth was speaking to you as an intimate—do you know how most of us would die for such words from her?—and you replied by thrusting a petition at her." Emme shook me. "She wanted to give *you* something, and you abused her generosity."

"But I thought it was virtuous of me *not* to be self-seeking!" Despair washed over me. "Oh, Emme, I should have listened to you and refused Anne. Now I have lost the queen's regard."

She tried to comfort me. "You are still a babe in the ways of this court. If you are lucky, perhaps she will overlook the whole business."

But the queen was not inclined to forgive or forget. She dismissed Graham from court, sending him back to Kent, and gave Anne a tongue-lashing that left her red-faced and tearful for days. Anne, in turn, accused me of betraying them and ruining her happiness, but Emme defended me.

"You should be glad she did not banish you," she scolded Anne. "She could have put you and Thomas both in the Tower."

"At least we would be together!" she wailed. "But now I shall never marry, and you, Catherine," she threatened, "will live to regret the harm you have done us."

"I already regret it," I said mournfully. "But since I intended no hurt, won't you forgive me?"

She would not, and she let everyone know that I could not be trusted. The other ladies shunned us both, fearing that our misfortune, like a disease, would infect them. They sent their own lovers away, and a virginal hush settled over the court, defying the turmoil beneath its surface.

Loyal Emme remained my friend. Anne found an ally in Frances, who also disliked me for some reason I could never discern. I waited on the queen with a humility so abject it pained me. If she noticed, she gave no sign. I lived in fear that one day her temper would flare up again and that I, like Graham, would be dismissed and disgraced. For I knew that Fortune's wheel never stops turning.

Elizabeth's court, which seemed a golden, glorious place when I arrived, was now like a forged coin—not worth a penny. I even thought about leaving. But where could I go and how would I survive?

Chapter 10

Shared Ambitions

Disconsolate, lacking friends and out of favor, I did what I could to alleviate my misery. That is, I dreamed of escape; I fantasized about love. I imagined walking with Sir Walter in Finsbury Fields or meeting him at a playhouse and weeping into his shoulder at the end of a tragedy. I pored over his letters and poems until I had memorized every line. But it only made me sadder that he no longer wrote to me. So I tied the pages up again in the embroidered handkerchief and hid the bundle in my chest. For solace I read the romances that passed among the queen's ladies, tales of shepherds in love with princesses and knights seeking their damsels. For a time they took me to another world.

But one night I found something far better, cast aside in the queen's bedchamber: a manuscript of the first voyage to the island of the Roanoke. I read it at once, devouring Arthur Barlowe's descriptions of the land so bounteous it was like paradise. I read about the innocent friendliness of the Indians and the chief's wife in her fur-lined cloak, with pearls hanging from her ears. How I wanted to meet her, to visit her bark house, to smell the air fragrant with unusual flowers and trees!

While reading I made an additional discovery. With the manuscript was a letter from Sir Walter. I held it to my nose but could smell no trace of his civet. I read the letter and found it contained verses exalting my mistress's virtue and recommending Barlowe's report. And an idea came to me, a plan whereby I might regain the queen's favor.

Best of all, it would give an opportunity to see Sir Walter again.

One day when the queen was abed with a ulcer in her leg, I asked Emme to come with me to Sir Walter's house, saying I had a favor to ask of him.

Emme's eyes lit up with curiosity, but she was also wary. "We must contrive a purpose for going out, or our absence may be questioned."

I grabbed a pile of old linens. "If anyone asks, we are delivering these to the embroiderer on the Strand."

So we left Whitehall with the linens, joining the crowds thronging the streets around Charing Cross. A ten-minute walk brought us to Durham House, where a footman said that Sir Walter was not at home. Emme and I walked back to Whitehall in silence. I decided my plan was a feeble, doomed effort.

"He was there, I am sure," I said. "But he does not want to see me!"

Emme's brown eyes were warm with sympathy. "He has a new love, and her name is Virginia," she said.

But the very next day I received a message.

My dear Catherine! I regret missing you. What was it,
I wonder, that brought you here after so many months'

absence? I beg the return of your delightful presence soon.
Nay, sooner. At once, if you could fly, angel.
  W.R.

My heart thumped at my ribs like a bird in a cage. Ralegh wanted to see me! I secreted the message with the others tied in the queen's handkerchief. Then I waited for an opportunity to go to him. I was careless with my duties, misplacing sleeves and partlets, but only Emme seemed to notice. Elizabeth's ulcer had improved and she could now hobble around her bedchamber.

"Go today," Emme urged. "You won't be needed to dress the queen until she can walk about more easily." She helped me into my green silk bodice and skirt that brightened my gray eyes. "Don't forget to fetch the linens from the embroiderers," she added with a wink.

Not half an hour later I was in the garden of Durham House, alone with Ralegh among the shaded bowers. The narrow paths forced us to walk close to each other, our arms touching from time to time. The scent of him and the clouds of purple lavender went to my head like new wine, and I could not order my thoughts. I found myself prattling to him about the queen's health.

Sir Walter stopped and put up his hand. "I do not wish to hear about the royal ulcer," he said with a wry smile. "Tell me about yourself instead. What you have been doing and thinking of late?"

Thinking too much of you. Reading your letters. Wanting to walk with you, just like this. I did not confess these thoughts, but a different truth. "What weighs on me now is the queen's disfavor," I admitted, relating the entire episode of Graham and Lady Anne. "So, to be plain, my position is precarious. I desire only to be back in Her Majesty's good graces."

"And I desire to be in yours," he said smoothly.

"What do you mean?" I murmured.

"You did not reply to my letters and poems these past months," he said in a tone of rebuke.

I looked at him in surprise. "But I have received nothing from you! Not since the handkerchief and . . . the poem that followed." I felt a wave of heat wash over my face at the memory of what he had written to me: *My America, north and south, I'd explore you with this hand, Claim you with my mouth.*

"Nothing? How can that be?" he said, frowning. "Then receive it now."

He leaned toward me, and I saw his parted lips, his teeth. Though everything in me longed to be kissed, I shook my head.

"No, I must not! The queen will be angry."

"She will not know."

Like a sapling in the breeze, I swayed toward Sir Walter until my lips just grazed his.

"That was no true kiss. Let me show you one," he whispered.

Clasping my shoulders, he lowered me onto a bench and sat beside me, his thigh pressed to mine. His nearness and his breath on my cheek sent a sharp tingling to the base of my spine.

"No, for I may not love without Her Majesty's permission," I said, pleading.

"You are here without her permission, are you not?"

"I was foolish to come. I should go now."

With a sigh, he released my shoulders. "But you may not leave until you have told me why you came."

"Oh, yes." I had been about to leave without even touching on my purpose.

"Was it simply to see me?" he prompted, sounding so hopeful I hated to disappoint him with an honest answer.

"I did come to see you yesterday—as a friend in need of your help. I wanted you to write a poem for me to give to the queen, something that might restore me to her favor." I sighed. "But it was a foolish idea, for if she learns I was here with you, I will lose my place altogether."

Sir Walter did not seem offended. He took my chin in his hand and tilted my head upward. "Rather, your coming here shows your courage," he said. "Many a man wishes to flout the queen's will in favor of his own, but dares not."

"Can you be you speaking of yourself?" I asked in disbelief. "I thought your wishes had been gratified by all the favors the queen grants you."

"Oh, Cat!" he cried, leaping to his feet. "I will confess my ambitions to you. I wish to go to the New World myself and govern it. I would bring all Manteo's people under my dominion and rule like Caesar during the golden age. I would dig in the earth with these hands and mine its wealth, enough gold and silver to make Virginia the richest colony in all the world. Every man in England would hail the name of Ralegh!"

Sir Walter strode back and forth proclaiming his ambitions while I watched in amazement.

"But Elizabeth makes me stay in England, a toy to entertain her! She appoints me warden of this, captain of that. All her favors, like ropes, only tie me down with heavy duties."

I could no longer contain myself. "Oh, Sir Walter, I also dream of going to the New World! Ever since I saw the maps in your library and your ships at anchor on the Thames. And the savage, Manteo— seeing his noble bearing and hearing him speak only quickened my curiosity. He is not much older than I am, and he has already traveled far and wide. Since reading Captain Barlowe's report, I want nothing more than to visit this land where nothing is corrupted and everything is free—" I broke off, breathless.

Sir Walter looked at me with an expression almost like pity. He sank down beside me, then lifted my hair from my shoulders, brought it to his face, and kissed it.

"You, Cat, you sleek, beautiful creature, are more innocent than America herself," he murmured, dropping my hair and touching my cheek instead. "You don't know how free you are. How fortunate!"

Moved by curiosity I touched his face, the straight, narrow nose, the furrowed brow beneath his curly hair. It was bold of me, but then I was no longer a timid Cat.

"We are both dreamers, are we not?" I said with a smile. "But you are the innocent one if you think that freedom is my good fortune. No, it is a fearful thing to one who has no family and no wealth. Without the queen's favor, I will starve."

Ralegh nodded. Then he looked over my shoulder and began to speak. "*Virginia, land of so much plenty, for your bounty I do hunger.*" He paused and thought for a moment. "*But on your shores you've placed a sentry, denying my poor love an entry.*"

"What do you mean by these rhymes?" I asked, hoping for a simpler declaration of his love.

"Why, it is the opening stanza of the poem you requested. The land of Virginia is the queen," he explained. "The bounty is the favor you seek. Write it down."

From inside his doublet he handed me a pencil and a piece of paper. They were warm from being next to his body. I wrote down the verses.

"This is like a poem you sent me," I said, unable to hide my disappointment. "Were those meant for the queen, too?"

"No, that is my style, to be allegorical." He then gave me a hurt look. "What I sent to you, I meant only for you."

I held his eyes with mine, waiting for him to say more. I wondered if it was easier for him to write of love than to speak it.

"Hold now, I have a second verse coming on," he said.

I wrote the rest of the lines as he uttered them, though the verses did not suit my circumstances. I would have to rewrite them or the queen would see Ralegh's style and I would be forced to confess the lines his. That could only lead to greater trouble.

I thanked Sir Walter for his efforts and took my leave with a decorum that belied the turmoil within me. I let him kiss my hand, which gave me not half the thrill of his lips near mine. But the moment for a true kiss had come and gone, because I refused it.

It wasn't until I was lying in my bed under the eaves, reviewing every moment of our meeting, that I wondered why I had not received the letters Sir Walter had referred to. Had they been intercepted? But why and by whom? Was someone trying to keep us apart? Perhaps it was a friend who wanted to protect us. Or an enemy who wanted to betray us. And why was Ralegh not more concerned about the stray letters? I considered that he had never written them, but pretended he had so I would think he had not forgotten about me. Did he, then, not love me? Oh, but he had so wanted to kiss me, and wasn't that all that mattered?

Mired in uncertainty, I did not fall asleep until the blackest part of the night, just before morning.

Chapter 11

Manteo, Friend of the English

My people live at the bright beginning of the world, the Dawn-land, where the sun rises from the sea and gives life to all things. We ourselves began long ago when a giant came from the sea and with an arrow split open a tree, and the first man stepped forth. I listened to this story many times as a boy. Now I wonder if the giant came in an English ship like this one. A canoe would not be big enough for him.

I thought about the giant-god every morning when the sun appeared behind the ship and at night when it disappeared into the water in front of it, drawing us toward Ossomocomuck. Finally, where the water met the sky, the islands appeared.

To protect my land, the gods surrounded it with sharp rocks hidden just beneath the water. I tried to warn the pilot but he said he would take no direction from a savage. So his vessel struck the rocks with a sound like an angry demon tearing into the wood. The sea poured in and the pilot cursed his god. I prayed to the sea-gods, who freed the boat and permitted it to land without sinking.

But as punishment for the captain's pride, all the wheat, rice, and salt in the ship's hold were ruined.

The English built their fort on the island of the Roanoke, near Wingina's village. Wanchese returned to his people. Gren-vill sailed back to London, leaving Ralf-lane to govern.

I led the English from one settlement to another on the mainland. John-white made drawings of the people and the dwellings and Ralf-lane gave gifts to the weroances. After leaving one of the villages, they discovered a silver cup to be missing. Ralf-lane made his men return there and he demanded the cup. The weroance denied that his people had stolen it. I knew I had to act or the fragile peace would break.

"Will you accept a gift of furs instead of the cup?" I asked the governor. He would not.

"*The English are angry,*" I then said to the weroance in his tongue. "*Send your women and children away for their safety.*" I thought this threat would make them give up the cup. But I was wrong.

"The women and children are leaving," said Ralf-lane. "That proves they have the cup and are preparing to fight for it."

I knew there were only a few warriors to defend the village. But before I could stop the English, they began to tear down the houses, looking for the cup. Finding nothing, they burned the houses. The fields also. Quicker than a hunter can flay a rabbit, the village was destroyed. Everyone had fled.

"The people will not forget this day or cease telling about it," I said to Ralf-lane, unable to hide my distress. He laughed, thinking my words were meant to praise him, not warn him.

The cup was not found among the ashes. I do not think the weroance had it, for if he did, he would have given it up to save his village. What montoac that cup must have contained, that the English went to such lengths to avenge its loss!

I learned about the white men by watching them from day to day. They were much like children. Quick to anger and to fight. Full of wonder. When they first ate the openauk, the wild potato, and pagatour, maize, their eyes grew round. Like children they could not take care of themselves. They could not hunt without startling every creature in the forest. They did not know how to track game. I showed them how to set up weirs to catch the whiskered *keetrauk,* which they named "catfish." They never tired of asking me where the gleaming pearls and the shining wassador were hidden. When I said I did not know, some accused me of lying.

Ill feelings grew between the laborers and the gentlemen, who would not build houses, dig the fort, or till the soil. Soldiers fought and Ralf-lane punished them by making them work with chains on their feet. Only John-white seemed content as he made his drawings of fish, plants, birds, and people. They were so true that my people were afraid, but I assured them that his pictures could not steal their spirit and cause them to die.

I no longer regarded the English as godlike. So they had seemed to me, gathered around their Kwin-lissa-bet. Here I saw they could be weak, foolish, and cruel, like any man. Still I was proud to be among them, for I was more esteemed than before. I translated the governor's words. He and the weroances both relied on me to conduct their business.

When Wingina heard me speak the stranger's tongue, his astonishment pleased me. I had montoac that even he, the great weroance, lacked.

Wingina said to me, "*Wanchese will not speak their language. He does not trust them. Why do you?*"

I said Ralf-lane and his men wanted to learn our ways. To trade with us, that we might both grow rich.

Wingina looked doubtful. *"I have permitted them to settle on my island so I may watch them."*

"You will see they desire peace," I said.

Wingina did not reply at first. He knew they were building a fort. He had heard about the silver cup and the destroyed village. This news had traveled throughout Ossomocomuck.

"The white man's weapons are powerful and deadly. And we have many enemies," he said finally. Wingina was known to be wise, and he would find a way to benefit from the English presence.

But by a mysterious fate, the English brought death to the Roanoke, though not with their feared weapons. After Ralf-lane's first visit to Wingina, ten villagers fell ill and died. Wingina sent for me. Wanchese was with him, and they were both afraid.

"It is proved the English can kill without weapons," said Wanchese. *"As they tried to kill me in London."*

"It was your own evil thoughts about the English that made you ill. I have no such thoughts, and I am well," I said to him, then turned to Wingina. *"They will not harm their friends."*

Wingina glanced at Wanchese then settled his gaze on me. He gave the Englishmen forty baskets of openauk and a large field planted with pagatour. Then he moved his villagers to the mainland, to a place called Dasemunkepeuc.

Wingina was wise but also crafty. In the spring he paddled to the island to inform Ralf-lane that an alliance of Chowanoc planned to attack Fort Raw-lee. Ralf-lane decided to act first. With thirty men he rowed upriver and surprised the Chowanoc village, seizing their weroance, Menantonon. This time I was able to prevent the English from destroying the village. Menantonon denied that he planned to attack the fort, saying it was a trick of Wingina to get the English to destroy the Chowanoc village. After a long parley with Ralf-lane, Menantonon saw what the English desired. He described a people who possessed wassador in such abundance they decorated their homes with it. Ralf-lane's eyes shone. He decided to go to this village, a seven-days' journey.

I suspected Menantonon, too, was lying. Even setting a trap. But I could not persuade Ralf-lane to turn back if there was a possibility of treasure. I had no choice but to guide them. Every village we passed was deserted. No food to be had. To keep from starving, the English killed and ate their dogs. Still Ralf-lane would not give up. When we came at last to the village, it was also abandoned.

"Where are the silver and copper Menantonon promised we would see?" Ralf-lane demanded.

"They are hidden within the hills themselves," I said. "No one knows where."

Without tools or food, there was nothing more Ralf-lane could do. By the time we returned to the fort, our stomachs were as hollow as dried gourds. Several men were near death. And Ralf-lane was full of rage at the deceit of the weroances.

"Wingina delivered us to his own enemies, hoping they would kill us. Then he and his allies could strike at the fort!" About Menantonon he said, "He sent us on a fool's errand, and told the people to leave their villages so we would starve."

I tried to soften his rage with reason. "The villagers may have been away hunting, according to their custom," I said. "What food they had, they took with them. There is hunger everywhere. For five years, the rains have been scarce."

I counseled peace and goodwill, for that was my duty to Raw-lee and his governor. But Ralf-lane's duty did not call for him to heed me.

Before they attack, the English do not prepare as we do. They do not paint or beat drums or dance to summon the spirits. Their leaders make plans in secret and the soldiers obey in silence. So I did not know Ralf-lane's intent. Had he told me his plans, could I have changed his mind? Would I have warned Wingina? Would the weroance have heeded me?

I was not with the governor and his men when they crossed the bay in their wherries. But I could hear, before dawn, the firing of muskets. Faint and distant. The day was long. The night even longer. The next morning the first boat returned from Dase-munkepeuc, and I heard Wingina had been shot twice. Despite his wounds he escaped into the woods. The soldiers could not keep up with him and left the chase. But one pursued him through woods and swamps for hours before Wingina's strength finally failed.

Ralf-lane came back to the fort in the second wherry, holding aloft the bloody head of Wingina. "Let them remember this deed, too, Manteo!" he said. He stuck the head on a pole outside the fort.

This did not call for a reply. But I thought, *They will remember. And you, in turn, will remember the terrible revenge that must come.*

As it happened, the English did not remain long enough for the Roanoke to take their revenge. A week after Wingina was killed, a fleet of English ships came to the outer islands. Their captain, called Francis-drake, was brought to the fort. He was tawny skinned from being so long at sea and under the sun. He spoke of such strife between the weroances of England and Spain that Ralf-lane feared no supply ship would be able to reach the island.

I could see the governor desired to return to England but was ashamed, for he had failed to find riches for his kwin. He and Francis-drake decided the captain would take away the weak and troublesome men and leave supplies to sustain the rest.

While the ships were being unladen, a fierce storm broke. Winds roared and demons stirred up waterspouts that reached to the sky. The demons threw men from the decks into the sea. Tore down the hills near the shore and flung up new ones. Smashed ships against the shoals and sent them under the waves. Men and women with skin as black as charred wood washed onto the sand. They were slaves taken by the captain in a far land. The storm lasted three days.

Ralf-lane decided to leave the island. Everything useful was brought to the remaining ships when the angry winds rose again. John-white's drawings flew into the waves. Also the basket of pearls for Kwin-lissa-bet. I was aboard the *Francis* when the spirits spewed it from the tempest onto a calm sea. There were men who never made it to the ships and were left behind.

The captain studied his maps to determine where the winds had come from. But I already knew. Wingina's powerful conjurors had raised the storms that drove away the English. In this manner they avenged the death of their weroance. I began to wonder if the montoac of the natives was stronger than that of the English after all.

Was it a mistake for me to have befriended the English? Would I be punished for it? At least the gods had allowed me to survive. For now.

Chapter 12

From the Papers of Sir Walter Ralegh

A Letter from Lady Catherine

Sir Walter, I have made a poem for Her Majesty, which I copy here for your eyes also. (It is not the one you composed, but one that befits my humbler state.) It is crammed with fine praise, and I am pleased with the rhyme. Thus:

As that new domain, the VIRGIN land,
One part of your kingdom, submits to you;
So I, one maid, from mine own hand
Submit this praise that is your due:

All desire but few deserve
A place in your affection.
All I seek is but to serve
You, joying in my election.

My life I trust you to preserve
By granting your protection.

And when from pleasing you I swerve,
I beg for your correction.

A poem is a powerful thing, I find. What my tears and
pleas did not accomplish, my verses did. She calls me her Cat
again! I purr! I am content, save for one thing I lack: your love.
Alas I, too, find it is easier to write my feelings than to
speak them.
Your affectionate
Cat. Archer

What does she mean by that last sentence? Does she accuse
me? Why should one speak words, when actions will do more? Is
writing not an action?

My Catherine pretends humility, yet is proud of her verses.
They are indeed passable. Amazing, that a maid should show a
poet's wit! I like her even better.

Memorandum

30 July 1586. Sir Francis Drake has docked in Plymouth with
half his fleet, some cargo pillaged from Spanish colonies in Florida, and all my colonists.

Damn Ralph Lane. I never gave permission for him to leave
the island, or his pack of sorry dogs, slinking home with their tails
between their legs. What fears did Drake, that dandified pirate,
arouse to make him abandon all our efforts there? Lane protested
he had been abandoned without supplies. But on the first of May I
dispatched Grenville with a relief ship. Damn him, too, for sailing
around robbing Spanish frigates for his own profit! The delay has
cost me my colony.

The queen is angry with Grenville and with Lane, whom she

has dismissed from her service. The fool Tarleton, drawn like a vulture to carnage, mocked their failure in Virginia—and my own. "They are no men, if a hundred of them cannot subdue a single virgin, but run away when she throws a tempest."

10 August 1586
Dear brother Carew,

By now you have no doubt heard of my setback. Reassure our investors they have not been defrauded. Do not heed the malicious reports of those disgruntled men who magnify the dangers of Virginia. No worthwhile enterprise is without risk, and those who take chances most deserve to be rewarded.

Thomas Harriot still has a favorable view of our prospects for success, citing the many resources, including the healthful uppowoc (which the Spanish call tobacco). He has no doubt that in time even greater riches will be discovered—if not by us, then by Spain.

He is writing a treatise and John White works on his drawings. Those that survived the storm strike the mind with their strangeness, yet convey our common humanity. My favorite is the depiction of a dancing conjuror, who but for his nakedness resembles Dick Tarleton. When published, Harriot's report and White's drawings will induce more men to try their fortunes in that land of wonders.

For true it is that the appetite for newness is never sated. Fashions change with the wind, and anything exotic is desired by all the moment it appears. Thus I may yet hope that my Virginia, a blushing maid dressed all in feathers and furs, will attract many suitors.

Your brother, Walter

Memorandum

Concerning Manteo. I did not expect to find such worthiness in one of the savages of Virginia, but Manteo daily surprises me with his excellent judgment and quick mind. His command of our tongue is better than a Frenchman's, and happily he lacks their affectation of speaking through the nose.

Concerning the Indians and the best means of governing them, he concedes they are divided by long-standing grudges and their alliances shift constantly.

"Do they understand their prosperity depends on their submission to the English queen and her deputies?" I asked.

Manteo hesitated. "We understand laws that are just. We understand the English are very powerful."

I said I was angry at Lane for the killing of Wingina and asked if he thought it had been justified.

Manteo thought before replying, for it was his nature to be circumspect.

"It is better to be feared than loved, so I have heard."

I was astonished to hear him quoting Machiavelli like a statesman. Harriot's lessons have been wide-ranging indeed.

The business of diplomacy had made me crave a pipe, so I asked Manteo if he had some of that uppowoc. Smiling, he produced two pipes and placed some shredded leaves into their bowls. We lit them and drank in the fragrant smoke. I could feel the ill humors being purged from my body. Assuredly my next voyage will meet with more success.

A dream. I saw my Catherine with the stem of a pipe in her mouth. The pipe became my fingers touching her puckered lips as we breathed together the ambrosial smoke. Like the Indian women in John White's drawings, she wore an apron of deerskin at her waist and nothing more. Her long black hair fell forward, hiding nature's twin delights. I started up in my bed and the vision fled. Dismayed, I arose and wrote her a passionate letter, for I could not confine my thoughts within a verse.

1 September 1586. Another plot to kill Elizabeth has been uncovered by Walsingham's network of spies. The king of Spain and the Jesuits promoted it and Anthony Babington—a known papist—was to carry out the deed. Fourteen others stand accused of treason. An intercepted letter proves that Queen Mary endorsed the plot. At last she will be tried for her treason. As for Babington, he lies in the Tower awaiting his due: hanging and disembowelment.

10 September 1586. Now some whisper the evidence against Mary was forged and Babington framed. Indeed, why would Babington turn traitor? He has too much to lose: lands, title, all his wealth—which the queen will now certainly give to Walsingham.

15 September 1586

To John White

Painter-Stainers Guildhouse, London

I request your attendance at Durham House to discuss your role in a proposed third voyage to Virginia. You know Grenville landed at Roanoke just after your departure in the hurricane and left fifteen men to defend the fort. Their numbers must be reinforced at the earliest opportunity.

Thomas Harriot and the savage Manteo affirm you are a man more disposed to peaceful understanding of the natives than to violence against them. As well, they testify to your love for Virginia, which favorably distinguishes you from those malcontents who complain about the hardships there.

The queen requires my service in her lawless counties of

southern Ireland. Thus while my own ambitions tend toward Virginia, I must obey Her Majesty, on whom all our lives and fortunes depend. May God continue to preserve her.

Yours sincerely,
Sir Walter Ralegh

Chapter 13

Bold Dreams

Sir Walter's amorous letter set my cheeks on fire. I cannot imagine wearing a deerskin about my waist. What gives men such thoughts?

I hid the letter among the others tied in the wrinkled handkerchief. I had stopped thinking of it as the queen's handkerchief, or even Ralegh's. It was mine, a token of his love. The queen had Sir Walter's loyalty, but his heart was given to me. Mine was the memory of his kiss, his hands touching my hair and face. And mine was the knowledge of his secret ambition to rule Virginia himself.

How hard it was to keep this all within me! Not to betray, by a slipped word or letter carelessly laid, that I loved Sir Walter. No doubt everyone thought my happiness resulted from being in the queen's graces again. Anne, however, was still out of favor and aggrieved because of it.

"It's not fair that Elizabeth should forgive you and not me," she complained one day as we sat in the gallery with our embroidery. "I have served her longer, and we are cousins." She stabbed at the cloth with her needle.

"But *she* is the queen's Cat," Frances said, narrowing her eyes at me. "Don't you know you can throw a cat from a wall and she will always land on her feet?"

"What are you jealous of, Frances?" Emme said. "You have the queen's ear."

"Yes, and I'll wager you have shared more confidences than any of Walsingham's spies," I said. "Whatever you disapprove of, you cannot help but reveal."

Anne turned to Frances. "Was it you who turned the queen against Thomas Graham?" she accused.

Frances did not even look up from her needlework. "Why do you blame me? Do you think she didn't know about you and Graham already? Anyone with eyes could see you were in love with him."

"Just be warned," said Anne, her eyes flashing. "If either of you dares to take a lover, I will tell the queen and see that you suffer as I do!"

"Catherine is the one you ought to watch," said Frances coolly. "She is often distracted, and I have heard her reciting poetry when she is alone. She must be thinking of a secret love."

I felt my pulse quicken. Again I wondered what Frances knew about Sir Walter and me. But I would not bear her smug teasing.

"Don't bother to watch Frances," I said to Anne. "No man will ever fall in love with her." I tossed aside my needlework and left the gallery.

Later I complained to Emme, "I am weary of these games we play with each other."

"You could endure them before you fell in love with Sir Walter," she said.

"Hush! I am *not* in love with him," I lied. "He only helped me write some verses for the queen."

Emme shook her head. "It's as plain as the nose on your face, to a friend who knows you well."

"Do Frances and Anne suspect?" I whispered.

"I don't know," Emme said. "But you must be more discreet and hide your feelings. Sir Walter is the queen's favorite, and she would be most angry to learn of your love."

"But it is so unfair!" I burst out. "He is half her age. She will never marry him or anyone else. Why shouldn't I be free to love whom I will? Why shouldn't Anne marry Graham? Are *you* content to let the queen rule your feelings?"

Emme shrugged. "That is the way of our world."

"When you are in love, you will not be so sanguine."

"I have thought about this," said Emme. "I will let the queen choose my husband, and then I will choose whom to love. It may be my husband, or it may be another. For once a woman is married, the queen can no longer rule her heart."

I regarded Emme with astonishment. I wished I could be as practical and sure of myself. She was a sturdy bark navigating the rough waters of the queen's court, while I was a shallow wherry, always in danger of capsizing.

That summer the queen was peevish, prone to outbursts and harsh accusations. Walsingham scurried through the halls, his beadlike eyes darting back and forth, and Robert Dudley was often in the queen's privy chamber. When an ashen-faced Earl of Shrewsbury was called in, we knew the furtive business concerned the Scottish queen. Then Shrewsbury's former page, one Anthony Babington, was arrested for plotting to assassinate Elizabeth and put Mary on her throne. After being hanged, Babington—still alive—was disemboweled, then quartered and beheaded. Balladeers sang the news of the gruesome death, which made me sick to think about. The damning piece of evidence against Mary was a letter written in her hand, approving the plot. The wily queen smuggled out her correspondence in a box hidden in a cask of beer, but the wilier Walsingham discovered it.

I ran to the chest where my own letters were hidden. They were still there, resting beside a pair of too-small shoes atop a hornbook from my childhood. Usually I placed the bundle beneath the hornbook. And the knot in the handkerchief seemed looser. Had I tied it carelessly? I undid the knot, thumbed through the letters, and assured myself nothing was missing. I folded the handkerchief and placed it in the toe of a shoe. I tied a ribbon around the letters and hid them inside my mattress. I determined to burn them at the earliest opportunity, for the Babington affair had frightened me.

The Scottish queen stood trial for her treason, which upset my royal mistress so much one would have thought she, not Mary, was to be judged. She could not eat. I set a platter of stew before her, but she pushed it away so violently it spilled all over my skirt before hitting the floor, where the dogs fell upon it.

"She sought every opportunity to betray me. She must die," Elizabeth said to the dogs. "But she is my cousin, my own flesh and blood!" She slammed her palms onto the table and stood up, shouting for Lord Burghley, her secretary of state.

I stood in the shadows, holding my breath, while the queen argued with Burghley.

"Mary is an anointed queen. If I consent to her execution, I am guilty of regicide. What will stop my own people from granting me that same death?" she said, her voice shrill.

The dogs crept to my feet, cringing there.

"She must die," Burghley insisted. "As long as she lives to give hope to papists and other disgruntled subjects, your life will be in danger."

But Elizabeth would not consent, and the matter remained unresolved.

That fall, Sir Walter and I used such caution in our courtship that our letters were few and brief, carried by his valet or another of his trusted servants. One or two came by way of Emme, though I forbade her to take any risk for my sake. Meanwhile I lived in anticipation of Accession Day, the November holiday when all the realm celebrated the anniversary of the queen's coronation. I knew I would see Sir Walter at the jousting and feasting. For days on end bells pealed, fireworks exploded, and the glow of bonfires lit the sky. In the streets hawkers sang ballads and psalms celebrating the queen's deliverance from the evil conspirators.

Awaiting the start of the tournament, I stood in the tilt gallery at Whitehall with Elizabeth and all her ladies. The gallery over-looked the tiltyard, on the far side of which stood a colorful pavilion hung with banners. Spectators filled the galleries surrounding the yard. I watched as the knights arrived—some in glittering chariots and artful disguises—to greet the queen before riding to the tilt-yard. I tried to guess which one was Ralegh. My gaze was drawn to a knight in burnished armor engraved with twining leaves. He carried a bow and arrow in one hand and a leafy branch in the other. When he removed his helm with a flourish, I saw that it was Sir Walter.

A cry of delight escaped me but no one marked it. Everyone's attention was on the splendid figure climbing the stairs to greet the queen on Ralegh's behalf. He wore loose leggings of chamois and a tooled silver gorget around his neck. Above his ankles were matching silver greaves. His wide brown chest was bare, showing the raised markings on his skin. Streaks of red paint decorated his cheeks and his long hair was plaited with feathers. It was Manteo! I could not take my eyes off him, not even to gaze on Sir Walter below.

"The Savage Knight greets you, O great English weroance," he said, then began to recite:

> *"From the New World he hails,*
> *Virginia she is named,*
> *And in her forests, rivers, and dales,*
> *Your virtue is proclaimed."*

He mispronounced a word or two but not a single lady laughed. He ended with a plea to let him—that is, Ralegh—go to Virginia and *"with the touch of my own hand, bring under your sway all that wild land."*

Our applause sputtered like fire doused with water, for Elizabeth was not smiling.

"The messenger pleases me," she said. "But tell your master I like not his message."

She held out her hand for Manteo to kiss. I watched in fascination as he took her small white hand in his tawny one and brought it to his lips.

Manteo then retreated down the stairs to join Sir Walter, who spurred his horse, scattering gravel as he galloped toward the tilt-yard. Entering the lists, he unhorsed his first opponent, who clattered to the ground and lay there trapped in his armor. Ralegh struck the shield of his second opponent so hard his lance shivered and cracked, and he raised the broken shaft toward the gallery. Was it a salute or a show of defiance? I glanced at the queen, who smiled as if the triumph were hers.

When the tournament ended, we hurried to dress Elizabeth for the banquet. Her damask gown was set with pearls and rubies, and she wore a matching headdress and a ruff made of Belgian lace. She glowed from the jewels and from the admiration of her knights. Concerns of state seemed far from her mind. At the feast I drank a little wine and danced with Emme and Frances while hoping to catch Sir Walter's eye. I laughed myself to tears at the antics of Dick Tarleton, who pranced around on a hobbyhorse, mocking the tournament. I sipped more wine and its heat rushed to my face, making me bold. While dancers performed a masque, I glanced around the audience until I saw Sir Walter. He looked in an ill humor, frowning with his arms crossed over his chest. When he met my gaze he raised his eyebrows and pointed to the dancers. But I wanted to watch him, not the masque.

When the musicians had played their final notes, I made my way through the crowd until I was standing beside him. My arm brushed against his sleeve. His fingers grazed the back of my hand, then my palm. The touch was light but the shiver of desire went deep.

"Why do you look so unhappy?" I asked in a low voice.

"You saw how Her Majesty rebuked me at the tournament. She will not support another voyage to Virginia because the last one failed."

I had heard Ralph Lane's men were more interested in fighting and destroying villages than in building a colony, and they had killed an Indian leader.

"That was your own fault, Sir Walter," I scolded him. "For there was no man's wife or mother or sister among your colonists to restrain their bad natures."

"What do you mean?" he asked, turning to face me.

"A colony peopled by soldiers and adventurers with no stake

in their common welfare is a colony that must fail. A man with a wife and a family will be more inclined to live peaceably with the Indians than to provoke a war with them."

Now Sir Walter had drawn me aside. "Go on, Cat. Tell me more," he said.

"Has it occurred to you that you must have women as well as men for your colony to thrive? Why, how else will you multiply the queen's subjects?" I felt myself blush. But I was excited, too, as the idea unfolded inside me. "Perhaps, Sir Walter, if the queen saw you intended to settle Virginia with families who would make a livelihood there, she might change her mind." I saw his face brighten. "And if you were to insist on going there yourself, rather than sending a lieutenant to govern, she would see you are serious about its success." My voice had risen, and heads turned in our direction.

The queen had also noticed us. She lifted her cup.

"Too much wine? Time for a sip of water instead?" she said, looking from me to Ralegh.

For a moment I was confused, my wits clouded by the wine. I saw Frances sneering and Anne with her hand over her mouth. Finally I realized the queen was rebuking me. And claiming Ralegh for herself.

Lightly as a dancer, Sir Walter stepped to her side. "I shall pour it out myself and slake Your Majesty's thirst," he said.

Now Emme was beside me, tugging me down onto a stool.

"Didn't I tell you to be more discreet?" she whispered. "Why, the whole court saw how he looked at you!"

But I did not care. The idea I described to Ralegh was blossoming further, and with it my hopes. He would persuade the queen to let him go to Virginia. I would flee the court and, disguising myself if necessary, board his ship. At sea I would reveal myself, Sir

Walter would declare his love, and we would be married. He would govern the Indians wisely, and I would be the first Englishwoman to live in that paradise, the New World, united with my heart's desire.

It was a lovely dream.

Chapter 14

Fortune's Wheel Turns

My hopes of escaping to a new life sustained me throughout the difficult months of winter. The queen was always in an ill humor from her many ailments. Chief among them was an abscess on her gums from a rotting tooth, which she refused to have pulled because it would leave a gap in her smile. The tooth prevented her from eating and she was peevish with hunger and pain. Also, her breath smelled foul, so it was unpleasant to be near her. Not a day went by when she did not revile one of us. I even saw Frances leaving her chamber in tears.

Only one person, Dick Tarleton, dared to jest in her presence. I had brought the queen a drink of mint and parsley to sweeten her mouth and there he was, strumming his lute.

"My royal mistress suffers a great abscess on her body politic. She will not be well until the Scottish queen is lanced and bleeds," he said.

I held my breath, expecting a tirade, but she only waved him away.

"Begone, fool," she said wearily. "I would be alone now."

So he plied his wit among the ladies as we sat doing needle-work and listening to Lady Mary read from a book of sonnets.

"Pish! Poetry is lies," he said when she paused to turn the page. "And who is more fond of poetry than lovers? Believe no man who swears he loves, and believe no man who rhymes his love. There-fore, believe no man."

Frances smiled. Anne, beside her, looked forlorn.

"By your logic, Dick, we should not believe you," I said. "Unless you are no man."

"Better to be no man than woe-man," he said, winking.

"It is a woman's woe to be in love with a lying man," said Emme.

"My lover was no liar," protested Anne. "And my woe is to be separated from him."

"All lovers are liars; they love to lie in secret," said Tarleton. "Yet beware of hiding love. I know a lady who hid her love so well that when she went looking for it she could not remember where she put it." He grimaced. "Someone found it and stole it away."

I started, pricking myself with my needle. Were the fool's jest-ing words meant for me? I thought of Sir Walter's hidden letters. I had not burned them after all. Once I had tried, crouching before the hearth at midnight with the bundle in my hands. But I could not destroy those scented pages with their words of love, the verses crafted solely for my eyes.

As soon as Dick Tarleton skipped out and the ladies were gos-siping again, I slipped away to the dormitory. Reaching into my mattress, I felt for the bundle of letters. Only dry rushes scratched my fingers. I groped further, checking every corner. Nothing. I pulled the rushes out and scattered them all over the floor in des-peration. No letters. Had I put them back in my chest? I threw it open and rummaged to the very bottom, but the familiar bundle was missing. I reached into the old shoe, where I had stuffed the handkerchief. It was empty. I threw it aside. There was no mistaking the terrible truth: the evidence of my secret love had been stolen.

"Who has done this to me?" I wailed into my hands. Then I recalled the day I had found the contents of my chest disturbed. The correspondence from Sir Walter that had never reached me. How careless I had been! All along, someone had been watching me, intercepting Ralegh's letters, and waiting for an opportunity to steal the rest from me. Was it Anne, avenging my role in Graham's banishment? Was it Frances, spying for someone or just being spiteful? What would the thief do with the letters? Try to betray or blackmail me? I wished I had overcome my vain desires and burned the letters months ago.

I put the stuffing back in my mattress, cleaned up the dormitory, and pondered my choices. To accuse anyone would lead only to denial; even to ask questions would raise suspicions about me. It was better to pretend nothing was amiss and watch my companions closely. But in the days that followed, no one confronted me with the letters. Neither Frances nor Anne behaved as if she were guilty. Nor did the queen treat me any differently, and I concluded she did not know of the letters. I considered warning Sir Walter, but I was afraid even to put ink to paper, lest the letter be intercepted.

After a week I could stand the suspense no longer, so I told Emme about the theft. As she listened, her eyes grew wide with innocent dismay. At least I knew that she could never have taken the letters.

"Remember, they are written in Ralegh's hand. When they come to light—that is, *if* they do—you must deny you returned any of his favors," she advised. "Let him explain himself."

A terrible thought occurred to me. "Emme, what if someone has seized the letters I wrote to him?"

"If he is wise, he will have burned them."

"And I was a fool and did not!" I lamented. "Though I meant to."

But Emme only pursed her lips and shook her head.

When weeks had passed without incident, Emme asked if I had burned the letters after all.

I thought back to the night I had sat before the fire with the letters in my hand. "Perhaps I did and was too tired to remember it," I mused. "For they did cost me many a sleepless night."

But still I was doubtful and tense, as if on tenterhooks. Fortunately the queen was too occupied with matters of state to notice a distracted maid. Her Privy Council was pressing her to decide the fate of the Scottish queen. Every day brought new rumors that Mary had escaped from prison or the Spaniards had invaded England. I thought Elizabeth would break down with the strain. One night she screamed in her sleep and we all rushed to her chamber in fear, only to discover that she was having a nightmare about her cousin.

I had a nightmare, too, in which pages of the missing letters and poems fluttered around me. I tried to catch them and hide them under my skirt while the faces of Frances, Anne, Lady Veronica, Dick Tarleton, and even Emme leered at me and Sir Walter danced with the queen. I awoke with tears on my cheeks, feeling alone and despairing. At least the Scottish queen, though betrayed by a letter, had loyal friends about her.

Indeed I pitied the poor Queen Mary. Elizabeth finally signed the warrant for her death, and on the eighth day of February she was beheaded in Northamptonshire. I noted the date because it was my birthday, which should have been a joyful occasion. But the celebrations that broke out all over London, with bursting fireworks and burning effigies, only filled me with grief for the dead queen. Yes, she had conspired against England's sovereign queen. But

I, too, might take such desperate measures in order to free myself from prison. How had Mary borne it for twenty years?

I had served the queen now for almost four years, and what had I to show for it? A nickname. Some nice clothing, daily food, and a bed to sleep in. Yet I hardly felt secure. Constant worry attended me. I had seen my mistress shift her favors like a weathercock whirled around by contrary winds. I had few friends and the court was a stewpot of envy, backbiting, and deceit. Now someone near me held a dangerous secret—a bundle of poems and an embroidered handkerchief—that could ruin me and Sir Walter. His downfall would be the result of my own carelessness.

After Queen Mary's death there was no rejoicing in Elizabeth's chambers. Her eyes were puffy with weeping and lack of sleep. One morning while we were dressing her, she tore off her ruff and threw it at me.

"Take this damned frill from my neck. It torments me!"

I had starched the thing to a perfect stiffness, but the narrow sticks sewn into the ruff had poked her, leaving red marks on her neck.

"And take this gown off me. I will wear black for my cousin."

Emme and Frances hurried off to the wardrobe while Lady Veronica and I undressed the queen. She stood shivering in her smock.

"I shall have to answer to God for this," she whispered to her reflection in the glass.

"Hers was the sin. Your Majesty is just," murmured Veronica.

"My councilors tricked me," Elizabeth continued, giving no sign that she had heard Veronica. "The warrant was delivered without my knowledge. Walsingham always wanted her dead. It was his doing."

I was stunned. Had Walsingham defied Elizabeth and murdered the Scottish queen? How could he have dared to do so?

Elizabeth started. "Say nothing to anyone," she said sharply. "Forget those words, which came from my grief." She turned from her glass and looked closely at Veronica, then at me. "I may trust my own ladies, may I not? You will never lie to me?" Her tone was more pleading than commanding.

As she stood there without her wig or her makeup, I saw her simply as a woman like any of us, but older, with bad teeth and graying hair.

"You know I am true," Veronica assured her.

The words stuck in my throat, but I forced them out. "Nor will I deceive Your Majesty, for I love you." And I bent down to retrieve her cast-off garments.

When the queen summoned me to her chamber one evening, I expected her to request a cordial or a cup of milk or a book from her library. Her back was to me as I curtseyed and greeted her.

She whirled around and began to revile me. "You crook your knee to me, Catherine Archer? You with the wayward, crooked heart."

My heart clenched to hear her say my true name, and with such a dire tone.

"What do you mean, Your Majesty? My maiden heart is true."

"*Are* you a maid?"

"How can you doubt that?" I cried, sinking to my knees.

And yet I knew the answer. I heard a rustling and, without even looking up, I knew she was holding Sir Walter's letters. Whoever had stolen them had waited until the Scottish queen was dead and Elizabeth could turn to new intrigues.

She unfolded a page and read aloud, *"At a table spread with treats, One tasty morsel tempted me.* Did Sir Walter bite that morsel? On the lips?" She threw the letter aside and picked up another. *"Double words do double duty, Praising one and another's beauty.* This is what I think of your double dealing!" She ripped the page in half. The two pieces fluttered to the floor in front of me. She read from a third letter—one that had never reached me—crumpled it, and threw it at me.

"How did you come by them?" I asked in a hoarse whisper.

"No, how did *you* come by *this*?" She flourished the embroidered handkerchief in front of me.

"Sir Walter gave it to me," I said, forgetting Emme's advice to deny everything. What was the point in lying now? "And those letters are mine, too," I added.

For a moment the queen was silent. I think she expected me to deny the letters. "Everything is mine," she said coldly. "Get up."

I obeyed. Her eyes, level with mine, flashed with anger and hurt.

"You deceived me, Catherine. I expect to be betrayed by papists and Spaniards, even by my own cousin," she said. Her voice trembled, then grew firm again. "Not by those I have entrusted with the care of my own person."

Her words stung me, so unjust did they seem. I knew I should beg her forgiveness, but for what? Nothing in those letters could harm her.

"How do I betray you by loving another?" I heard myself say. "Are you the only one who can be loved?" I went on, more boldly still. "I can love Sir Walter without diminishing the love I owe Your Grace."

"Sir Walter cannot be yours. He. Is. Mine!" She threw the words at me one by one, like a handful of stones. "I have made him from nothing and lifted him over the others." Her forehead and cheeks were bright red with anger. "You were also nothing until I favored you. But I see you have entirely forgotten that."

"No, I have not forgotten," I said forlornly. I could see my good fortune sinking like a wrecked ship. What was left for me to cling to but my pride? So I looked my queen in the eye and said, "I would gladly be nothing again, and thus be free to choose my own love."

"So be it," she said, shaking with rage. "You will not serve me or feel the warmth of my favor ever again. You are nothing to me." She threw open the door and shouted to her guards, "Take her to the Tower!"

The Tower? Too stunned to protest, I let the guards lead me away. Over my shoulder I could see the queen feeding pages into the fire, its red glow illuminating her face.

I never saw my royal mistress again.

Part II

Chapter 15

In the Tower

It was not the queen's grand barge that carried me down the Thames to the Tower but a creaking wherry pitched to and fro by the waves. Garbage bobbed on the water and a drowned cat floated by. I leaned over the side and retched, sick with misery and dread. I had left Whitehall without being allowed to say good-bye to anyone. I took with me only what I could fit into my small trunk, the one that had held the letters that undid me. Water sloshed around my feet. The wherry passed the wharf where we disembarked on my first visit to the Tower. It slipped under a rusted portcullis known as the Traitor's Gate, where the filth of the river gathered, and bumped against a jetty green with slime. Climbing out of the wherry I slipped and nearly fell in the water, but the guard caught me. And so, like a criminal I entered the Tower, my sodden skirt dragging behind me, my heart like a great stone in my chest.

My prison was a small room furnished with a bed, a bench, and a table. It had a single high, narrow window. If I stood on the bench I could see through it to a simple paved courtyard below. Though the room was damp, there were rush mats on the floor and a fireplace. It would have been comfortable under different circumstances. The bed was even hung with faded curtains. Someone of high status had been confined here before me. Was it the conspirator Babington? I imagined his head on a spike over the Tower gate, a warning to all England. Entering by the water, I had thankfully been spared that sight. Yet there was little else to gladden me in the room, and nothing to do but to wait there and ponder my fate.

When the heavy door closed behind me and the bolt on the other side fell into place, I began to weep loudly. Magnified by the bare walls, the sound was frightful, like the roaring of the lion in the queen's *menagerie.* So I cried noiselessly, letting the tears trickle down my face. I cried over the cruelty of my mistress and because I realized I no longer loved her. Soon I had no more tears.

In this notorious prison, I was surprised not to be mistreated. A guard delivered my food, took away my chamber pot, and brought me clean water for washing. My soiled linens were laundered, though they were returned to me none too clean. I asked for something to read, and the guard brought me a Bible well-thumbed by other prisoners. Thinking to try my hand at another poem, I asked for ink and paper but he shook his head. He may as well have been mute. Every few days he led me outside, where I was permitted to walk around the courtyard. I had no visitors and no one to talk to.

The long days passed into weeks. I felt spring arrive in the air that blew through the narrow window. I missed Emme and Lady Mary. Had everyone forgotten me? I wondered if Sir Walter had felt the queen's wrath. Was he also in the Tower awaiting judgment? What crime had either of us committed? Surely there were malefactors more dangerous than an outspoken maid and a knight who sent her amorous verses. I expected the queen would release me once she thought I had suffered enough.

And what then? When I thought of her fury, I had no hope she would ever forgive me. Even if by some miracle she did, I could not return to her service as if nothing had happened. Nor could I bear being sent back to the country to live in disgrace with my uncle's family. I began to think I preferred the lonely Tower to the queen's palace or my uncle's house.

But what I most desired now—to go to Virginia with Sir Walter—seemed impossible. And the letter that I finally received from Emme made my vain dream vanish altogether.

My dear Catherine,

I have cried over you nearly every day since you were taken away. I was in the hall and overheard what you said to Her Majesty. (Your brave words are already legendary among the ladies.) I wish I could visit you in that dreadful place and console you, for there is no happiness without a friend nearby. But I dare not. The queen will permit no one to speak of you. It is dangerous even to write this.

Unfortunately, your W.R. did not suffer as you do. No, she still dotes on him, so much that she has made him Captain of her Guard and he must stand by her at all times. It is unjust that he should be rewarded while you are punished. I have told him that he is a coward who does not deserve your love.

Catherine—I know who stole your letters. Indeed she makes no secret of it. You will not be surprised that it was Frances. She took them first to Anne, offering her the chance to betray you, but Anne would not touch them, saying, "Do it yourself." Now Anne weeps with guilt for what has happened

to you. She admits she did not stop Frances because she
wanted you to lose W.R. as she did her T.G. She wants me to
tell you she wishes she had taken the letters from Frances
and burned them.

I do not need to ask Frances why she betrayed you. Of
course she envied you your nickname. She also hates lovers,
because she has none. (Does she think spying will make the
queen love her?) And she envied our friendship, yours and
mine, from the day you arrived. Now that you are away, she
thinks I must be her friend again. But I will not speak to her.
Indeed she is hated by everyone. So you see we are all in a
turmoil here over you. If only none of this had happened, or
that I had happier news to write—

Come what may, never forget your dearest friend, E.M.

I held Emme's letter to my cheek. I was grateful for the pains
she had taken to write and pleased to think of Frances being hated.
I began to fill my empty hours dreaming up plots to torment her.
Though I had little hope of ever being able to enact them, it gave
me a little comfort to reflect that I had plenty of wit, while Frances's
would fit within her thimble. Still, she was in the queen's favor, and
I was in the Tower.

If Emme could manage to write, I wondered, why couldn't Sir
Walter? Surely his every waking moment was not spent beside the
queen. While she slept, could he not write to me? While she was
awake, could he not persuade her to release me? There could
be only one reason he did neither of these things: he did not love
me. Rather, he loved the queen. I flung myself on the bed, overcome
with fresh tears. So let him enjoy his doubtful reward, waiting on
the aging Elizabeth all his days, bearing her changeable moods

and incessant demands! My love had turned sour, and disappointment rankled in me like a wound.

Some days after receiving Emme's letter, I had a visitor at last:
the gray-bearded Earl of Leicester. He was red-faced and short of
breath from climbing the stairs. When the guard admitted him,
then closed the door without bolting it, I expected to hear I was
being released. But Leicester looked morose.

"I've come at Her Majesty's bidding," he said.

"I thought so." My voice sounded hoarse from disuse. "No one
would dare come otherwise, because of the manifest danger I pose."

"I am sorry for your plight, my lady. You do not deserve it," he
said gently.

"Does Sir Walter deserve his? That is a harsh punishment, to
be made Captain of the Guard," I said with a mocking smile.

"Walter Ralegh is an ass!" Leicester's face turned purple.

I stared in surprise, then remembered he had long been the
queen's favorite. He must be jealous of Ralegh, who was younger,
handsomer, and now far more favored.

"She gave him all of the traitor Babington's estates. He has never
been wealthier," he grumbled.

"Has the queen decided to give me anything?" I asked, anger
growing in me. "Will I be released?"

"That is the matter of my visit," he said, letting out a long sigh
that did not bode well for me.

"She will not put me on trial—or will she?" I asked.

"God, no!" he said. "You are no traitor. She would not dare."

"Does she mean to return me to my uncle in Wiltshire?"

"Alas, I wish that were her will. But it is a harsher fate she has
in mind for you, one that I would spare a lady of your tender age
and upbringing—"

"Just tell me, please!"

He clasped his hands together and his eyebrows lifted in an expression of grief and sympathy.

"Sit down, my lady, for you look pale."

"I will hear my fate while standing on my feet," I said, losing all patience with his wordy delays.

"Her Majesty has decreed your banishment! A ship sails tomorrow and you, my lady, are to be on board."

My thoughts leapt with a fearful anticipation. I saw vessels moored at Billingsgate, swarming with sun-browned mariners loading cargo for distant parts of the world.

"Destined for? The ship goes where?" I asked, unable to put my words together.

"To a barbarous place, that one day, through the presence of those such as yourself, may develop into a civil society—"

"Not Ireland!" I cried, thinking of warring peasants and forsaken bogs.

Leicester held up his hand and shook his head sadly. "My lady, that would be a mercy. No, it is the colony on Roanoke Island. I am sorry for you."

He looked away and thus did not see the smile spreading over my face. I felt like dancing a jig.

"But who? Why? How did this come about?" I asked, hardly able to believe my good fortune.

He turned to me and replied, "You have Ralegh, that horse's ass, to thank for your doubtful and dangerous freedom."

Chapter 16

From the Papers of Sir Walter Ralegh

Memorandum

13 March 1587. C.A. was a very foolish maid not to destroy those letters and then to defy Her Majesty. I know where I must worship and how to pray for mercy, and thus was spared the Tower. Then, to my surprise, she gave me Babington's estates, which even I expected Walsingham to receive. He falls while I rise; such is the way of this world. The income will permit me to send more colonists to Virginia.

The bigger prize, the captaincy of her guard, seems to me more punishment than reward. It keeps me at the queen's side like a dog on a chain. The other night she called upon me to scratch her back, saying she had an itch that could not be satisfied. What could be more humiliating? Yet this would be a most desirable office were my C.A. nearby. Think how easily we might meet, even pass the night together.

Ah, my mistress knows exactly what she does. She keeps C.A. locked up to punish me.

25 March. Today I have been so altered in my thinking I hardly know myself anymore.

The maid called Emme has been continually frowning at me, and I was determined to know the reason. So, passing her in the hall, I asked if her lovely forehead pained her.

"'Tis the sight of you that pains me," she said. Then she drew me into the empty wardrobe, where she began to denounce me as a rank opportunist and a villain. "My friend languishes in the Tower while you proudly prance around here in your new livery," she said, with a disdainful eye toward my suit.

I defended myself, saying Lady Catherine's indiscretion had caused the queen to be embarrassed, and once Her Majesty's mood recovered, she would no doubt return.

"And how long will that be, for one who is innocent? The indiscretion was all yours, Sir Walter Ralegh," she said, scorning my very name. "My friend loved you truly, but you only feigned your love in verses."

I admit she startled me. "She loved me, you say? But she refused my kisses. We barely touched one another."

"An honorable man considers the lack of looseness to be a virtue in a woman," Emme said coldly.

I thought I knew the marks of love in a woman: the desiring looks, the coy refusals followed by the revelation of a bit of the breast. Now I am not sure. Catherine is not like any woman I know.

"Sir Walter, right now you should be at the queen's feet, begging her mercy on Catherine's behalf. I am forbidden to speak about her, but you are so close to Her Majesty's heart you could ask her for anything." Every word of hers rebuked me most harshly.

I thought of the estates and other favors that could yet be withdrawn, putting the Virginia expedition at risk, if I displeased my queen now. As I hesitated Emme struck again.

"Do you know Catherine stood before the queen and proclaimed her love for you? Was that not brave? Had you a similar courage, you might be a man worthy of her love. But you are not."

She pushed me out of the wardrobe and into the hallway, where I stood as if paralyzed.

Now I cannot sleep. I see my Catherine resolute before the queen, defying her with her words. Like a fool expecting the king to see truth in his antics. I did not know the maid possessed such greatness of mind.

What could she gain by her defiance? Nothing. She lost everything rather than deny her love for me. I must adore her for it, though she despise me. Indeed I despise myself. I threw her into the lion's den while I sat at a fine table feeding my self-regard. I deserve to be flayed alive.

I swear, never again will I, Sir Walter Ralegh, be such a damnable villain in matters of love, but behave with the highest honor.

Poem

That pearl I careless cast away
Now o'er my heart asserts her sway,
And I am vowed, at any cost
To revive her trust, that I have lost.

10 April 1587. All my good intentions come to naught before my canny, heartless queen. I meant to deal honorably in the matter of C.A. but was forced into the path of deceit.

I asked if Her Majesty was prepared to forgive the poor maid, who was young and inexperienced and had no one to protect her.

"She had me. That would have been enough for any young lady in the kingdom," she retorted. "Do you dare plead for her?" Her words carried a tone of threat.

"I do, for she does not deserve her misfortune." Remembering Emme's accusations, I added, "I confess I misled her with my affections."

"How could you affect her? She is low and base. Did I show you too little love?" she asked, now petulant.

"I have repented of my infidelity to you, my sovereign mistress," I said, trying to sound humble. "Not you, but I, loved too little." The flattering words were like chalk in my mouth.

But she smiled and I went on with my calculated lies, saying I desired to be free of the maid's charms and only a great distance between us would keep me from temptation. She seemed to take my bait.

"When do your ships sail for Virginia?"

"At the end of this month, God and Your Majesty willing." Then I pretended to be startled. "Nay, I see the drift of your thoughts! That would be too cruel. I've heard the maid has a fear of wild animals. I pray you, send her to Ireland instead."

Her eyes narrowed at me. "Ireland is too near. I have decided to send her to Virginia."

That had been my intention all along, for I knew how Catherine longed to see the New World. I feigned dismay to hide my delight. But then she played her trump card on top of mine.

"As for you, my Warter, find someone to govern the colonists in your stead. I cannot permit you to go to Virginia. Ever." She smiled with satisfaction. "It is too far from me."

I had lost the game.

21 April 1587
To Capt. John White,

> *The voyage will proceed, although I am prevented by a*
> *...than my own from governing Virginia with my*

own hand. Therefore I designate you as my lieutenant governor with authority over matters of law, military discipline, and the ordering of civil society.

Your first duty will be to relieve the fifteen men left by Grenville to safeguard the fort. Second, remove everything of use and value from the settlement and depart for Chesapeake, where the land is open and fruitful, the bay more easily navigable for trade. There you will establish a permanent settlement and name it "Ralegh." Supply ships will be dispatched to that region.

Manteo is to be installed as Lord of the Croatoan and Roanoke. His loyalty and judgment give me confidence he can govern his fellow savages and persuade them to peaceful relations with us.

For you and your assistants, Simon Fernandes, Ananias Dare, et al, I have had coats of arms devised, making you gentlemen, that all may know the colony will be governed by men of good standing.

I also entrust to you one Catherine Archer, who, through no fault of her own, has displeased Her Majesty. She is a maid most virtuous and dear to my heart, besides possessing a rare wit for a woman. Enclosed are the wardship papers and the monies to support her for as long as she shall need your protection. I desire that she be a free woman of sufficient means, servant to no man or woman, until she shall choose a husband of her own liking.

Yours,

Sir W.R.

P.S. Please hand the enclosed letter to the Lady Catherine <u>before you sail</u>.

To the Lady Catherine Archer
My dear,

    To convince you of my truth, I will be plain. I have erred, not in loving you, but in failing to recognize and hence defend my feelings for you. My wrong has been shown to me by your true friend, the Lady Emme.

    Sorrow consumes me at the thought of your suffering. Her Majesty punishes me with a daily bondage which is inescapable at present. But I have dealt for your freedom in terms I pray will bring you happiness. The queen thinks your exile a harsh penalty (to both of us). I think it may satisfy the curious part of you that hungers for adventure.

    As for the part that used to regard me, I dare not presume it remains unchanged. I have proved myself unworthy of you. And yet if you deign to love me still, I would swim the seas to join you and be the truest man in all of Virginia.

    If you cannot forgive me, I wish you to find a worthy husband among the brave men seeking their fortunes in Virginia. John White has been entrusted with the means to enable you to live comfortably there.

    Send me a reply before the Lion *sails. Until then I will live in hope.*

    Your penitent servant,
    Walter Ralegh

Chapter 17

The *Lion* Sails

I stood on the wharf on a morning in late April, ready to begin a new life. I shaded my eyes against the sun. After so many weeks in the Tower, the light seemed painfully bright, the noises sharp and loud. The air smelled of fish and tar, wet ropes, and the promise of adventure. Before me was a freshly painted ship with three masts so tall I had to crane my neck to see the tops.

"She's called the *Lion*," said the guard who had brought me from the Tower. The sight of the ships made him talkative. "By the look of 'er she'll carry about 120 tuns." To my questioning look he replied, "A tun is a hogshead that'll hold 252 gallons of wine. She's a merchant ship, but ye will see the gunports there 'tween the decks, four on each side. She's got two anchors and a spare; just don't lose 'em all." He laughed and went on. "A Spanish galleon be much greater, but not so swift or steady; should ye meet one on the high seas it'll be like a bear that's tied to the stake, with the hound nipping and tearing at it until he brings her down."

He glanced at me. I must have looked pale. "Don't mean to

frighten ye, lady. I'm saying the *Lion* here be like the dog that can run from the bear."

I gulped at the thought of being attacked by Spanish ships. "Doesn't the bear sometimes kill the dog?" I said.

"In the arena, you mean? The queen loves the sport, don't she. Bearbaiting." The guard launched into this new topic while I studied the smaller ship moored beside the *Lion*. Three gunports faced me. I wondered how many guns were mounted on the Spanish merchant ships.

"Would the Spanish attack a ship carrying only men and food and building supplies?" I asked.

In reply, the guard pointed to the soldiers standing on the quay wearing helmets, brass gorgets over their leather jerkins, and swords at their belts.

"Them will protect ye. There be dangers on land even if ye escape those at sea, that's for certain."

I turned away to watch the ships being loaded. With seeming ease, workers slung great bundles and firkins on their shoulders or backs, treading the narrow planks that led from the wharf to to the ships' decks. Men shouted to one another, and cargo thumped and banged the decks as it was lowered into the hold. Two men struggled to push a cannon onto the *Lion*. A soldier lent a hand while the others leaned against a barrel and watched. The boarding planks threatened to break under the weight. A cart carrying a blacksmith's forge nearly crashed to the quay before it was brought under control.

I saw my fellow voyagers gathering. Some wore woolen cloaks and the plain garb of tradesmen and carried their possessions in bundles. Others were dressed like gentlemen fresh from court. My attention was drawn to a wide-shouldered young man who carried himself like an eager child. He smiled at me and I saw he was simple-minded. I returned the smile, thinking he was an unusual sort of colonist. An older man I took to be his father put a hand on his shoulder to calm him.

I wondered what these men would think of me. Would I be accepted among them, and on what terms? I watched servants carry bedding, pots and pans, and even furniture on board. I had few possessions and no money. Would I have to work as a servant to earn my livelihood?

"Get yourself aboard now, lady," said the guard. "They'll be weighing anchor before the tide turns."

But I hesitated, suddenly unwilling to leave the country where I had lived my entire life. Though I had no one who desired me to stay, it pained me to go away. The prospect of being the only woman in a colony of men—and a servant to boot—also filled me with misgiving. How could Elizabeth, who had treated me like a daughter, consign me to a future so uncertain, even unsafe? I lingered on the wharf, growing ever more reluctant to board the ship. And then I saw a woman and a young boy going up the plank. Another woman followed on the arm of her husband. Her belly was round with an unborn babe. Apparently Sir Walter had decided to plant a colony that could grow and flourish. I would not be the lone woman after all.

"I'd give my eyeteeth to be young again," said the guard, watching the colonists board. "Think of the fortunes they'll make." He summoned a shipman to carry my trunk, and I boarded the *Lion* without looking back.

From the ship's deck, which was not so wide as it appeared from the wharf, I looked over the expanse of the city. I was glad to be freed from the grim, gray Tower and hopeful as the church spires that rose above the thatched roofs. Whitehall Palace, where I had lived for four years, was invisible beyond the bend in the river. The barges and wherries plying the Thames looked small and insubstantial.

"Get below! Move on! My ship is no place for women."

The voice belonged to a man with face and hands as brown and creased as shoe leather. He wore a black doublet with Spanish lace at the neck and sleeves.

"Simon Fernandes, be careful how you speak around the ladies," said the man with the large-bellied wife. He took the scowling pilot's hand. "Ananias Dare, Governor White's son-in-law," he said. The two men measured each other with their looks.

And then I saw behind the pilot a tall, familiar figure. He was dressed in a well-cut doublet and hose and soft leather shoes. His hair was bound at the nape of his neck and his skin was as tawny as that of Fernandes. It was Manteo. I had but a moment to wonder whether Ralegh was also on board, when Ananias Dare took my arm to guide me belowdecks. My unwieldy skirts tangled in the ladder and I pitched forward, landing in a scene of utter confusion. The between deck was piled waist high with cargo, leaving only the narrowest of walkways. The passengers spread their mattresses, blankets, and belongings atop the cargo, marking their spaces for the journey. Dare's wife had claimed a desirable spot near an open gunport that provided light and fresh air. The mother and her young son were hanging a cloth from the beams to curtain their sleeping pallet. The berths fore and aft were reserved for the ship's officers and the gentlemen of the colony. Near the stern, a rough-looking seaman—an Irishman, judging by his accent—and a soldier were arguing, the soldier saying he refused to lie next to a papist.

There were perhaps forty people in the hold. They spoke to each other as kin and neighbors of long acquaintance. I was keenly aware of being the stranger among them. Clothed still like a lady,

I must have looked quite out of place. I found a spot near the hatch that led to the ship's hold and spread out my cloak, for I had not even a mattress to lie upon. I thought of Emme and all the nights we had slept next to each other. Would I ever see my friend again? Lying on my cloak, I waited for the tears to come, but my eyes remained dry. Not until the ship drifted from the dock and the current began to carry her down the Thames did the tears slip down my face, and I knew what I had hoped for was impossible: that Sir Walter would board the ship, declare his love, and sail with me to Virginia.

I wiped my tears and shook myself awake from this dream for the last time.

The *Lion* was en route to Portsmouth to pick up more passengers when the ship's boy came below and, to my surprise, called out my name, saying the captain wanted to see me. Everyone's eyes were on me as I followed the boy up the ladder. Compared to the lodging below, the captain's cabin was spacious, containing a sleeping berth, a table covered with a carpet, two chairs, and an open chest of maps and charts. On the wall hung pieces of armor and instruments of navigation such as I had seen in Sir Walter's library.

The captain had graying hair and a kindly demeanor. He introduced himself as John White and took my hand in his. I noticed the ink-stained fingers and realized he was the very painter Ralegh had sent on the first voyage.

"Sir, I have beheld with wonder your drawings of the New World, and they made me long to visit this paradise called Virginia," I said.

Captain White smiled at the compliment and picked up a sketch on the table as if he wanted to show it to me, then put it down and broached his business instead.

"As the deputy governor of Virginia, I would consider it an honor if you would become a member of my household there," he said. "Along with my daughter, Eleanor, and her husband, Ananias."

"You require a servant, then?" I said. John White did not look like a harsh master. I could do far worse.

"No, you will not be a servant, but more like kin," he said. Seeing my confusion, he continued, "I have been given a sum of money to cover your passage and establish you in the colony."

"By Elizabeth?" I could hardly believe the queen had shown me both mercy and generosity.

"No, it was Walter Ralegh's doing," he replied. "He said he felt an obligation to you." He turned and fumbled among the papers on his desk until he found a sealed letter. "He asked me to deliver this to you. I apologize for the delay. The ship's business has consumed me."

I left the cabin clutching the letter and stumbled into Manteo. My face met his doublet and I blushed as red as an apple, remembering the sight of his bare chest with its raised markings. He quickly righted me and withdrew, but not before our eyes met and he gave a nod of recognition. Without a word he passed into the cabin, and I sank down on a pile of sails. I realized I had crushed Sir Walter's letter in my fist. I unfolded it, read it quickly, then leapt to my feet.

Send me a reply before the Lion *sails,* he had written. It was too late; London was behind us. When we landed in Portsmouth I could dispatch a reply. But what would I write? I pored over the letter again. On the first reading, it had seemed plain and dutiful. Now I discerned a flame of feeling, more honest than passionate. Reading it a third time, I noted the self-regard in his complaints about his own suffering. Yet he signed himself as a humble penitent. I did not know what to think of it. Why had he waited until my very last moment in England to admit his wrong and attempt to know my mind? Was he afraid of my reply? Perhaps he did want me to find a husband in Virginia and thereby release him from any duty to love me.

My speculations seemed fruitless. I would never know what Sir Walter's letter truly meant. And I was in such turmoil I did not even know my own mind. So I would not reply until I could write something truthful.

We docked at Portsmouth, where twenty or so farmers, laborers, and women waited with their belongings. Some were taken on the smaller flyboat and the rest boarded the already-crowded *Lion*. They received a sullen welcome, and out of pity I made room for one Jane Pierce, a single woman of about twenty-five. Like me, she had no family, but she had a mattress and kindly agreed to share it with me.

At Plymouth, the last port before the open seas, we took on casks of fresh water and lay at anchor for several days, waiting for favorable winds. I borrowed paper and ink from John White and ruined it all with striking out what I had written. If Sir Walter loved me, he could follow me to America. All he had to do was board one of his own ships. He had the means. But did he have the will to leave his estates, his honors, and his royal mistress—to exchange them all for love?

Only time would tell the answer.

Chapter 18

Dangers and Discoveries

On the eighth of May, the winds turned favorable and Fernandes decided to sail. The gunports were sealed for the voyage, leaving the hold dark and smelling of tar. Ten men strained like oxen against the bars of the capstan, turning it slowly to lift the anchor. The sails were unfurled and caught the wind, flapping like the wings of a mythical dragon. All the noises were new and sounded strange from belowdecks: waves slapping the hull, the ship creaking in all her seams, and seamen shouting in a language of their own. The ship rolled from side to side, sometimes with a gentle motion, sometimes lurching violently. Unable to quell my sickness, I retched into a common bucket. The hold stank of vomit and waste. I lifted my face to the hatch, trying to breathe fresh air. When it rained, the water leaked through the canvas cover and soaked our skimpy pallet.

We were in such misery that John White allowed us to come onto the deck in small numbers, despite the objection of Fernandes. The pilot glared at the women from under his dark brows and shouted oaths at any man unfortunate enough to be in the way of

a crew member. Soon the sickness abated as we became accustomed to the pitching of the ship.

On the twenty-second of June we anchored at the island of
Santa Cruz, where John White would purchase sheep, plants, and
salt for the colony. For the first time in six weeks I stepped on
land, but could barely stand upright because of the weakness in
my legs. On the sand was a turtle of immense proportions, its claws
bigger than a man's hand. The slow creature was no match for the
soldiers, who killed it at once, hungry for the meat. Its blood stained
the white sand.

The swift birds fared better. Their feathers flashed red, yellow,
and green as they darted, squawking, among the trees. John White
called them parrots, and the tree with purple blossoms a *lignum
vitae*. The men went off in search of fresh water while the women
bathed and washed clothing. The boy Edmund turned cartwheels
and dug in the sand while his mother, Betty Vickers, tried not to
smile. She was probably a Puritan, with her plain clothing and
prayer book always at hand. The governor's daughter, Eleanor, let
her thick golden hair down and washed it in a bucket of salt water.
Despite the weeks of deprivation, her belly had grown since we
first boarded the ship.

A sweet scent floated upon the air, its source a green, applelike
fruit. The children eagerly collected these, as we had not tasted
fresh fruit in many weeks. Eleanor threw her damp hair over her
shoulders and accepted one from little Edmund, who sniffed his
own uncertainly.

Moments later I heard Eleanor cry out, "My lips! My mouth!
They are on fire!"

At once her tongue began to swell up. She put her hands to her
belly, and I could see terror in her eyes.

Dimly I remembered once eating a leaf of cow parsley and my

mother trying to get me to vomit. I showed Eleanor how to put her fingers in her throat until the contents of her stomach spewed out, and I held her head while she shuddered afterward.

Panic spread as more became sick. Edmund had swallowed the fruit and his face and hands were inflamed. "Not my son; oh God, don't let him die!" Betty prayed, clasping him to her.

Hearing the cries, the men came running, their weapons ready. Manteo broke open the stem of a plant that oozed an oily salve, indicating it was to be spread on the inflamed skin.

Ambrose Vickers, Betty's husband, began to complain. "Why didn't John White warn us about that fruit? It is his duty to protect us."

George Howe, one of White's assistants, grabbed Vickers by the collar and hoisted him off his feet. "Shut your trap and fetch some water for these suffering folk."

George's son, the simple boy, had bitten into the fruit, but was unharmed.

"It was bad. I spit it out. It did not hurt me. It did not hurt Georgie Howe," he said again and again, proud of himself. It was a strange relief, to see such a sturdy youth smiling amidst so much distress.

By the following afternoon, the effects of the poison had worn off. No one died, and Eleanor did not miscarry. John White cautioned us against eating anything he did not provide. He seemed surprised that we had been so reckless. But in this new place we were like children in need of a strict father, while John White seemed to be an indulgent one.

Eleanor was convinced I had saved her life and her unborn babe, and thus I acquired a friend.

"I know you must think it foolish of me to sail in my condition," she said. Her cheeks and lips were still swollen from the poison. "But I love my father, and since my mother died, he has no one to take care of him. He came home from his first voyage nothing but bones. Were it not for me, he would spend all his time drawing and forget to eat."

This admission did not increase my confidence in John White.

"How did you persuade your husband to make the journey?" I asked.

"It was not me, but five hundred acres of land that induced him. Few of these men would have left England were it not for the promise of land. And my father offered to make Ananias one of his assistants. They were granted coats of arms, so they are both gentlemen now."

"And that makes you a gentlewoman," I said.

She smiled. "I care nothing for titles. I only want my child to be safely born and thrive."

"Virginia is fertile and the climate healthy. We should all thrive there," I said.

I told Eleanor only a little about myself. I said that my parents were dead and I had served the queen, who granted my wish to see the New World and put me under her father's protection. I admitted I knew Sir Walter and had often heard him describe his plans for the colony. It was not the full truth, but why should I admit to being disgraced? I was free to hide or reveal whatever I chose.

Eleanor seemed to be in awe of me. "I am so fortunate. You are like a sister to me already," she said.

I was as pleased as she was.

Once Eleanor befriended me, the other women began to show me respect as well. They were hesitant to address me, perhaps because they did not know what to say to someone who had waited on a queen. I asked them not to call me Lady Catherine, but simply Cate. Still, I felt like a stranger among them, for they were all related or had grown up in the same parishes. Betty Vickers had lost two infants and a young child to the plague, leaving only ten-year-old Edmund. Her husband was a hardworking journeyman, but with little hope of advancement in the London guilds. Seeing the opportunity to become a master woodcrafter in the New World, he had sold all his family's possessions to finance their voyage.

Not all the men on the voyage would become landowners in Virginia. Some were indentured servants who would work for their freedom. Many were soldiers paid to guard the colony. Besides myself, the other unmarried women were servants, except for one widow of independent means. The number of colonists traveling aboard the flagship, the flyboat, and the small pinnace was a hundred and fifteen, including seventeen women and eleven children.

Leaving Santa Cruz, where White failed to obtain sheep, plants, or salt, Fernandes sailed to the island named St. John. There we also encountered trouble. The men found freshwater, but they drank so much beer that nothing was gained. Three soldiers who were supposed to be watching for Spaniards were found imbibing. White had them whipped and chastised the others, but they were all too drunk to care.

The pinnace was already anchored at St. John. Among her passengers was a soldier who followed me with his eyes, which made me uneasy. Soldiers were generally rough and unsavory. He drew nearer and was about to speak when I said, "You are too bold. I do not wish to know you."

"Lady Catherine, do you spurn an old friend?"

I peered at him. "Who are you?" There was something

familiar in his stance. "Thomas Graham?" I said, incredulous. For he was no longer "the fool of fashion" as Dick Tarleton had once dubbed him. He had traded his slashed doublet for a common jerkin, and his face was covered with a reddish beard. He looked sturdy and vital.

"At your service." He bowed. "Do you wonder why I am I here?"

I knew Graham had been almost penniless when the queen sent him from court. I also remembered how he had admired Ralegh's treasure-laden ships docked along the Thames.

"You must be seeking your fortune like everyone else," I replied. "Do you mean to settle in Virginia?"

Graham laughed. "I've no longing to live among savages. I will save my earnings, maybe look for gold, then return to England with the means to marry my Lady Anne."

Swept with fresh regret, I said, "I'm sorry I could not help you and you had to become a soldier."

"Lady Catherine, your intentions were the best, and I bear you no ill will."

I nodded, grateful. "I call myself Cate now," I said.

"Then, Lady Cate, do not be sorry for me. This is an adventure that puts me among the finest of men." He gestured toward his companion. "Why, this fellow spent ten years at Colchester prison for murdering a farmer. I'm afraid to beat him at a game of dice!"

The man grinned but without mirth. "It was for stealin' not killin'. But I didn't do either."

Then Graham grew serious. "My dear Cate, it is I who am sorry for *your* plight."

"Do not speak of it, please," I said in a low voice. "I do not wish anyone to know I was imprisoned like your dice-playing friend."

Graham leaned closer and lowered his voice. "I will be discreet. But as we find ourselves in the same circumstance, we ought to be friends."

"Being a woman, my circumstance is somewhat different and more perilous than yours," I said, drawing back. "We are being observed, and I do not wish to be the subject of gossip."

"Truly, reputation is as precious to a soldier as it is to a lady. Worth more than gold," he said, bowing like a courtier. "I would be reputed the bravest man in the Americas; Anne will marry me even if I am penniless. Damn, even the queen will love me then."

Despite myself I smiled. I decided Graham's character was much improved by soldiering.

Just then a commotion broke out, and I saw the Irish seaman and his unwilling bunk mate sprawled on the ground. John White stood over them, his face pale with rage. Everyone had stopped what they were doing to watch the unfolding drama.

"I've had enough of your quarreling and insubordination!" White shouted. "I'm giving you a choice. You can take your flogging, or you can leave the company now and see how long you'll last on this island."

His threat was a dire one. Many of the mariners said the island was peopled by savages who stuck bones through their noses and ate the flesh of their enemies.

In reply, the Irishman spat on the captain's shoes. White drew back his foot as if to kick him, but the Irishman was too quick, scrambling to his feet and fleeing into the brush. The other rogue followed him. Thus, without a word, they chose their fate.

The boatswain threw two bundles overboard and they were quickly plundered.

"See what I found in Darby's sack!" cried a man, holding up two strands of beads with brass crosses dangling from them.

Murmurs went through the crowd, as everyone affirmed the Irishman was indeed a papist.

Roger Bailey, one of White's assistants, laughed harshly. "We are well rid of that Catholic dog," he said. But it was Bailey, with his sharp yellowish teeth, who resembled a dog,

Next to me, Graham shook his head. "It was unwise of Captain White to let them go," he murmured. "He should have had them flogged and thrown into the bilge instead."

I was surprised by his harshness, but set it down to a soldier's love of discipline. Soon, however, I understood what he meant. The evidence of Darby's religion and the presence of Spaniards in the islands led to rumors that the Irishman was a traitor.

"That fellow has been to Virginia before," said Ambrose Vickers. "He knows where the fort is located. Why, for a little money, the villain would betray us to the Spaniards around here. We will never be safe on Roanoke Island."

I found myself defending the seaman. "I do not think Darby was disloyal, even if he was a papist," I said. "Perhaps he only brought the beads to have something to trade with the Indians." Ambrose and the men looked at me in surprise, and I realized they were unused to having a woman—even a lady—speak in their company.

The next day the ships weighed anchor, leaving Darby and his bunk mate to their uncertain fates. The idea of conspiracy had been planted, making everyone sober and fearful.

To make matters worse, John White and the pilot argued. Their raised voices drifted down through the open hatch. Eleanor was concerned for her father, so together we crept up the ladder and onto the deck. The boatswain dared not admonish her because she was White's daughter.

"We *must* land at Salinas Bay for livestock and salt," said the captain, bursting from his cabin. "Or we will reach Roanoke without enough supplies to survive for long."

Fernandes was at his heels. "At this time of year, the currents, the reefs! It is too great a risk to the ship."

"This time of year," said White, whirling around and stabbing his finger at the pilot's nose, "you prefer to be on the high seas, for your own profit. But if you hasten this voyage and thus endanger my colonists, you will have Ralegh and the queen herself to answer to."

Fernandes only laughed. "I tell you, we will find these goods in Hispaniola. I have a friend there."

"I think your friends cannot be trusted," White said, then strode to the ship's rail and stood with his hands crossed over his chest.

It dismayed me to see our governor overmastered by his pilot. Our fortunes were dependent upon his. If he failed in his purpose, we would all be lost.

"You must speak to your father," I said to Eleanor. "Fernandes considers his own interests. He does not care about the success of our colony."

"I will," whispered Eleanor. "When he is calmer."

Soon we were sailing the northern coast of Hispaniola, which appeared like a distant tuft of moss, green and low. The ship did not go ashore as Fernandes promised. White did not order him to land, or if he did, the pilot ignored him. Thus we still lacked salt and livestock, and White remained grim. We encountered no Spanish vessels, and the islands disappeared from view on the sixth of July. Two weeks later, Hatorask, on the outer banks of Virginia, was sighted. Everyone scrambled to the decks, where there was great rejoicing. Eleanor and her husband embraced, the baby in her belly keeping them some distance apart. The hardiest soldiers wiped tears from their eyes.

Our voyage had been brought to a safe end. But our trials were only beginning.

Chapter 19

From the Papers of Sir Walter Ralegh

Memorandum

12 May 1587. The *Lion* has departed Plymouth and I have had no reply from the Lady Catherine. Perhaps she did not receive my letter? No, it must be that her reply was lost. I see the sodden pages adrift upon the furrowed sea. Alas, I shall never know her mind.

My heart beats with a passionate remorse. If only I had delivered the letter myself! But I was afraid to face her and now am punished for my cowardice.

24 May 1587. I live the dream of every man in England. Who does not desire to behold the virgin queen at the hour of her awakening, all the day long, and in the last moments before sleep? I see her in her shift, her bosom drooping like a withered bloom. I see her scalp beneath her white hair. I watch her grimace, limping on an ulcered leg, and feel compelled to offer her my arm. This is a husband's intimate office, not mine.

I think I never will marry. Does every man fear to find his ardor cooled by the sight of frailty? By a beauty exposed as stark plainness?

There was nothing false or painted about C.A.'s beauty. Even now I see her lips and cheeks of a natural coral hue, her dark thick hair—all her own. Ah, in years hence it will show strands of silver, and lines will mark her face like tributaries on a map. The thought does not repulse me. Why? Because I will be old as well.

I cannot forget her, though an ocean widens between us. Does she sit in John White's cabin and take her fill of stories from him, as from a father's lips? Does she gaze upon the swarthy Fernandes and wish to sail with rovers and adventurers?

It was her lively imagination—so like my own—that I loved in her. And now it has wandered from me, to wonder new thoughts.

And I am, though never alone, lonelier than can be imagined.

Poem

I hope for what I have not,
I would come, but may not.
Of my wounds you care naught,
Because the pain you see not.

13 June 1587. At the banquet for the Dutch ambassador Her Majesty called me her second Sir Philip Sidney. It was the highest praise, for this soldier-poet lately slain in the Netherlands is England's greatest hero. Before everyone, she demanded a sonnet, which I created extempore:

Let us honor fair Astro-phil
(Fall'n on the battle's bloody plain)
By meeting his enemy, Spain, full well
In Virginia, across that watery main.

The queen bade me sit at her right hand, while Walsingham gave me the blackest of looks. He is still angry I received the Babington estates. Alas, I would almost give them up to obtain what I have not: my freedom, my own will, and true love.

1 July 1587. Outside the privy chamber, Walsingham stopped me with these words: "Do not forget I am the architect of Her Majesty's policy with regard to Spain. Your efforts must not interfere with mine."

Is he so full of envy he does not welcome my enterprise of challenging Spain in the New World?

Fie upon his threats! The old spymaster does not command me.

I wonder how he can hear anything with that cap pulled over his ears?

24 July 1587
Dear brother Carew,

Her Majesty's summer progress will take her through Devonshire. I may not leave her side, so you must contrive to visit me. You will recognize me by my puffed-sleeve tunic the color of a Valencia orange, and a plumed hat too ostentatious even for my taste. Do not laugh at me or I shall thrash you as if we were boys again.

I swear no man is more hated for being loved than I am. The queen has granted me the monopoly on broadcloth, and every man who suffers the loss of his trade because of it hates me. I wish she would love me more by hating me more. It is a paradox, I know; oftentimes things most contrary are both true.

By now the Lion *and the pinnace have landed at Chesapeake. There must be no time lost in sending a supply ship, but I am all of out funds. Go to our investors and praise*

*Gov. White's abilities. Remind them of the innumerable pearls
and the veins of copper awaiting our discovery, by which we
shall all be made richer than King Croesus.*

Your brother,

Sir W.R.

Chapter 20

A Dead Man

The tides ebbed and flowed around the *Lion*, anchored near the inlet at Hatorask. But after so many weeks of confinement we still could not leave the ship. John White, Ananias Dare, Manteo, and forty soldiers had set out in the pinnace to retrieve the soldiers Grenville had left at the fort. When they returned we would sail the short distance to Chesapeake and settle there.

While we waited, I borrowed an eyeglass to peer at the sand-covered hills, where grass and gorselike bushes grew. They were not as green and lush as I had expected. A seaman, gesturing with pitch-stained hands, explained this was a barrier island holding back the sea from the mainland that lay across the shallow bay beyond it. With the glass I searched the sea, hoping to see a great fish with fins like sails or the rare leviathan, creatures I had seen only in pictures. I was impatient to be on land, but it was a pleasure just to stand on deck and feel and taste the salty wind. I found myself wishing Sir Walter were beside me. Did he envy me, that I would see Virginia before him and help to build the colony he longed to govern?

I wondered what it was like for Manteo to return to his own land. Would he tell his people about great city of London and teach them English? Would they still accept him now that he looked like an Englishman? I smiled to think of the horrified looks that would greet us if we all returned to London dressed like savages.

When the pinnace returned, it carried the same forty men who had gone out the day before.

"Where are Grenville's men?" called Roger Bailey from the deck of the *Lion.*

"They were not at the fort," shouted Ananias in reply. "But we will search until we find them."

"No, son, we sail for Chesapeake now. We will return later," said John White.

One of the women started weeping, for her husband had been among those left on the island.

Then Fernandes announced from the quarterdeck that none of the men would be allowed to board the ship again. But he demanded to see White and sent out a rowboat to fetch him.

At this the men in the pinnace grew restive. Ananias insisted on getting in the rowboat with White. I wondered about Fernandes's purpose. The governor climbed the rigging and jumped to the deck, his face red with exertion and rage.

"What is this? Send the boatswain back to fetch all the men in the pinnace," he demanded.

Without replying, Fernandes disappeared into the cabin, and White and Ananias could only follow him. Again we heard their angry voices. Eleanor clung to my arm. I knew she had not spoken to her father as she promised. Now trouble was in store.

John White emerged from the cabin and without preamble said, "Fernandes has elected to return at once to England because of the lateness of the season and the storms he is anxious to avoid."

He frowned and his eyes flashed. But the storm on his brow was evidently not the one Fernandes feared.

"Thus we are obliged to stay at Fort Ralegh—"

Roger Bailey interrupted him. "What happened to Grenville's men? Did the savages get them?" He pointed to Manteo standing in the pinnace. "He must know. He is one of them."

I admired the way Manteo stood erect, not even glancing at the accusing finger.

"We have women and children with us," said Ambrose Vickers. "We can't stay here if we're likely to be attacked."

His words caused murmuring among the others and White raised his hand to silence it.

"There is still a fort. We will reinforce it and build up the existing houses." He paused, then said with emphasis, "And *because* of Manteo, we have friends among the Indians."

I did not understand why the men were angry with the governor and not with Fernandes, who stood before the cabin door as if he owned everything inside. I wondered if he would have dared to treat Ralegh as he treated White.

Vickers, too, noticed the pilot. "Wasn't he ordered to take us to Chesapeake? And now he refuses. That's mutiny!" he shouted to his fellows.

John White stepped so close to Vickers their noses were almost touching. "The weapons are on this ship and my soldiers are in the pinnace. Shall *you* fight Fernandes and his seamen for control of the ship? Shall we begin this venture with bloodshed?" His voice was low and tight. "Not while I govern here."

Vickers seemed to consider his choices. His shoulders slumped. "Governor, I am at your service," he said. But his tone was sullen.

"Men, to your tasks," said White. "Unlade this ship."

The slow business of transporting goods to the island

commenced. Bailey oversaw the rebuilding of the shallop, a large rowboat with a mast and sails that had been stored in pieces in the hold. The pinnace and the shallop sailed back and forth over several days. Fernandes watched the operation in silence from the forecastle deck.

The women and children were the last to leave the ship. We climbed down into the shallop, which Ananias guided through the inlet and along the leeward side of the barrier islands. There in the shallows were thousands of sleek cranes with long necks and thin legs. As we passed by, they rose as one into the air. The flapping of their wings sounded like sails unfurling in a gale. Jane sat on one side of me and Eleanor on the other, our elbows linked, as the shallop entered the wide bay. We were all silent with expectation, even little Edmund, and Betty's lips moved as if she was praying. The island of the Roanoke loomed larger as we drew near. Its shore was dark and dense with trees, their roots like fingers planted in the water. I peered into the swampy thickets and wondered what man or beast could survive there. I wondered if Grenville's men had been killed by Indians and thrown into the black water or attacked and carried off by the Spanish.

Ananias sailed around the island to a more hospitable landing point, where the pinnace was lashed to some trees. A path had been cleared from the sandy shore to the fort. The site was already a hive of noisy activity, with men cutting down trees and milling the timber by hand. Others were repairing the palisade, a tall fence made from roughly hewed planks. From a forge erected in a clearing came a rhythmic clanging. A grinning Georgie Howe walked by, carrying a cask on his shoulder. Perhaps his mind was weak, but his body was strong and his temperament always sanguine.

But where was Fort Ralegh? I expected to see a high stone wall and a tower within. The soldiers were shoveling sandy dirt into wheelbarrows and dumping it on a high mound. To my dismay, I realized the fort was no more than an irregular earthen wall. Most of it had slid into the ditch around it, and the soldiers were shoring it up again. Inside the fort was a single building, the armory. I watched as three soldiers heaved a gun from its carriage onto a wooden platform built atop the earthworks. I was not reassured. Every city had its defenses; even peaceful London was surrounded by a wall. But here the houses were located *outside* the fort, and new ones were being built outside the palisade. If the Spanish attacked, or the Indians who were not Manteo's friends, we would be at their mercy unless we were fortunate enough to be inside the fort.

I regarded the settlement, too, with dismay. The dozen cottages built by Grenville's men had fallen into decay. Their doors sagged and the rush roofs were collapsing. Weeds grew waist high and melon plants with their thick, wide leaves twined like snakes through the windows. Ananias was already repairing the largest cottage to house the governor and his family. It had two rooms, one with a wooden bedstead, the other with a hearth and a rustic table. I wondered where I would sleep.

Eleanor, undeterred by the disorder, was already scrubbing the grimed hearth. She grunted and sweated with the effort.

I was not meant to be anyone's servant in Virginia. But watching Eleanor working in her condition made me ashamed, so I took a broom and began to sweep. Beneath the dried leaves and twigs there was no floor. I stared at the packed dirt in dismay.

"We have mats somewhere," Eleanor said, wiping her brow on her sleeve. "But not enough for both rooms."

"I will find some rushes to strew on the ground," I offered, thinking of the tall grasses I had seen near the shore.

I set out on a narrow path that led toward the shore beyond the landing place. It was hot and still in the woods, and my shift and bodice clung to my body. Even my legs were damp with sweat. The clangor of the settlement grew faint, until all I could hear was the sound of my own breathing and the insects buzzing around my face. I wondered why I did not see the exotic creatures and plants John White had painted in such detail, the red fruits hanging in clusters of leaves, the yellow and black butterflies. The countryside around Wiltshire was more beautiful than what I could see of this island. The queen's garden had flowers of every hue and was not so full of insects. I brushed past brambly shrubs that snagged my skirt. If I walked long enough, perhaps I would come to the Eden I had imagined.

I had gone far from the settlement when it occurred to me that I should not have ventured out alone. I began to wonder about the savages. If they were friendly, as White claimed, why had they not greeted us when we landed? Could they be hiding and watching me even now? I turned in a circle, smiling and holding my palms upward in a gesture of innocence. For some reason it made me feel safer. Then I heard a whispering that rose and fell. I froze until I realized it was the waves lapping the shore. The sound recalled to me my task, and I made for a patch of rushes near the water. I had not thought to bring a knife to cut the rushes or a cord to bind them. The sharp grasses cut my hands, so I wrapped them in my petticoat and pulled at the rushes until I had more than I could carry. Then I took off my sand-filled shoes, hiked up my skirts, and waded into the water, crouching to bathe my raw and aching hands.

The inlet was so still, the water so clear, I could see fish large and small darting in the lee of the rocks, an entire colony beneath the water's surface. One was greenish in color, with fins as elaborate as a lace ruff. I was about to reach into the water and grasp it, when I beheld out of the corner of my eye a sharpened stick resting against a log, the point stuck in the stream bed. It seemed Providence meant for me to catch a fish that day.

Careful not to stir up the water, I took a few steps closer and reached for the stick. That is when I saw, behind the log, the figure of a man. His legs were in the water, the rest of him lying on his back over a rock. His chest was bristling with arrows, and his bloody head had been staved in.

Chapter 21

I, Manteo, Try to Keep the Peace

I heard the woman's voice, faint and far away. I thought of Ahsoo, the maiden who sang so beautifully that the river became alive with leaping fish. They labored so hard to reach the music, even swimming against the stream, that many died on the journey.

I ran toward the sound, leaping like one of those fish. The woman was not singing but screaming. I readied my bow.

An English maiden with dark hair stood in the stream. She held a fish spear like a weapon. Her eyes were wide with terror. When she saw me she lowered the spear, but the fear did not leave her eyes. I recognized her as the maid who had fallen into me on the ship, the one who had served the English weroance. And I saw the dead man in the water.

"Are you hurt?" I asked. She shook her head. Seeing her tremble, I wanted to touch her, to reassure her. But I only said, "You are safe now."

The soldiers were just behind me. The one named Grem picked up the maiden and carried her until she could walk by herself. They also took the body back to the fort.

The dead man was George-howe, one of John-white's councilors. His head was beaten in with a club. Sixteen arrows stuck in his chest. I recognized the bone points and feathering on the arrows.

"This is the work of Wingina's warriors," I said to John-white.

"A year later, and they seek revenge?"

I nodded. Did he think the Roanoke would forget the killing of their weroance?

I let the English see my anger at George-howe's killing, so they would know I was blameless. Instead they blamed John-white, because he had told them the native peoples were friendly. They looked at him with one question in their eyes: *Can you keep us safe?*

It was my idea to ask Weyawinga what she knew about the fifteen lost men and the killing of George-howe. So I guided John-white and twenty men to Croatoan, a two-day trip by boat. My breast was filled with gladness to be returning home. The English would see how my kin would welcome me. My people would see that John-white and his men respected me. *Look how far they have come to understand our ways and live among us,* I would say. And my people would be proud to be allies with the English and receive their powerful gifts.

But as the shallop came near the shore, war cries rolled toward us on the wind.

"We are betrayed! It is Manteo's doing," Bay-lee shouted. The men fired their muskets in alarm, and John-white shouted for them to stop.

I stood in the bow of the shallop and called to my kinsmen, *"It is I, Manteo! We come in peace."* I leapt into the water, putting myself before the muskets. My grief was great that they distrusted me.

But the English lowered their weapons. Hearing my voice, my kinsmen came out from their hiding places and welcomed me with smiles and embraces. When all the men had come ashore, they led us to the village.

Weyawinga, my mother, greeted me as a fellow weroance, then embraced me as her son. Yet I could see that my English clothes dismayed her, so I removed my shoes and put on a deerskin.

"We must feed the English with great ceremony, to gain their trust," I said to her.

A feast of squashes and nuts and venison was prepared. We smoked uppowoc until the men were content.

I translated between the tongues as John-white asked Weyawinga about the missing soldiers. She said they had been attacked by warriors from Dasemunkepeuc and Secotan.

"Are you certain?" John-white asked. "They are not allies of one another. And the Secotan chief and his wife received us warmly and allowed me to draw them and their village."

There was no mistake, my mother insisted. *"The peoples who once fought each other conceived a hatred for Ralf-lane and his warriors that has drawn them together for their protection."* She also said Wanchese now led the Roanoke.

John-white thought for a moment, then said to Weyawinga, "You must take this message to all the peoples of Ossomocomuck: in ten days, we will receive them at Fort Ralegh and assure them of our peaceful intentions. If they accept our friendship, we will forgive the wrongs of the past."

My mother agreed to this, and I left with the English. John-white was pleased at the success of our visit. But Bay-lee said he did not want all the strange chiefs to come to their island.

The day of the meeting came and passed into night, and none of the weroances of Ossomocomuck came to the fort. Only Weyawinga sent a councilor. It disturbed me that no one else had come. Why did they not show themselves?

"The Indians are not interested in peace," said Ana-nias the brickmaker. "Indian" was their term for all the native peoples together. "Therefore it is time for war."

"Let us wait. Our time is not their time," said John-white.

"While we wait, hoping for peace, they are readying for war," the brickmaker argued.

Bay-lee said, "Indians cannot be trusted. You heard Weyawinga say they have united against us. We must destroy them."

I knew the governor did not want a war, but he was not strong enough to prevent one. His councilors wanted to show their strength and repay George-howe's killing. It was Bay-lee's plan to attack Dasemunkepeuc, Wingina's village. He and John-white and I would go with twenty soldiers. So on a moonless night, the silent pinnace crossed the sound. I hoped I could persuade Wanchese to surrender and thus prevent a war. A smoking fire showed us the village. The soldiers attacked just before dawn and the surprised villagers fled into the woods. One warrior turned to fight and Bay-lee shot him. I ran up to him, expecting to see Wanchese.

But the warrior bleeding from his back and gasping for air was not Wanchese. He was one of my kinsmen, a Croatoan.

"Call back your soldiers!" I shouted to John-white.

Then I demanded of the injured warrior, "Have the Croatoan turned against the white men? Are you an ally of Wanchese?"

His eyes rolled up in his head and he was still.

Soon we understood our terrible mistake. Ana-nias captured a warrior named Tameoc, who said that Wanchese and the Roanoke who killed George-howe had left Dasemunkepeuc. Tameoc's band of Croatoan, fifteen in number, had moved in to gather the corn and pumpkins left in the fields.

"*Why did you not recognize your own people sleeping around the fire?*" said Tameoc, rebuking me angrily.

My heart was cut with an arrow of grief, but I hid the wound. I would not show weakness before Tameoc or the English. But I said to John-white that we must offer hospitality to Tameoc's kin if we wanted their forgiveness and friendship.

So after the slain warrior was buried, Tameoc's band came to Roanoke Island. John-white received them in his house. He gave them bright cloth and vessels of iron and copper. His daughter fed the men from her cooking pot and the women and children sat outside and ate. This pleased them because it was also their custom.

The maiden who had discovered George-howe's body lived at John-white's house. I heard the governor call her Ladi-cate. Through the open door I watched her serve the women and children. All were silent, having no common language. Ladi-cate sat among them as they ate. Her eyes never strayed from their faces. Her hair, black as a raven's wing, shone in the sun. I wondered what it would be like to touch it.

During the feast I praised the fallen warrior to Tameoc, saying John-white regretted his death. I reminded Tameoc these were not the same English who killed Wingina, but they still planned to punish Wanchese for killing one of their own. Tameoc agreed not to become Wanchese's ally. When the Croatoan left, I was satisfied I had brought peace.

John-white was also pleased. He announced I would be made Lord of Roanoke and Dasemunkepeuc, with authority over all the native people. To be a weroance was a gift beyond my deserving. But I accepted it as the hero accepts everything that befalls him on his journey, the good as well as the bad. At first I wondered, *How can I persuade the native peoples to trust the English when they will not trust each other?* But I knew both parties needed me to make themselves understood. No one but I could be the maker of peace.

Before I could become a lord, I had to be baptized. John-white explained this ceremony of water would be a sign of the English religion taking root among us. I agreed, for I had learned about their beliefs from Hare-yet and found many likenesses to my own. They believe in one chief god, who is the creator of the sun, moon, and stars. Like us, they believe that after death a man's spirit either dwells with their god or in a fiery pit, which they call "hell" and we call "*Popogusso*." They also petition their god in order to to receive good things.

So I let John-white lead me into the water and call upon the spirit to enter me. Afterward he laid on my shoulders a mantle trimmed in fur and beads and feathers.

I had become a lord. A weroance. I waited for the montoac to fill me.

Chapter 22

A Birth

For a long time I was haunted by the sight of George Howe's body pierced with arrows, his head smashed like a melon. Almost harder to bear, however, was witnessing young Georgie's grief. When he saw his father's body, he tried to wake him up. When his father did not stir, Georgie began to howl. It was terrible to hear: the deep voice heaving and sobbing. Joan Mannering, his aunt, tried to soothe the giant boy. But his wordless lamenting went on until his father's body was buried and Georgie could no longer see him. Then from time to time he would stop people and say, "My papa is in the ground, where the worms are. Do you think it is cold under there? Georgie is not cold." But he shuddered anyway.

"Your papa was a good man. And you are a good boy," people would say, then hurry away to keep the innocent boy from seeing their own sadness, their own fear.

George Howe had gone crabbing by himself the day he was killed. Immediately the governor forbade anyone to leave the settlement alone or unarmed, and the guard was doubled at the fort and around the palisade. Everyone said I was lucky to be alive myself.

But I wasn't frightened. I thought because I held no prejudice against the Indians, they would not harm me. Perhaps the shock of finding George Howe had only numbed me to danger and fear. Eleanor was more blunt; she said I was crazy.

The raid on Dasemunkepeuc was carried out to end the threat from those who had killed George Howe. When White and his men returned, they brought several Indians to Fort Ralegh. Thinking they were captives, the soldiers rushed to seize them. All the women retreated into their houses to peer from the windows. I stood outside the governor's house, too curious to think about hiding. I saw Jane Pierce also watching from her garden.

Georgie followed the Indians, his eyes wide with interest. He did not know who they were, or that they might have killed his father, so he was fearless. His aunt dashed out from her house and pulled him roughly inside.

Governor White gave orders for the soldiers to lay aside their weapons.

One of his assistants, who had stayed at the fort, was unwilling. "You left to seek revenge and return with the enemy in tow?" he asked, his hand resting on the pistol tucked in his belt.

White looked at him sharply. "We erred in our attack," he said. "These are friends of Manteo. They did not kill George. Leave your pistol and join us."

The man shoved the weapon into his boot and followed the governor and the Indian men into the house.

Five women, one of them stooped with age, and two children remained outside. The women had markings that encircled their upper arms in a design so intricate it reminded me of Venetian lace. They wore deerskins over their loins like aprons, but above the waist they were naked. They did not scruple to cover their breasts with their hair, as I would have done.

"Shall we give them our shifts?" I said to Eleanor, then wondered if that would offend them.

Eleanor didn't reply. She was busy stirring the kettle, peering into it as if she had lost a jewel in the soup.

The women's faces looked fearful. Their eyes darted about though they held their bodies still, like deer sensing danger. A child of about four, completely naked, clung to his mother's leg. Her hand grasped his dark hair as if she was afraid of losing him. A young woman with smooth skin had light brown eyes that reminded me of Emme's. I smiled, and so did she.

"Cate," I said, touching my bosom with both hands.

The young woman giggled.

The mother with the little boy touched herself with her free hand. "Takiwa," she said.

I was beside myself with delight. I, Catherine Archer, was speaking to the Indian women! What would Sir Walter think? Why, Elizabeth herself would be pleased by my manner of greeting her newest subjects. There were so many things I wanted to say. I made the motions of feeding myself and raised my eyebrows. The women nodded and rubbed their stomachs.

"Eleanor, they are hungry," I said.

"I can see that," she said. "Look how thin they are."

While the women and children ate, I smiled and nodded my encouragement. I saw Jane Pierce approach and motioned for her to join us, but she shook her head, watched for a time, then went back to her garden. Eleanor was finally able to look up from her pot and even gave some glass beads to the old woman, who divided them with the others. Not to be outdone, I took a piece of lace from my sewing basket and tied it around the arm of the young woman, whose name was Mika. She pointed to the other women's arms and began to talk very fast. I think she was happy with my gift, and I was pleased we could understand each other, even without words.

"Wouldn't it be wonderful if we could speak each other's language?" I said to Eleanor. "We could learn more about them than any scholar or explorer—being only men—could ever discover. Maybe I will write a treatise, and it will be published in London."

"Cate—," Eleanor began. She grimaced. "It's only the heat, I think."

But the Indian women knew better. They pointed to Eleanor's belly and began to speak to each other and nod. The old woman made rocking motions with her hands, and held up her forefinger.

Very soon, she seemed to say.

In John White's house, Eleanor and her husband shared the good bedstead and the governor and I slept on small cots, the three beds all separated by curtains. I could not get used to sleeping in a room with men. It seemed improper. Moreover, they snored and passed wind all night, making the air noisome and keeping me from sleep. The arrangement afforded little privacy for dressing or washing myself. I missed the comforts of the queen's palace, especially the water closet. Here on the island everyone used a common pit with a hut set over it. Emme and Frances would be horrified.

When I could not sleep at night, I would sit on a stool outside and gaze at the multitude of stars, feeling wonder and sadness and longing all at once. I mused about the Indians, or I thought of Emme, or I imagined Sir Walter waiting on the queen and strolling in his garden. I recalled the familar cries of hawkers in the streets, the sound of footsteps on flagstones, the smell of the queen's favorite sachet. Sometimes I fell asleep there, lulled by the strange buzzing and clicking of a thousand invisible creatures. Then I would wake up and return to my bed feeling calmer and able to sleep des_t the discomfort.

One night, shortly after the visit by the Croatoan, I awoke to hear groaning from Eleanor's bed. I knew what was happening. I pulled back the curtains. Eleanor lay pale and sweating, her nightgown twisted, her belly as large as any of the pumpkins ripening in the fields.

"Help me, Cate," she pleaded.

Ananias had gone to fetch the midwife, and in the next room John White had built up the fire under a pot of water. All I could do was hold Eleanor's hand and wait.

Alice Chapman, the midwife, bustled in and waved away the governor and Ananias. She commenced knitting, unmoved by Eleanor's groans. In the morning as news of Eleanor's labor spread, the women came by; Jane Pierce brought spare linens, Joan Mannering, a jug of mulled wine, and Betty Vickers, nothing but unhelpful advice.

"The first one always takes a long time," she said. "I'll pray for your deliverance."

My hand was soon bruised from Eleanor's constant gripping. By late afternoon her face was ashen, her lips raw with biting. She was so tired she could not bear down when Alice told her to.

"I'm going to die, I know it!" she wept.

"You won't die," I said, though I was far from certain.

"But if I do, will you take care of my baby?"

"Of course we will. Now push," said Alice sternly.

"Not Alice; *you*, Cate," Eleanor insisted, then let out a sharp cry.

I could see Alice was becoming worried. Finally she reached inside Eleanor, who screamed in pain. Moments later she withdrew a pair of feet.

"Cate, press down on her belly," Alice said, her voice urgent.

\d, *don't let me kill her,* I prayed silently, and put my
ʌnor's tight, sweaty belly.

ˈer!" said Alice.

.., and something yielded within Eleanor. At last the baby
slipped into Alice's hands, its skin as pale blue as the veins under
my skin. Alice bent over it, and moments later the tiny creature
let out a high, thin wail. Eleanor began to weep with relief.

John White was the proudest man on Roanoke Island. The
first English child born in the New World was his very own granddaughter. Ananias hid his disappointment that it was not a son.
But there was such rejoicing for the deliverance of the mother and
daughter that it seemed all our hopes would be rewarded, our
troubles and fears banished.

At her christening, Eleanor's baby was named Virginia.

Within a month of our coming to the island, Fort Ralegh was
secure and all the houses habitable. Wells had been dug and lined
with barrels to catch rainwater. Horses that had run loose on the
island since Ralph Lane's sudden departure were captured and
put in new stalls. The chickens were producing eggs. Hundreds of
trees had been cut to build the palisade and the sunny clearings
turned into fields.

Manteo showed the farmers how to plant the seeds in small
hillocks placed a few paces apart, so the beans would grow upright
around the stalks of maize. Between the hillocks they planted
squash and saltbush for flavoring. But the farmers spent as much
time arguing as hoeing, debating whether the sandy soil would
yield healthy grain and whether the crops would ripen before the
winter, since they had been planted so late.

Meanwhile it rained two or three times, and pale green seedlings appeared.

In John White's house, I slowly grew used to the different routine. Eleanor recovered her strength quickly, and though she nursed Virginia for hours on end she still managed to do all the cooking. I swept the house clean and beat the dust out of the bedding. Sometimes I held the baby or rocked her cradle and thought about how to invest Sir Walter's money: either in fragrant cedar for furniture or the uppowoc plant, which could be dried and shipped with less expense. Because the governor would accept no payment for my board, I became the laundress for his household instead. It was a task that would have been too menial for a queen's maid, but I was no longer placed so high. The one job I refused to do was grubbing in the dirt with a hoe.

I also traded on the only skill that was mine alone. The village women were pleased to have their ruffs bleached and stiffened by the same hands that had fixed the queen's ruffs. And so I worked on many a ruff in exchange for pies and jellies and small favors. But the garments made our necks perspire in the heat, and as time went on we seldom wore them. I had less neckwear to launder and starch, but the baby made up for it with an abundance of dirty linens.

I did not mind washing them, foul though they were. I was simply glad for little Virginia's presence. She was the treasure of our entire village. She had struggled into life and was flourishing, despite hardships beyond her infant awareness.

Chapter 23

A Sudden Departure

A month had passed, then five weeks, and Simon Fernandes still had not left Hatorask. The *Lion*, though anchored out of sight, cast an invisible shadow over the colony. In the hands of the mutinous pilot, the ship was a sign of John White's failure. It reminded us we had not reached our destination of Chesapeake, and getting there was now beyond our means. Yet while the ship stayed, there was the possibility of escaping the strangeness, hardship, and danger of the New World and returning to what was familiar. Once she sailed, we would be truly alone. And it would no longer be possible to send a letter to Sir Walter.

I still had written no reply to the letter I received aboard the *Lion*. Now I had little time for shaping fine phrases to convey feelings I was not even sure of. I still yearned for him, so I believed. Maybe I only yearned for what was familiar and comfortable simply because it was now lost to me. My thoughts were too confused for words. However, I did write to Emme that I was well, leaving unsaid almost everything that mattered in this new place, because it was simply too much for a single letter. I gave the letter to the boatswain, who promised to deliver it when he reached London.

Fernandes may have been ready to sail away in pursuit of treasure, but both the *Lion* and the flyboat required caulking and repairs. Fernandes also needed wood for fuel and fresh water for the return voyage. But John White would not allow his men to assist the pilot, and the seamen were not welcome at the fort. Whenever they came to the island to cut timber or gather pine resin, fights broke out. Nearly every day malefactors were put in the stocks.

Finally the governor called a meeting of all the colonists. His house being too small, the meeting was held outdoors. He sat at a table with his seven assistants flanking him. There had been nine, but George Howe was dead, and Fernandes was excluded. Manteo, now a lord, was away on some embassy.

The men sat on stools or stood with their arms crossed, the women behind them. Eleanor cradled the sleeping Virginia. Georgie Howe sat on the ground, rocking from side to side in silence.

"What is that cursed ship still doing here?" Ambrose Vickers burst out. "If Fernandes won't take us to Chesapeake, he should be on his way."

Ananias nodded and turned to the governor. "Truly, that ship is a beacon to any vessel plying the coast. Fernandes could lead the Spaniards right into this bay."

John White raised his voice over the grumblers. "Fernandes and I are in disagreement, but he is not a traitor, I'll warrant you."

"We might try again to persuade him," said Roger Bailey. "With arms if necessary." He looked around to measure his support.

I shook my head in disagreement. The time for taking back the ship had been the moment Fernandes first defied the governor. Now it was too late.

"There will be no bloodshed," said White firmly. "Going to Chesapeake was always a risk. We would not have had time to prepare for winter. We are here now and must make the best of it."

"Since Ralegh expected us to settle at Chesapeake, he will send his supply ships there," said Ananias. "Then what shall we do here?"

White thought for a moment and said, "We have much to accomplish in the next months, but with time we shall be self-sufficient."

He had not answered Ananias's question. Several of the men stirred with dissatisfaction.

"We have less than you think, Governor," said Roger Bailey. "Much of the grain rotted on the voyage, and we have used more of the building materials than we expected. I have been an army quartermaster, and I can tell you our stores will hardly last the winter."

"How many of us will die then?" asked Ambrose Vickers. "I know I'll not let my wife and son starve."

"Or be slain by savages," said one John Chapman. He was Alice's husband and an armorer by trade. "I am not the only one who does not trust Manteo. Lord of Roanoke indeed! When he returns it will no doubt be at the head of an army of Indians."

Alice glared at her husband and I could see there would be an argument between them later.

"The Indians. They came and slew my papa. I saw the arrows in his chest. Oh, my poor papa!" wailed Georgie, his big frame shaking. "They will come back for me next."

A sense of alarm spread through the crowd as if a hornet buzzed in our midst. Eleanor's arms tightened around baby Virginia, who awoke and began to cry.

I could barely restrain myself from speaking aloud and murmured to Eleanor, "The governor should stand up to Chapman and Bailey and forbid such talk."

Eleanor pursed her lips. "It is not a woman's place to judge a man."

"Governor, what are you going to do to about the Indians?" Chapman demanded.

"This meeting is adjourned. Go to your houses," Bailey ordered, though he did not have the authority to do so.

"If there is any trouble, the offender will be arrested," said the governor. His voice did not carry over the din.

That evening John White consumed his supper in a dismal silence no one in the household dared to break. Afterward he placed his portable desk on his knees and drew a picture of his grand-daughter while she slept. He would not even look at Ananias, who remained seated at the table. I took my needle and thread to a ripped seam, wishing I were a man and could speak about govern-ment. Hadn't the queen once said I would make a good councilor? I glanced at Eleanor, hoping she would speak to her father, but she kept her head bent over her own sewing.

I took a deep breath. What did I have to lose by speaking up? "Governor, it pained me today to hear how the men spoke against you and Manteo. Would you not be justified in punishing their sedition?"

I heard Ananias's cup hit the table.

"Cate!" The loud whisper of warning came from Eleanor.

Only John White did not seem surprised. "Everything is new to them, and they are uncertain and afraid," he said, continuing to draw.

"Then you must reassure them," I said. "All of us look to you to keep us united in our purpose."

To my surprise, Eleanor said, "It is Roger Bailey and Ambrose Vickers who lead the malcontents."

"Silence, wife!" said Ananias.

Eleanor stood up, her needlework falling from her lap. "I would chain them to the bilboes if I were you, Father!" Then she sat back down and began to rock Virginia's cradle rapidly.

"You might remind them of what you encountered before, and the negotiations that brought you safely through danger," I suggested.

He seemed to consider my words. "There are new difficulties I did not expect or even imagine," he said with a sigh. "The native inhabitants have changed toward us." He closed his drawing table and stood up, signaling that the conversation was ended.

At least he did not chastise me for speaking.

The next day the seven assistants called on the governor. Ananias came down from the roof he was tiling to join them. I retreated outside, lingering by the open window so I could overhear them, as I had often listened at the queen's door.

Roger Bailey was their spokesman. "Fernandes informs me that he is now prepared to sail," he said. "One of us must return to England with him to ensure sufficient supplies are dispatched here, not to Chesapeake, before winter."

"Excellent," White said. "I will draft a letter to that purpose for Fernandes to carry."

"You misunderstand, Governor," said Bailey.

There was a long pause. Then White replied, "Indeed, perhaps we should not trust Fernandes. Roger, you must be the one to convey the letter."

"John, we have already decided you should undertake this business," said another of the assistants.

"But I am the governor here!" White's voice rose. "I am charged with protecting the queen's subjects. Choose another among yourselves."

"We have considered the others," said Bailey. He cleared

his throat. "You are the only one who can be trusted to return here."

I understood the plan. The assistants knew how much the governor loved this New World, almost as much as he loved his daughter and granddaughter. So they would use Eleanor and Virginia as hostages to ensure that he would bring the goods to sustain us all. Moreover, while appearing to entrust a vital task to him, they were in fact ousting him.

"Is it so desolate and disagreeable here that none of you would return?" said White in disbelief. Then his tone became scornful. "I thought my men were made of stronger stuff. Or are you all afraid of Fernandes?"

There was silence. Were the men ashamed? Was even Ananias against his father-in-law?

"You are my councilors only. You may advise me on a course of action, but you may not command me. This decision is mine!" White's voice was trembling with rage. "I will render it tomorrow. Now I dismiss you all."

The assistants, including Ananias, left. After a few minutes I slipped into the house again. John White sat at the table staring at his hands. He knew his men had lost confidence in his leadership. I could imagine the lowness in his heart.

"I am sorry, Governor," I said. There was no use pretending I had not overheard their conversation.

"How can I leave them?" he asked, sounding forlorn.

"Someone must go," I said. "And no one is more likely than you to move heaven and earth to bring back what we need."

"My daughter," he said, his voice faltering.

"I will take care of Eleanor and the baby and see that they come to no harm," I said. But I wondered how I could keep myself or anyone safe in this unpredictable land.

He nodded gratefully.

"People are fickle," I said. "When you return, they will welcome you as a hero. Though some of them may have less reason to celebrate if they are hanged for treason."

He looked at me with a wry smile. "You are wise and well spoken for a woman. The queen should regret sending you away. But I think her loss will someday be judged Virginia's gain."

I warmed at this praise, yet I would have traded every word of it to have John White stay at Fort Ralegh.

The next morning, Governor White called all the colonists together and announced he would sail back to England at once. He demanded an inventory, an accounting of the colony's assets, and a list of its requirements. He ordered his assistants to preserve his maps, papers, books, and drawings, as they were of great value to him and to posterity. By asserting his authority in this way, he was trying to conceal that it had already been taken from him.

"Your welfare has been entrusted to me by God and by England's queen," he told the assembly. "And I promise I shall fulfill my duty to every one of you. It is not my desire to return to England. But I have been persuaded by my assistants that I am the best man to convince Sir Walter Ralegh to supply our needs." He paused before resuming his speech. "There is some urgency, I grant you. And there is danger, for the growing hostility between England and Spain makes sea travel hazardous. Thus I understand why others . . . declined to make the voyage."

The colonists glanced from one assistant to the next, wondering who had shown fear. Bailey and Ananias looked uncomfortable.

"Know, all of you," the governor said, "I will not rest until I return, for my sole purpose will be the relief of this colony." His voice broke, then gathered strength again. "I have decreed that in my absence, my seven assistants will govern with equal voices, and all matters are to be decided by the greater number of them."

I thought that unlikely. Some voices, like Roger Bailey's, were always louder than others.

"Let there be no dissension, but only a unity of purpose and goodwill among you," he concluded.

It was a worthy speech. Some of the women dabbed their eyes. I clapped my hands and others joined in. A few people smiled, showing a forced cheerfulness. But the malcontents could not remain silent.

"When will we go to Chesapeake and settle?" called Ambrose Vickers. "We cannot trust the savages around here."

John White replied with vehemence. "I said before, this is not the time. You have only the pinnace, which is too small to carry much. If you divide yourselves to make the journey in stages, or go by land, you increase the danger to everyone. I will return with ships and men and arms. In the spring we will move to Chesapeake." He stared down the line of the men standing to his right. "This is my decision, to which my assistants have consented."

But by the warning tone of his voice, I suspected that the men were hardly of one mind.

The governor's household was also divided. Eleanor wept and begged her father not to go, to send another man, and to stand up to the scheming Roger Bailey. John White pleaded with her to be brave, and anyone with a heart would have wept to hear them. I held little Virginia and wiped my tears on her dress. She was not even mine, and still I could not imagine parting from her. Poor John White! When Ananias returned, Eleanor released her fury on him, saying he had betrayed her father and thus was no longer welcome in her bed. He shouted at her but managed to refrain from striking her. Then he left the house to lodge elsewhere.

Retreating to a corner of the tempest-tossed house, I wrote a hasty letter to Sir Walter, my words flowing like water over a broken dam. The time was short, for Fernandes would sail with the morning tide. I gave the letter to John White to deliver and thanked him for his kindness to me. His face was grooved with sadness.

That night three of the assistants rowed the governor to where the *Lion* and the flyboat were anchored. Our little household was headless, the colony leaderless. And I was mindful of a suppressed longing my pen had reawakened, the desire for Sir Walter's familiar voice and his touch.

Chapter 24

From the Papers of Sir Walter Ralegh

Memorandum

8 August 1587. There is a new favorite at court—the Earl of Essex, Leicester's stepson. Leicester, grown too old for the queen's love, slips the boy into his place, knowing she will not be able to resist the hot-blooded pup. He is barely able to grow a beard and skilled at nothing but playing cards.

2 September. Essex dared to thumb his nose at me. I seized his collar and promised to answer the insult later.

18 September. The queen was entertaining her knavish boy in her chamber when I heard shouting and a crash from within. I flung open the door and entered the chamber with a sergeant behind me. "I cannot serve a mistress who would be in awe of such a man," Essex was saying. He held a broken wine vessel, its contents spilled over the queen's dressing gown.

Seeing me, he said in a tone of contempt, "Speak of the devil, and he comes!" Then he put his hand to his sword hilt, and I arrested him by the arms.

"It is treason to draw in the the presence of the sovereign," I said.

"Let me go, ape! My lady, order him to release me," the arrogant youth commanded.

"Nay, hold him still," she said to me, much angered. Then to the boy: "You speak and act too boldly for a subject of mine." She struck him across the face with her fan, leaving a red welt. "Let this be a lesson to you. You rise by falling."

She pointed to the ground and he duly fell to his knees. Then she laughed, saying to me, "Let him go and leave us alone."

Essex is fortunate that Elizabeth is smitten. For less offense than his, many a luckless creature has been sent to the Tower.

21 October. With the prospect of a Spanish invasion growing more likely, the queen has appointed me to raise armies and strengthen the coastal defenses of Cornwall, Devon, Somerset, and Dorset. She also tasks me with converting merchant vessels for the use of the navy and enforcing the Privy Council's ban on shipping from all ports.

Thus I am released from guarding her private person, that I may guard her public body—the realm of England. This is a duty that befits a man of action.

20 November 1587. Received a most unexpected visitor today—a sea-roughened, bone-thin John White. The news from Virginia is dismal: my colonists left at Roanoke Island, the need for supplies immediate, and the governor forced to seek relief himself, his voyage so fraught with misfortunes that he was at sea for months and returned home more dead than alive.

What ill luck attends this venture! I explained to White that the threat of war, the ban on shipping, and my own lack of funds prevented me from sending a relief ship.

White was not sympathetic. "I came through that battlefield

alive. Surely Her Majesty can spare a thirty-ton bark. Remind her that the lives of her subjects are at stake, even women and children." Here his voice faltered. "They have consented to live in her new colony despite the dangers. They must not be abandoned there." His eyes, deep in his weathered face, shone with weary desperation.

Then he told me of the killing of George Howe, the shifting loyalties of the natives, and wondered whether even Manteo could succeed in reconciling them to us.

"But the most pressing need is for food," he said. "In the month I was there, the Indians would not meet with us or trade for food. They know there is not enough for them and for us." He rubbed his forehead as if it pained him. "Moreover, we may have planted too late to reap before the winter. My family may be starving even now."

To hide the regret that swept me, I began to arrange the weapons in their racks. I thought of all those who had sailed seeking the chance to become wealthy in a new world. I told myself they had chosen the journey, its risks as well as its rewards. But my Catherine had not chosen her fate. She was banished to Virginia because of me. Now what undeserved miseries does she endure?

"How fares your ward, the Lady Catherine?" I asked.

"She is useful to my daughter and beloved of her and the child," said White, smiling for the first time. "She has no fear or hatred of the natives, unlike many of the colonists. I was pleased to see how she welcomed the Croatoan women, giving them pieces of lace with which to adorn themselves." He paused, reflecting. "Truly, if she were a man, I would wish her to be one of my assistants."

So speaking, John White made me see my witty and lovely C.A., a pale rose among the tawny savages. I must find a way to succor her and the others.

"I cannot permit the colony to fail after so much has been invested," I said. "Let me speak to Her Majesty and summon you after."

As he left, White placed a letter in my hand. I knew at once it was from C.A. The page was crinkled as if it had gotten wet and the ink had run in places. I put my lips to the letter and thought it tasted of salt. The spray of the sea? Tears? I hoped to read, at long last, a protestation of love or a declaration of sorrow at our separation. Perhaps a poem to prove her affections.

Oh, the letter did strike me strongly, though in a most unexpected way.

Dear Sir Walter,

I have often composed in my mind the phrases in which I would praise this New World. But there is little to be written in favor of seasickness, the hellish climate, and other discomforts. Nor have I any matter for a sonnet, but enough for an elegy upon poor George Howe, deprived of his life by sixteen arrows and several blows of a club. But I must keep to my point.

My purpose here is to inform you of injustices committed upon the bearer of this letter, John White. It is bold of me, a maid of honor now disgraced, to appeal on behalf of a gentleman and bolder still to charge others with wrongdoing. But I have the liberty of one who has nothing to lose, and so I presume upon our past affections and your present influence with the queen.

First, Capt. Fernandes has defied the authority of our governor. I and many others witnessed his brazen refusal to carry us to Chesapeake. The reason he gave—that the season was too far advanced—was contradicted by the five weeks he remained at anchor offshore. In my judgment, Fernandes is a traitor determined to ruin this colony. Some even think he is a secret papist in league with Spain.

Simon Fernandes, whom I have trusted on so many voyages—a mutineer loyal to Spain? He is Portuguese and thus an enemy of Spain. He is no more a papist than Walsingham. Indeed, Fernandes has been Walsingham's man ever since W. saved him from hanging once. Can it be that Walsingham uses Fernandes to ruin my colony? To kill my fame and all my credit?

Seeking more evidence I read further, but found little satisfaction.

> *Second, in the matter of our governor's departure, it is evident his assistants have conspired to remove him from his office that they might rule instead. To preserve the appearance of concord, the governor has consented to this second mutiny. In my judgment Simon Fernandes, Roger Bailey, and Ananias Dare ought to be hanged and the others thrown into the Tower.*
>
> *John White may have his faults as a governor, but they do not proceed from a lack of kindness. Those who usurp his power seek only their own good, and they act from ignorance and ill will that will surely lead to war with the native peoples.*
>
> *Because I have been mistreated by those I had reason to believe cared for me, it pains me to see Gov. White betrayed. I beg you: do what is necessary to restore just rule to your Virginia.*
>
> *Come yourself and govern this colony that hungers for leadership and this heart of mine starving for lack of love's food. Or we shall all be lost.*
>
> *Yours, Catherine Archer*

Truly, it cannot be tolerated when the governed decide to rule themselves and throw off their governor. It must be the savagery of that place that makes men descend from their civil upbringing to a beastly state in which the strong devour the weak. I should have made a statesman—not a painter—their governor. But no other man of merit and experience would consent to return there.

Shipping bans and Spanish pirates be damned! I will go to Virginia myself and teach them all what it means to obey. My iron hand once put down the Irish rebels and it shall be raised again over these wayward subjects. As for my duties of fortifying the coast, my deputy can perform them as well as I can.

For my Catherine calls me, and I will answer. No royal threat or command must hinder me from the embrace of my fair, my own, my sweet Virginia.

Chapter 25

I, Manteo, Am Tempted by Wanchese

When I returned to my home as Lord of Roanoke and Dase-munkepeuc, I wore my English mantle. The trim glittered in the sun, making me look like a god. *"See how great Manteo has become!"* my people said.

"I am still Weyawinga's son," I replied. A hero must be humble and pay respect to his weroance and to his mother. I said the English had honored me in order to show their love for the Croatoan.

My village was changing. The children still ran in and out of the longhouses all day until they fell asleep. But now they played with English dolls and fought over them. The women decorated themselves with glass beads and bright cloth. Some warriors had knives and axes with iron blades. These differences led to envy and bad feeling. One of my kinsmen wore a piece of armor for which he had given a basket of mussel shells that he said contained pearls but were in fact empty. He was pleased with the trade, but I warned him that the English would not be friends with those who deceived them.

Death had also changed my village. Where Ralf-lane and his men had gone, a great sickness followed in their wake. A hundred Croatoans died. Many times that number in the villages of Osso-mocomuck. The elderly and little children fared worst, and the women who cared for them. Now some of my kinsmen had no wives or children. They also thought I had died or been stolen by the wind gods when I went away on the English ships. But when I came back a lord, they believed my journey had caused them to be spared greater losses.

Dolls, beads, and death. These were not the gifts I wanted for my people. Was I to blame for the sickness because I brought Englishmen back with me? No, I realized they would have come anyway, bringing their goods, their weapons. And their sickness.

So far I had brought nothing valuable to my people. Not rain to make the maize ripen. Not grain and spices from distant lands or new plants to fill the fields in summer and feed us in winter. Would the people of my village one day be forced, like Tameoc's band, to wander from place to place in search of food? What must I do to make them prosper again?

I visited all the Roanoke villages between Pomeioc and Dase-munkepeuc with the message that the white men desired friend-ship. Wingina's people had left Dasemunkepeuc after killing George-howe and built a new village. I went there to parley with Wanchese, who was now their weroance. It was a dangerous envoy, but my robe of office gave me the spirit's protection.

Wanchese greeted me coldly and regarded my robe with con-tempt. I said the English wanted to know why he had killed a man who had done them no harm.

"In war one must slay or be slain," he said.

"We were not at war with you."

"*We? You are one of them now, are you, Manteo?*"

"*No. I am a Croatoan,*" I said. Even being a lord would not change that.

"*Have the Croatoan forgotten the white men killed Wingina?*"

"*This leader is not the one who killed Wingina. But his men are preparing to take revenge for the death of George-howe. And for the soldiers killed at their fort before John-white arrived.*" I wanted to make Wanchese afraid so he would offer payment and terms of peace. I wanted to go back to John-white and say I had prevented a war.

But Wanchese looked angry, not fearful. He said the soldiers had come to his village and forced women to lie with them. The women died, and others whom the soldiers had not touched. I saw the scars from his own disease still on Wanchese's face. If hatred and ill will had caused Wanchese's sickness, what explained the deaths of people who had never seen a white man to hate? People who were innocent of evil?

Wanchese said his warriors and the Secotan had killed the soldiers and burned their bodies to destroy the disease. "*Now all the weroances are grateful to me.*"

This was startling news, that the soldiers had violated the Roanoke women. John-white would have put the men to death for it. I could not blame Wanchese.

"*Did they stay away from the council that John-white called because they feared a sickness?*" I asked.

Wanchese said with a sly smile, "*The peoples of Ossomocomuck do not heed John-white or Lord Manteo.*"

Then I understood that Wanchese had prevented the weroances from meeting with John-white. Did he threaten the ones who wanted to make peace? Why? Because he wanted power only for himself? I think he was envious of me because the English preferred me from the beginning.

Now Wanchese was speaking to me as if I were a mere boy.

"Manteo, you do not understand the doings of men. The English are buying your faith with empty honors. They try to buy us with beads and copper, but I am not deceived. I know they plan to betray us."

Wanchese's words were like seeds on damp earth. I felt doubts growing within me. Some of the colonists hated all natives. John-white said he wanted peace, but why had he brought so many soldiers, if not to make war on us?

"I have been across the water like you and know the English are many," said Wanchese. *"We must make them fear to come here. We will unite and show the white men our strength. Kill them before they kill us."* He gripped my arm. *"And if you do not join my alliance, you and your people will suffer."*

My anger rose. I would not be threatened by Wanchese. I was a weroance by the power of the English kwin, whom I had vowed to serve. I could not betray that vow and keep my honor. Nor would I let my people submit to Wanchese.

"What are you asking me to do?"

Wanchese replied, *"Deliver the English to us."*

My heart drummed inside me. I thought of John-white's kindness to me. His daughter and the child. The brave maid with the dark hair who had found George-howe's body, yet welcomed the Croatoan to her house. How could I deliver them to Wanchese? To their deaths?

"Would you destroy the women and children too?" I asked.

Wanchese only shrugged. *"Show me where they are weak, that I may know when to strike."*

I, too, could be a deceiver. *"Give me time to consider how this can be done,"* I said.

I went back to Roanoke filled with uncertainty. When I arrived, John-white was gone and I was greeted with cold, mistrustful stares.

Chapter 26

The First Winter

Edmund Vickers was lucky to be little and have no worries. He dashed through the fields shouting and waving his arms. It was his job to keep the crows and deer away from the crops, and he thought it was a fine game. Sometimes Georgie would join him, and I would smile to see the large boy capering like a court fool while little Edmund clapped his hands. Not a whole village of scarecrows, however, could have made the maize grow taller. Only rain would do that. But not a drop fell in all of September, and the spindly stalks turned brown. When at last we plucked the ears and stripped the husks, the kernels were as small and sparse as baby's teeth. After a portion was set aside for planting in the spring, what remained was enough to last only two months.

The beans fared a little better, but most of the squash had rotted on the vine when the frost came. Everyone blamed the planters, who said it would not freeze because of its thick skin.

Whenever two people met, they talked about the weather and debated how many days it would be until the governor returned, and whether his ship would take the southern route or the more direct but dangerous northern one. All agreed he could not reasonably return before December. As winter drew closer, Betty Vickers would kneel down right in her garden or in the middle of the street and pray out loud for deliverance.

John White's house was still the meeting place for the assistants. Ananias had returned home and made peace with Eleanor. He even began to listen to her advice. "He owes me that much," she said. When I had an opinion, I would tell it to Eleanor, who would pass it to her husband, who might raise it with the assistants. He seemed to regret his part in ousting John White from the colony.

But Ananias was not strong enough to stand in the way of Roger Bailey, who took leadership of the assistants. At once the dispute resumed over whether or not to remain at Fort Ralegh. Bailey wanted to disregard the governor's instructions and move the colony to Chesapeake. Ambrose Vickers and many of the colonists were also of this mind. But three assistants thought it wiser to remain on Roanoke Island and await relief. One of these was Christopher Cooper, who of late had set himself openly against Bailey.

"Our governor won't return. We are on our own," insisted Bailey.

This made Eleanor weep, and she used all her persuasion, including tears, to convince Ananias to wait for her father's return. Thus he voted with Cooper and two other assistants to remain at The fort, leaving Bailey and his two supporters furious at being outnumbered.

"We'll take this matter up again," said Bailey darkly.

When Manteo had returned from his envoy to the Indians, he was surprised to find John White gone. Bailey and Ananias gave no explanation and made him feel so unwelcome he had gone back to Croatoan. Now that winter was approaching, they summoned him back and offered kettles and axe blades in exchange for food. Manteo opened his hands and said the Croatoan had no food to share.

"I don't believe him," said Bailey. "He wants us to starve." He said this in front of Manteo as if he lacked understanding.

Ananias continued to probe Manteo about which Indians had food, but Manteo said the harvest had been poor everywhere. I listened, stirring the kettle in which the soup was already thin.

"What good is he to us?" Bailey asked Ananias, then turned his back on Manteo, dismissing him.

Manteo said nothing to defend himself. I was ashamed of Bailey and wanted to show Manteo we were not all so lacking in respect.

"Perhaps Lord Manteo will help us repair the broken weirs," I heard myself say. "Then we can at least catch fish and dry them for the winter."

There was a silence in which I could hear Bailey seething.

For a moment Manteo's eyes met mine. Was it surprise or gratitude or simple interest that I glimpsed there? I turned back to my kettle, not daring to look at Bailey.

I heard Manteo say, "It would please me to do this for my friends."

Ananias clapped his hands, breaking the tension, and proceeded to discuss the broken weirs with Manteo. It was not long before they were fixed and several of the men had learned how to maintain them and build new ones. Trust in Manteo was renewed as the colonists saw him working for our benefit.

John White did not return even by Christmas. Dabbing away her tears, Eleanor prepared a meal of game, dried fish, and pudding made from eggs, suet, and precious dried figs. It was a meager feast compared to the rich pies and beef I had grown used to at court. The guests were fewer, too: Georgie and his aunt Joan, and John Chapman and Alice, who was now nursing an infant son. The babies' cooings lightened the somber mood. The Chapmans brought Thomas Graham, who showed off the new gorget Chapman had made for him and tried to cheer everyone with tales of his exploits in London. I did not wish to remember those days. Alice reported the widow was ill. We were all thinner than we had been in the summer. I had to pin my skirts so they would not slide down my hips.

Christmas night the prayer service was held in the armory, the only building large enough for so many people. The preacher read a gospel and recited the litany. When he prayed for God to preserve all who travel by the sea, he fairly shouted. And we called in return, "Hear us, good Lord!" as if God were deaf. And then, crowded together on the hard benches, we listened to a two-hour sermon, interrupted once by Betty Vickers crying out, "God bestowed the Magi's gifts on his infant son. Surely he will provide for us!"

Alice had little patience for Betty's piety. "What use did Jesus have for gold, frankincense, and myrrh?" she murmured to me.

"Only a midwife would say such a thing," I whispered back.

"We could use those riches now," said Eleanor. "The gold alone would make our men wealthy enought to forget all their troubles."

"No, they would only fight over it like dogs over a bone," said Alice. She was probably right.

By this time the preacher had stopped his sermon to glare at us. I heard Eleanor giggle and I smiled despite myself.

One January day, Tameoc and his band of Croatoan came to the village. There were eight of them, wrapped in furs that were white from the falling snow. Manteo was away, so there was no one to translate. But their need was clear, even without words. Mika's eyes were large in her thin face. Takiwa held her small boy in her arms.

Ananias and Roger Bailey went out to meet them but kept their distance.

"We have no food!" shouted Bailey. "Go home."

"Bad sickness," Tameoc said, pointing to the child.

"No medicine either. Go away," said Bailey, waving his arms.

Ananias started to plead with him, but Bailey went back into his house and bolted the door. From shame or fear of sickness, all the doors in the village remained closed.

The Croatoan turned and left, and Ananias came inside.

"Surely we can spare something," said Eleanor. Ananias shook his head, and they began to argue.

I opened the cupboard. On a plate were six cakes, made from ground maize. I put four of them in my apron and ran until I caught up with the Croatoan. They ate the cakes right there where they stood. Takiwa fed her boy small bites with her fingers.

"I am sorry I can't do more," I said, holding out my empty hands. I blinked away tears brought on by the biting cold. Mika smiled and touched my arm, and the others nodded to show their gratitude. For days I wondered where they had gone for shelter and whether the boy had recovered.

Winter began to claim its victims. One after another they were buried on a hill near the village. The widow died from a weak heart and hunger, a planter from poisoned blood after his foot was cut by an axe, two soldiers from a fever that killed them so quickly they were buried with all their clothes on. No one even cut the buttons from their shirts or took the purses from their pockets, for fear of being contaminated. Then a laborer was chained to the bilboes for lewdness because he dared to piss within sight of Betty Vickers. He was left there overnight because he had no friends or kin to plead for him, and he froze to death.

But worst of all was the hanging and what led to it.

John Chapman had paid Georgie to guard his shop against thieves. But when a sword he was crafting for Roger Bailey went missing, he hauled Georgie before the council. It was the boy's aunt Joan who brought everyone to the scene with her cries.

"Only yesterday he touched it and made an admiring noise over it," Chapman charged. "He is the thief."

"He is an idiot. How do you expect him to know right from wrong?" said Christoper Cooper.

"He is innocent; the boy is innocent!" protested Joan, her hands raised in appeal.

"Did you take the sword?" demanded Ananias. "What did you do with it?"

Georgie shook his head and spittle flew from his open mouth.

Bailey pulled a knife from his belt. "Do you know the penalty for thievery?" He grabbed Georgie's hand, pinned it to the table, and put the blade to the back of his wrist.

Joan screamed and fainted. Georgie's eyes were wide with terror. I could not believe Bailey was about to cut off the young man's hand!

"That was my sword you stole," Bailey said and drew the blade across the skin.

"Stop! Where is the proof?" I heard myself shout, but my voice was drowned out by Georgie's howls as blood welled from the wound.

"They killed Georgie's father!" the boy wailed. "They shot him in the chest with arrows. He was full of blood too. Now he is in the cold ground. Georgie is cold." He shivered and turned pale.

I started forward but Eleanor grabbed my arm.

"Do not intervene, Cate." And then she called to her husband, "Do something, Ananias!"

But before Ananias could act, Christopher Cooper grabbed Bailey's arm. "Stop this torture," he said. "Search the boy's house first. Search every house."

While Bailey and Cooper faced off over the shaking Georgie, Ananias and the other assistants began to search for the sword. They came back dragging a soldier I recognized as Graham's gaming companion, the one who had spent ten years in prison.

"State your name," said Cooper. He leaned closer to the man and sniffed. "And why are you drunk in the daytime?"

"He was on guard in the fort," said Ananias, trying to be helpful.

"James Hind, sir," said the soldier belatedly. "This is my own sword, I say."

"A known thief," said Bailey. "*And* drunk while on duty."

"That is not the missing sword," said Chapman, peering at the hilt of Hind's sword.

"If he didn't steal it, he most certainly stole the ale, for each man's share is but three ounces a day," said Bailey.

"Why, he is determined to punish *someone* today," I said, not scrupling to lower my voice.

James Hind swayed and blinked at Bailey. "Are you calling me a thief? I am a man of honor, you scoundrel, and I shall prove it!" And with that he drew his sword and lurched toward Roger Bailey, who fell backward.

The crowd gasped with one voice. Every man, woman, and child knew the punishment for drawing a weapon upon the governor or his assistants was death. James Hind was undeniably guilty, so he was seized and put in the bilboes until he could be executed. Georgie was forgotten.

I had never been to a hanging. I knew noisy crowds gathered at Tyburn in London, shouting and jeering from the time the malefactor appeared until his lifeless body was carted away. I had no desire to see James Hind hanged. But I went along with everyone else to the gibbet that had been hammered together at the entrance to the fort. People were sober and wary, even doubtful about what they had seen. Had the man deliberately struck at Bailey, or had he only stumbled drunkenly while showing the sword to his accusers? For his part, James Hind shouted his innocence until the noose choked off his words and the breath behind them.

When James Hind was dead, the mystery remained unsolved. The sword John Chapman had been making for Bailey was not found anywhere near Fort Ralegh. I wondered if Bailey himself had taken it and then created the entire scene to demonstrate his power over us. No doubt he made many people afraid of him, but he only made me hate him.

Chapter 27

I Rediscover My Dreams

Roger Bailey began to lay out plans for the colony to move to Chesapeake, and no one dared contradict him, not even Ananias or Christopher Cooper. He came to John White's house whether or not he had business there and put his feet up on the table as if he were the master. When he left, Eleanor would rail against her husband, calling him a weakling. Then little Virginia would start to cry and Eleanor would put her to her breast and rock back and forth, weeping herself. I felt sorry for all of them. But I decided when we got to Chesapeake, I would use Sir Walter's money to build my own cottage. And Roger Bailey would never be allowed to set foot inside the door.

One day I was alone in the governor's house when I heard Bailey at the door. I slipped into the bedroom, hoping he would go away. His footsteps sounded inside. I heard him blow on his hands and knew he was standing at the hearth. The fire gave me away. If no one was at home, it would have been banked for safety.

Bailey was standing in the bedroom doorway, trapping me inside.

"You should not be here," I said, determined not to show my alarm.

"Were you expecting someone else? Thomas Graham, perhaps? Pah, he is nothing but a common soldier. You should grant your favors to one more suited to you—a gentleman." He tapped his chest.

"You, you . . . are a vile . . . *worm!*" I was so angry I stammered. "Graham is more a gentleman than you will ever be."

He laughed, baring his yellow teeth. "See how she defends her paramour."

"He is not my lover, and you I despise."

He raised his eyebrows. "So you were the queen's *maid*? More like her bawd, I'll warrant. I know why you were sent away from court."

"You know nothing," I said. "Now let me pass." I tried to get by him but he grabbed my wrist.

"And you are too outspoken to be a decent woman. But I will teach you a lesson or two. First, how to obey a man." He pressed me to the wall. His eyes were fixed on my bosom.

Now I was afraid of Bailey, but my hatred of him was stronger. "Unhand me now or I will scream rape. Surely you know the punishment for that."

To my surprise he dropped my arm and stepped back. The penalty for rape was death.

"You need to be married, and you can't do any better than me," he said.

"I would marry the rudest savage in all Virginia before I would ever let you touch me as a husband," I said, pouring all the disdain I could summon into my words. "Now get out."

"You'll regret your pride, vain wench," he said with a sneer. He turned to leave and on his way out kicked over the governor's chair. It crashed onto the hearth and became singed by the fire before I could manage to set it upright.

All my limbs were trembling, and I fell in a heap on the floor, resting my whirling head on the seat of the chair I had rescued from the fire.

That night Eleanor noticed the bruises on my wrist, so I told her about Roger Bailey's indecent demands. She struck her cooking ladle against the tabletop so hard Virginia began to cry in her cradle.

"Damn him! You are not the first to be undone by that man."

"I did not lie with him, you understand. How can you even think I would?" I said. "Who else has he tried to violate?"

"I have had it in confidence from Alice that Jane Pierce is with child by him, but she will not say he raped her because she wants to marry him."

"Jane? How could she want to marry Bailey?"

"We are not as wellborn as you, Cate," said Eleanor testily. "Jane hires herself out as a servant to earn her living. Bailey took more from her than her cooking. And now, to keep from being disgraced, she *must* marry him."

"Yet he dares to come to me and say I should marry him," I said, more indignant than ever. "At least I told him what a vile worm he is."

"That was hardly wise," she said with a rueful shake of her head. "You saw what he did to Georgie and that unfortunate soldier."

"Roger Bailey is not my governor," I said. "He is a tyrant, and I pray he will come to a bad end."

"So you have no man to govern you," she said with a wry smile. "I should envy you, Cate."

I thought about Sir Walter and how I had imagined marrying him. Would I have been happy to let him govern me? Did all wives consent to be ruled by their husbands? If so, marriage was no different than serving a king or queen. As a wife I might never have the freedom of my own will.

"I am fortunate to be no one's servant," I said. "I have no mistress or master, and I will have no husband either, if Roger Bailey is the best Virginia can offer."

"Don't worry. No man here will have you for a wife because you are so willful," said Eleanor, teasing me.

"I *have* gotten my will. I wanted to come to Virginia," I mused. "It is certainly not paradise, but if life were like heaven, dying would be a disappointment."

At this, Eleanor laughed and I did too. We laughed as we had not for months, so consumed with cares had we been. I started to feel light, like the flakes of snow that fell through the air. I might be hungry and thin, but I was still alive. I was not free from care, but my will was free. My place in this new, harsh world was mine to fashion. My dreams, which had lately grown dim, now filled my mind again, like unrecognized shadows that, with the dawn, show their bright, true shapes.

But then I thought of poor Jane Pierce, my companion aboard the *Lion*. Now pregnant by Roger Bailey, what contentment could she dream of?

Eleanor unlocked her father's trunk. I laid aside the jumbled maps and sea charts, sketches, journals, and old invoices until I saw a sheaf of papers titled *Thomas Harriot's Vocabulary of the Algonkian Language*.

"This is what I was looking for," I announced. "I will learn to speak Manteo's language."

Eleanor merely raised her eyebrows, then turned to watch Virginia, who was learning to creep across the floor.

Harriot's pages were full of strange markings, and I soon realized he had created a new alphabet for the Indian sounds. Using the key and other notations, I was able to make sense of it. Then I practiced speaking out loud.

Ananias complained about the "savage sounds" I was making. "It's not proper for a woman to be a scholar," he said. "Put that away."

"You do not rule me," I said lightly. Eleanor laughed, for that phrase had become our joke, and Ananias had the goodwill to smile too.

"Perhaps you should also learn Algonkian," I said. "Someone besides Manteo should be able to speak to the Indians. He cannot always be at hand to translate."

Ananias's good humor dissipated and he stamped out of the house. Eleanor gave me a look of distress.

"He can barely sign his own name," she said. "Most of the assistants can read and write a little, but they couldn't begin to study those papers."

"Well, they can learn the language from Manteo. I dare not. If I so much as nod to Thomas Graham, people think he is my paramour. Can you imagine how the gossips' tongues would wag if I were to seek out Manteo for conversation?"

"What I can't imagine is that you, Cate Archer, would let the suspicions of others guide your behavior," she replied.

I thought for a moment. "You are right, Eleanor. Why should I let others hinder me with their disapproval? It will not keep me from befriending the Croatoan women, which is my purpose in learning their language." I had not stopped thinking about their plight, which my fellow colonists preferred to ignore. "Mika reminds me of someone I used to know. And Takiwa's son—perhaps he still needs medicine. I can speak some Algonkian now. I want to go to them." Restless, I paced back and forth in the narrow room. "Does anyone know where they are living?"

"Ananias thinks they are still at Dasemunkepeuc," she said reluctantly. "But how will you get there? You're not thinking of going alone?"

I had a sudden thought. "Thomas Graham! He pledged to help me before." I grabbed a wool cloak Eleanor and I shared.

"Wait! You propose to go off in the company of a soldier for the purpose of relieving a band of Indians? Have you no care at all for your reputation?" She threw up her hands.

"This is Virginia, not England. A different decorum applies here," I argued.

"Not in the matter of a woman's virtue," she said firmly. "Soldiers are known to be rogues."

My face was hot, my mouth dry. "As I have no plans to win a husband here, my virtue is no one's concern but my own. And Thomas Graham is no rogue, but a better man than any of those false-made gentlemen who usurped your father's authority."

Eleanor drew back as if I'd slapped her. "You dare to accuse my husband? And you speak ill of my father, too." Tears came to her eyes.

"I'm sorry," I said, suddenly contrite. Eleanor and I had never quarreled. Now I stood to lose her friendship.

"I think you *do* need a husband to rule you and curb your tongue. Graham may be just the man," she said coldly and turned her back on me.

I went to the armory, where the soldiers were oiling and polishing their muskets, and asked to speak with Graham. A few of the men leered at me, but I ignored them. Graham only laughed at their lewd jests.

"Come, fellows, you know I love the fair Lady Anne, not this sun-darkened Ethiop," he said.

"Was that necessary?" I said when we were out of doors. "My hair may be black, but I am no Ethiop."

He smiled. He really was quite charming. "Queen Cleopatra was Ethiopian and a renowned beauty. How may I serve you, my Cate?"

I said I wanted to hire him to row me to Dasemunkepeuc and protect me while I visited the Croatoan.

"You need not pay me. I will relish the adventure," he replied.

"I have the means, and I will pay you," I insisted. "For this is also a business investment. I want to learn how the women make the designs they paint on their skin. Then I will sell those designs to weavers and embroiderers. You know how London loves a new fashion in cloth. And the Croatoan would prosper by the trade."

Graham did not reply for a long while. No doubt my plan sounded like an insubstantial dream. But I would find a way to make it real.

"I know why Ralegh loved you now," he said, admiration in his voice. "You are a woman after his own heart."

"I was after his heart," I admitted ruefully. "But I doubt he loved me. If he did, I would not be in this bind. If he loved this colony, he would have sent relief ships by now. He would be here to govern it himself."

I had never spoken about my feelings for Sir Walter to anyone besides Emme. But our shared exile led me to confide in Graham.

"Now it no longer matters whether he loved me or I him. I am no longer after his heart, but something more . . . lasting, I suppose."

Graham nodded, looking into the distance. No doubt he was thinking of Lady Anne.

I told Alice Chapman of my plan to go to Dasemunkepeuc and

asked her to come because of her knowledge of the ailments of women and children. Moreover, her presence might discourage the gossips. I was not entirely careless of my reputation.

"But my babe is not yet weaned," she objected.

"Eleanor will nurse him for you," I replied. "And we will only be absent a few days."

"If it is to help women in need, you know I cannot refuse," she said at last.

We visited the apothecary, who kept his medicines in a cupboard in his house. Alice advised me to buy saltpeter, a few grains of which cured measles and many aches; syrup of poppy, which induced sleep in restless infants; and small bags of a foul-smelling herb which, infused in a drink, relieved fevers. As I made these purchases, her eyes lit up with anticipation.

"Will the Indians welcome us, do you think?" she asked.

I reassured her Tameoc's women would recognize me and I would be able to converse with them.

I did not ask Bailey's permission to go to Dasemunkepeuc and thus acknowledge his authority over me. But Ananias knew of our plans. He preferred us to wait until Manteo had returned from his embassy to the Secotan, but he did not stand in the way of our going. Graham asked Christopher Cooper to procure a wherry for us, and Cooper, out of curiosity, decided to accompany us as well.

The morning of our departure, a tearful Alice turned up at the door alone.

"Is the babe sick?" I asked with sudden fear.

"I cannot leave him. What if I never return?" She began to sob. "My son will grow up without a mother."

Eleanor went to comfort Alice. "At least you have some sense. Cate's plan is folly," she said.

"What is foolish about tending the sick and bringing them

medicine?" I said. "Alice, nothing can go wrong. Why not bring your babe and let the Indians see we are just like them."

Eleanor gave a horrified gasp and Alice shook her head. "I want to go with you, Cate," she whispered. "But the truth is, John has forbidden me. And he fills my ears with such tales of savagery I am almost afraid to leave my house."

As Alice could not be persuaded, I took the satchel of medicine and went to meet Graham and Cooper by the shore. The March morning was silent except for the the lapping of waves against the wherry. There were patches of ice near the shore.

"Alice cannot join us. Let's be off now," I said.

Graham and Cooper rowed while I held the tiller. The foggy clouds that rose from the water left a rime on their beards and on everything in the boat. I pulled my cloak tight around me for warmth. As we neared the shore, Cooper stood in the prow with his musket ready. I felt my stomach clench. Was this how our soldiers felt when they neared Dasemunkepeuc? Did they imagine warriors eyeing them from among the trees, ready to release their arrows? The shore was deserted. Graham led the way to the village. It consisted of a few dwellings shaped like loaves of bread and covered with reed mats. A thin wisp of smoke came from the roof of one.

"Maybe they will come out if you put down your weapons," I said.

Graham unshouldered his musket and laid it on the ground, while Cooper lowered his, but did not release it.

"Seeing a woman with us, they won't attack," Graham said.

Into the silence I spoke the words I had carefully rehearsed. "*I am Cate Archer. I come with medicine for the sick boy.*"

There was no reply from within the house, though it seemed occupied. Had they not understood me?

Cooper murmured something about an ambush but Graham dismissed him. "What are they waiting for?" he said. "We've been sitting ducks since the moment we landed."

"Let's search the houses for stores of food," said Cooper.

Before I had a chance to object, the mat was pushed aside and Takiwa stepped outside. A second face, thin with hunger, peered from the opening. It was Mika. Takiwa held up her empty arms. She let out a stream of words, most of which I could not understand, but I knew what she meant by them. Her son was dead.

My own eyes filled with tears, a better ambassador than any words. I stepped toward her and she motioned me into the house. It was dark inside but smoky and warm. As my eyes adjusted, I saw how spacious it was. The walls were hung with baskets, dried herbs, furs, nets, and quivers of arrows. The fire had been covered when they heard us coming, but the old woman rekindled it. I was offered a bitter-tasting tea, which I drank so as not to offend. My halting efforts to speak Algonkian had some success. I learned Takiwa and Mika were Tameoc's sisters. The old woman was their grandmother. She was weak but otherwise healthy. The other women were also kin. They had no food except acorn meal and a few strips of dried meat. Tameoc and the men had gone hunting. There had been no sign of Wanchese lately.

Mika was shivering and appeared feverish. I gave Takiwa the medicine and, remembering what Alice had told me, explained how to administer it. I said nothing about my plan to bring them prosperity, for to speak of my own dreams seemed a mockery of their misery. Before I left, Takiwa gave me a mantle made from fox furs, which they had in abundance. They would have traded these for food if there had been any. But in all the neighboring villages was nothing but hunger and sickness.

When we returned to Fort Ralegh, Bailey was angry with

Cooper and accused us all of insubordination. Ananias, however, persuaded him that to punish us—especially me, a lady—for aiding a few Croatoan women would cause many of the colonists to turn against him.

Alice was relieved to see me alive, and Eleanor said grudgingly, "I needed your help with Virginia."

There were two more deaths among the colonists before the snow melted and spring announced herself with birdsong and shoots of greenery. I was glad so many of us had survived our first winter in Virginia, and I hoped Mika was well again. I was eager to return to Dasemunkepeuc and build upon my friendship with the Croatoan women, the dream of which had helped carry me through the winter. With the coming of spring, hopes were rekindled that a relief ship would come, while Bailey and his supporters revived plans for moving to Chesapeake.

Bailey made no attempt to stop the visits to Dasemunkepeuc. He told Graham he hoped we would be killed for our troubles and thus end his. For my part, I was glad to escape the company of the anxious and divided colonists for that of the Indian women. Mika had recovered her health and was always glad to see me. She patiently corrected my errors in speaking, then had me repeat what she said. By this method my knowledge of Algonkian grew, and soon all the women could understand me.

Graham was always pleased to come along as my protector, though we encountered no dangers. Then I realized he had been watching Mika. As yet she wore a mantle against the cold, but in the summer months when all the women bared their breasts, would he stare all the more? Mika was of an open and generous nature. One day she gave me a small cup lined with mother-of-pearl. She gave Graham one also. He had learned a few words of Algonkian and he thanked her, which made her turn away shyly.

"You have not forgotten Lady Anne, have you?" I admonished him.

"No more than you can forget Sir Walter," he countered.

"But he and I were never to one another what you and Anne were—*are* to each other," I said. "Your affection was apparent and ours never spoken." I thought of Ralegh's letter I had read aboard the *Lion* almost a year ago. It had been full of regret and sorrow and even hope, but not love.

"I do not think of Sir Walter often," I admitted with some truth. It seemed vain to dwell on the past or wish for an uncertain future. When I thought of the touches, the words and the poems we had exchanged, it was all about the anticipation of love, the secrecy of it. Never the fulfillment, which might have ruined the pleasure itself.

"Now he and I belong to different worlds, as unalike as the sun and the moon," I said.

"But if he were to come to *this* world—," Graham prompted.

"We would all be glad, for we would no longer be in want. But where are the ships he promised?"

Graham shook his head. "Perhaps Ralegh has suffered financial ruin or lost the queen's favor. John White may have been ship-wrecked. The plague may have struck and carried off half the people of London. Or the Spanish have invaded England. The queen might be dead and King Philip on the throne, for all we know."

"Are you trying to frighten me, Thomas Graham?"

"No, my dear. But I do think I am unlikely to see an English ship or my Lady Anne again." He looked so forlorn I thought he might weep.

"Then we must make the best of our circumstances here and learn to live alongside the Indians," I said.

And so I continued my efforts to learn the ways of the Croatoan women. I followed them to the swamps where they gathered reeds and watched as they wove them into mats. They showed me which roots were edible and which ones would sicken me. I learned to identify huckleberries, cranberries, and mulberries, which I took back to the island and made into preserves. I picked wild peas and helped to harvest rice from a shallow lake; I ground nuts and acorns and even made bread out of them. All this knowledge I shared with the other colonists in the hopes that our second winter would not be as desperate as the first.

Mika and I became close friends. She loved to dress my hair, tying it behind my head after the Indian fashion. One day she turned up my sleeve and, using a dark blue dye, embellished the skin of my arm in a lacy pattern. I felt like one of the queen's ladies preparing for a masque. She offered to dress me in a deerskin like her own, but I did not want to bare so much of my flesh. I wished that Emme and Anne could see me and hear me speak the Indians' tongue as easily as they themselves spoke French.

While Graham and I were at Dasemunkepeuc the hunters returned, arriving as quietly as the fog that rolls in from the sea. Graham saw them first and called to me. I followed the women as they came out to greet the hunters, who were dragging the carcass of a deer on a sledge. To my surprise Manteo was with them, wearing not his English clothes but a deerskin around his loins and a torn shirt. At the sight of me and Graham he looked displeased.

And then I noticed Tameoc, his arm wrapped in a bloody cloth. It appeared to be the sleeve from Manteo's shirt. How had he become injured? My gaze went to his belt, from which a bloody patch of skin and hair dangled. I thought of the dead men's skulls atop the Tower gate in London. For the first time I felt a tremor of fear in the Indians' presence. Who had Tameoc slain, and how was Manteo involved?

But it was not only the piece of scalp that made me afraid. Also tucked into Tameoc's belt was a bright new sword. I knew it had to be the sword missing from Chapman's shop, the one James Hind had died for. Tameoc must be the one who had stolen it, and as soon as Roger Bailey found out, there would be trouble.

Chapter 28

I, Manteo, Meet the Moon Maiden

One of the legends my mother used to tell me has become part of my dreams. Now I cannot separate it from the dream. Which one is true? They are both as true as life itself. This is what I know.

One evening Algon the hunter was returning home from the forest when he came upon a group of maidens singing in a clearing. Among them was one who outshone the others in beauty as the moon outshines the stars. At his approach the fair maiden fled, leaving her companions behind. Algon's heart, which had risen with hope, fell with disappointment. The other maids tried to cheer him but he only begged, "Bring back the fair one." They replied, "We cannot make her come or go; she obeys her own will."

Every day Algon visited the clearing, hoping to see the maid again. He thought of her always, the Moon Maid with her bright eyes and gleaming dark hair. His ears strained to hear the song of her laughter. A month later he was rewarded with the sight of her. Again she fled, laughing as if this were a game. This gave Algon an idea. The third month he captured a hungry wolf. From his hiding place he released the wolf into the circle of maidens. They fled in terror, leaving the Moon Maiden facing the growling beast. Algon came forth and loosed an arrow into the wolf's neck. The beast turned on him, but with his bare hands he choked it to death. The grateful Moon Maiden fell into his arms and he carried her home. He treated her with kindness and she returned his love, but in secret she mourned. Large tears fell from her eyes and covered the ground with dew. Did she weep for her lost freedom? Had she loved another? She would not say, and Algon had to content himself, knowing he could never understand the woman he loved.

When I came with the hunters to Dasemunkepeuc, I saw the fair-skinned maiden among Tameoc's kinswomen. The one who had asked for my help with the fishing weirs, the one they called Ladi-cate. And like Algon, I was stricken at the sight of her beauty. But what was she doing in Dasemunkepeuc? Did she not know the danger? She did not flee like the Moon Maiden, though her eyes regarded me warily.

Takiwa dressed her brother's wound. I described how a party of Roanoke had attacked us for our food. Tameoc slew one of them, and now they would seek revenge.

Ladi-cate stepped forward and asked, "*Lord Manteo, are you not king of the Roanoke, by the authority of our queen?*"

It amazed me to hear her speak my tongue. "*The Roanoke follow Wanchese,*" I said, then went on in English: "Wanchese will not heed your kwin." What the English did not know yet was that Wanchese planned to destroy them. That he expected me to assist him. How much time did I have before he would fulfill his threats?

Ladi-cate pointed to Tameoc. "Can you not keep your own people from stealing from us?" She looked more distressed than angry. "Do you know what strife that sword has caused among us?"

Yes, I knew Tameoc had stolen the sword. I had rebuked him, but he refused to give it up. He believed the montoac in the shining weapon would bring him success in hunting. Now Ladi-cate demanded an explanation. But I did not owe her one. She was a woman, not one of the governor's assistants. I crossed my arms against her.

She glanced toward Takiwa and Mika, then turned back to me. Her eyes were wet as she pleaded, "Lord Manteo, if Roger Bailey and the others learn of Tameoc's theft, we will be friends no more, but enemies."

"Tameoc steals only to provide for his people," I said.

"I would not go to war over a sword, but I do not make the decisions," she replied.

This was a wise woman, I could see. The soldier Grem stood beside her, looking displeased. Would he tell Bay-lee that Tameoc was a thief and Manteo his accomplice?

"*Who are . . . you with, Manteo?*" Ladi-cate halted over the words, but her meaning was clear.

How could I answer such a question? For I am on two sides. I am the windward shore of the island and the calm one. I am the inside and the outside of the clay pot. Wanchese also demanded I choose. But how can I? There is but one island and one pot.

"I am Manteo of Croatoan, Lord of Roanoke and Dasemunkepeuc and servant of Kwin-lissa-bet."

Ladi-cate looked relieved. She even smiled. Not even Algon had such good fortune. Was this a dream? I struggled to keep my mind on the serious matter before me: keeping the trust of the English. Keeping Ladi-cate and her people safe. Would Algon have let the wolf devour his Moon Maiden?

"And as Lord of Dasemunkepeuc, I ask you to return to your fort," I said.

Ladi-cate's eyes grew wide with surprise to be spoken to in such a way. Then she bowed slightly as the English do before their kwin.

"*We will, Lord Manteo,*" she said.

"*For your own safety, Moon Maiden,*" I whispered to myself.

I went to Croatoan to find that Wanchese had threatened my mother if she did not join his alliance. She agreed to be his ally, deceiving him. She sent me to offer the English our best warriors if they would fight Wanchese in her name.

I went back to Fort Raw-lee. I told the assistants that sickness and death had weakened Wanchese and the Roanoke. That the English and the Croatoan together could defeat him. But I admitted this might provoke the Secotan and others to retaliate. In the men's faces, the desire to defeat Wanchese battled with their mistrust of me. I said I would show Wanchese that I—not he—was lord of the Roanoke by the authority of their Kwin-lissa-bet.

The assistants made me leave John-white's house while they debated what action to take. I waited by the garden gate. Doubted the truth of what I had said. Was it the kwin and John-white who gave me my power, or was it the gods? Had not my mother's people— and Wanchese's—dwelt here and called the land Ossomocomuck for many generations before the English weroance claimed it and called it Virginia? The priests had chosen my name. Manteo, "he who snatches from another." What did my name mean? How would I live up to it?

I did not realize Ladi-cate was in the garden until I heard her call my name.

"Lord Manteo, will you come in?"

I opened the gate and went to her. The gray mists that were her eyes seemed to enfold me, so I looked away from them.

"You did not go back to Dasemunkepeuc, did you?" I asked.

"You do not rule me," she replied with a smile.

I hardly knew what to think of a woman who would not heed a man's will. Even Weyawinga and Ladi-cate's kwin took advice from their male councilors. Was it my young age? Did Ladi-cate see that although I was tall, I had only lately entered my manhood?

"When I came here I said I would never dig in the dirt," she was saying. "But Takiwa gave me these seedlings. I will transplant them when we move to Chesapeake. If I did not go to Dasemunke-peuc, I would not have these new plants and Takiwa would not have the medicine that made her sister well."

She brushed off her hands and went inside, bidding me wait. I stood in the garden like a stone unable to move itself. Ladi-cate was talking to me without any fear. She was no Moon Maiden from a story, but a woman I might touch if I dared.

Ladi-cate returned with a notebook full of writing and pictures of our lodges and their furnishings, our food, ornaments, and more. She was proud of her book and let me examine it.

"It does not please the English men when you go among Indians," I said.

"No, nor many of the women," she agreed. "But I am not afraid, for Wanchese has not been seen since George-howe was killed eight months ago. Is it true he has moved inland because he is afraid of us?"

"If the assistants would heed me, they would learn the truth about Wanchese," I said bitterly. "The Croatoan are in danger and so are you. This is why I ask you to avoid Dasemunkepeuc."

Ladi-cate looked startled. Now I expected her to run away. But she did not. No, she beckoned me to her.

"Then you, Manteo, must come with me. Wanchese will not dare to harm you."

I could not say no to Ladi-cate. Already she had overcome my will. Oh, had I but ruled myself and her as well, how much suffering might have been spared?

PART III

Chapter 29

From the Papers of Sir Walter Ralegh

Memorandum

15 March 1588. Two items pertaining to my Roanoke colony: In Cornwall my fleet of six small ships, commanded by Grenville, prepares to slip through the embargo and sail for the island with supplies. Second, Thomas Harriot's report on Virginia is newly published, rebuking the malcontents who have spread their lies and praising the marvelous commodities of the land. I would expect a surge of investors and adventurers were a war with Spain not imminent.

29 March 1588. My plans are foiled. The queen's Privy Council has ordered Grenville to join my ships to Sir Francis Drake's fleet for the defense of the coast. Drake does not need those ships. It must be Walsingham who conspires against me. But now is not the time to defy the council, with the Spanish Armada preparing to invade.

2 April 1588. I have tried to question Simon Fernandes about the events of last July and August, but he will not satisfy me. And John White's sense of honor prevents him from speaking ill of his

assistants. His only ambition is to see his family again, while that of every other man in England is to rip out the heart of Spain in battle.

How then shall I weigh the charges in Catherine's letter? When I distinguish myself in this pending battle, I shall defy Walsingham and petition Her Majesty to permit me to sail for Virginia. There I will mete out justice and rescue my colonists. This must earn my lady's gratitude and, I dare hope, her love.

15 April 1588. I appealed to Her Majesty to hold back two of my ships because of defects that made them unsuitable for her war fleet. She gave me leave to send them to Virginia, saying none of her subjects should perish through her inaction. (By her response, I *know* it was Walsingham who stayed my ships.)

But my canny mistress again prevents my going, appointing me to her Council of War. It is a golden opportunity to shape her policy toward Spain. In my judgment we ought to take to the seas and attack the Armada, not sit like ducks and wait for the fox to attack us, which is Walsingham's strategy.

22 April 1588. Today the *Brave* and the *Roe* sailed from Bideford with John White and eleven passengers, including four women. I advised them to follow a direct northern route, despite the risk of contrary winds, to reduce their chances of encountering the Spanish.

15 May 1588. The pope has excommunicated our queen yet again and calls upon her subjects to depose her. The astrologists predict an apocalypse of storms, fires, and sinking ships. If only they could declare who will prevail and spare us the descriptions that serve no purpose but to terrify.

25 May 1588. The *Brave* and the *Roe* limped back to port after being attacked and boarded by the French. What irony, when all the fear is of war with Spain. Twenty-three were killed and White

injured in the head and shot in the buttocks. He is swathed in bandages from head to foot but swears he will sail again once his injuries are healed.

25 July 1588. A great battle is imminent. On the 19th the Armada was sighted and skirmishes reported. Now the Spanish war fleet nears Calais to join the Duke of Parma's army and then invade our shores. Her Majesty's navy follows with my own *Ark Ralegh* as the flagship: a wonder at 1,100 tons, 100 feet from keel to keel, with four masts and three banks of guns.

30 July 1588. In Calais harbor our fire-ships packed with wood and pitch sailed among Spain's galleons like nimble dogs baiting slow-moving bears. Winds fanned the flames, crippling the great ships and destroying their formation. It was a glorious rout, the godly David victorious over the wicked Goliath! Not a single English vessel was lost, and what remains of the mighty Armada flees northward, attempting to return to Spain by going around Scotland.

20 August 1588. Providence continues to assist our victory, raising winds that wreck the Spanish ships off Scotland and Ireland. The threat of Spain lifts like the fog. Our Elizabeth is justly celebrated as the greatest prince in Christendom. Ballads are sung all over London, and her speech to the troops at Tilbury camp repeated on every man's tongue. She said:

"I am resolved to live or die amongst you all, to lay down for my God and for my kingdom and for my people, my honor and my blood even in the dust. I know that I have the body of a weak and feeble woman, but I have the heart and stomach of a king."

I wish I had been there! According to reports, she was dressed all in white, armed like an Amazon empress, and rode among the troops on a white gelding.

I repent ever thinking ill of this virtuous virgin or resenting my duty toward her. It is the grace of God that gives her such courage and through her moves England to victory. May I live long enough to show her my regard, my grateful love.

Chapter 30

Serpents in Paradise

As a poem may beautify a plain mistress or feign love, so can a flowing discourse beautify a harsh wilderness. If Virginia had ever been the paradise described by the writers Barlowe and Harriot or the one painted by John White, it had fallen from grace in an astonishingly short while.

Did the *Lion* bring the serpent that corrupted the garden, or was it living here before we arrived? Did Harriot and White ignore it in their eagerness to promote the virtues of the land? Were they, with all their knowledge, as innocent as I was? For I believed my efforts to aid the Croatoan women would benefit us all. I hoped a desire for the common good would prevail over the cruelty and self-interest of men like Roger Bailey. Finally, to my grief, I believed Manteo's authority was enough to check the serpent Wanchese and his minions.

After killing George Howe in August, Wanchese did not strike until the following spring. One morning the fishing weirs were discovered pulled up from the riverbed and broken apart. Two weeks later the armory was raided and four muskets taken, along with bandoliers and gunpowder. The guards swore they had not been drunk or asleep, so they were only flogged. We could not afford to lose any more men by hanging. I wondered if Tameoc was one of the thieves. Graham had not revealed his theft of the sword. Of course the assistants suspected Wanchese, and the evidence that he was nearby made everyone alert and nervous.

But Wanchese was not the only serpent on Roanoke Island. In our very own settlement was a nest of them, stirring up discord and dividing us against ourselves.

Roger Bailey had decreed that the entire colony would move to Chesapeake. He sent Christopher Cooper and forty men to find a location for a settlement and begin planting. Ananias objected— as John White had—that the separation would make both parties vulnerable, but Bailey ignored him. So Cooper sailed in the pinnace, taking Manteo with him to smooth relations with the Indians. Ambrose Vickers was also in the party, for he was in favor of the move to Chesapeake.

While his father was absent, tragedy befell young Edmund Vickers. Playing outside the palisade, he stepped on an iron caltrops laid there to deter the Indians. The spike penetrated his foot, which became swollen, then gangrenous. His fever raged, red streaks shot up his leg, and the surgeon decided the entire limb had to be cut off. Alice and I were there to assist him when Betty, learning of his decision, began to rave and pray incessantly.

"Be silent, Mistress Vickers, for your own good," the surgeon admonished her.

"Hush, Mama!" the boy pleaded. His eyes were wide with pain and alarm.

"Leave her be; she is distressed," I said out of pity for her and the boy.

"But she is calling out to the saints!" the surgeon said.

"See if there are some spirits in the house. That may quiet her," Alice said.

I went to the cupboard and threw it open. There, nestled among some empty jars were candle stubs, a cross with a figure nailed to it, and a small statue of a woman in a blue robe.

Alice was looking over my shoulder. "The Virgin!" she whispered.

"Oh blessed Mary, Saint Joseph, and holy John the baptizer, save my son," cried Betty. "Afflict me instead, for I have done wrong by living among the ungodly—" Her words dissolved into tears and she dropped her head to her son's chest.

Thus it was revealed that Betty Vickers was a papist.

The surgeon, a man without prejudice, cut the boy's leg off out of mercy, but Edmund died in the night.

The next morning Bailey had every cupboard, trunk, and bedstead in the village searched. The yield was two Latin psalters, a set of rosary beads, another statue, and two brass crosses, all found among the possessions of Ambrose Vickers and his kin. Ambrose and his nephew had gone to Chesapeake, but the grieving Betty and her brother were brought forth and shackled.

"We have sheltered papists in our bosom, and therefore we do not prosper," shouted John Chapman angrily. His hair, which had turned white in the last year, flew about his head.

Murmuring rose and then the cries began. "Flog them!" "No, hang them!"

Seeing Betty in chains horrified me. I couldn't speak up, for I didn't even know what to say. It was one thing to object to the torture of a simpleton, another to defend an admitted papist. It was Ananias who demanded that judgment be postponed until Cooper's party returned, so Ambrose and his nephew could be questioned, too. Betty and her brother were put under guard. Little

Edmund was buried at the base of a tree far removed from the cemetery where George Howe and all those who died in the winter had been laid to rest.

A week later, eight men of the original forty-one straggled back to the island in a leaky shallop. Manteo was with them. Their tale was a disturbing one. They had reached Chesapeake without incident and begun their work. Then the eight men had gone upriver in the shallop to explore, and when they returned a week later, the pinnace was gone. Five bodies were found dead on the shore and in the camp. Christopher Cooper was one of the dead. Everything useful had been taken from the camp.

Bailey drew his conclusion at once. "It was the Indians. You have betrayed us," he said, confronting Manteo.

"Musket shot killed them," Manteo said, staying calm. "Their own betrayed them."

Griffen Jones, a Welshman and a farmer who was the leader of the eight explorers, nodded. "Manteo is right. There were malcontents among us. While we were exploring, they must have decided to chance a return to England. They shot the ones who tried to resist. And they didn't stay to bury their bodies," he said, his mouth tense with anger.

"But they had no provisions for a sea crossing," said Ananias in disbelief.

"With luck they could make the Azores in a few weeks' time and find passage on another ship," said Bailey. He clenched his fists as if to keep the rest of his power from slipping through his fingers.

"Who planned this? I want to know who betrayed us," said Ananias. "Now we've lost thirty-two men and the pinnace to boot!"

Thirty-two men. With those who had already died, I counted forty-five lost, almost half of our original number. Now there were barely enough men to defend the fort. On the other hand, there were fewer mouths to be fed if the next winter should prove harsh.

And then John Chapman suggested the conspiracy. "It was the papists who plotted this. Ambrose and his nephew are on that pinnace. They were in league with that Irish seaman and Fernandes from the beginning. Now they've sailed off to rendezvous with the Spanish." His face grew red and he tottered, making me wonder if he was drunk. "Mark my words, one morning we'll wake up to find ourselves murdered by the Spanish."

At this I stifled a laugh, drawing suspicious looks. Well, if people were going to stare at me, they might as well hear me.

"Mark instead what nonsense Master Chapman speaks, " I said. "How could Vickers or anyone have planned a rendezvous with Spain a year ago, not knowing the circumstances in which we would find ourselves now?"

Some looked away abashed, while a few nodded. Bailey and his allies regarded me with hostility.

"Moreover, being a papist does not make a traitor of a man—or a woman," I added in Betty's defense.

"But what if they *are* guilty?" someone shouted.

"Now is the time to find out," Bailey said, heading for the armory where Betty and her brother were being held.

Silently I berated myself for speaking out. Why could I not learn to hold my tongue? Now Betty would be judged by the four assistants who remained: Bailey, two lazy gentlemen who did his bidding, and Ananias.

Everyone crowded into the armory as Betty and her brother were brought forward. Betty's eyes were wide with dread and her lips moved in prayer. Bailey questioned her first, perhaps thinking she would confess easily. But she shook her head when asked to reveal the details of her husband's plot. Bailey held up a pair of iron pliers. Still she confessed nothing. He placed her fingers in the pliers and pressed. She gritted her teeth, and he pressed harder. I saw Ananias cringe. I stared at Betty's brother, willing him to confess in her stead, but his eyes were tightly closed. There was a crack of bone and Betty screamed the names of Jesus, Mary, and Joseph. Jane Pierce, far gone with Bailey's child, fainted. Alice and I carried her out and laid her on a bench. My own stomach was churning. I wished with all my being that Roger Bailey would be struck dead.

Georgie Howe stood by the door of the armory, rocking back and forth, fear in his eyes.

"Papa's in the ground. Georgie is cold," he said, although there was sweat on his forehead.

"Cate is cold, too, Georgie," I said.

After Roger Bailey broke three of Betty's fingers, her brother shouted out what everyone waited to hear: that he and Ambrose had conspired with Fernandes to betray the location of Fort Ralegh to the Spanish. I was certain he lied, except in swearing that Betty was innocent. Still, Bailey decreed that they would be taken to the mainland, rowed upriver in the shallop, and left to fend for themselves. It was a sentence of death, more cruel even than hanging. The punishment stunned everyone, and Bailey had to carry it out himself to ensure that it was done.

I simmered with rage against Bailey and all the assistants. A sense of my own guilt and helplessness plagued me. Every one of us, I felt, had been complicit in making the Vickers family scapegoats for our fears. The only innocent one was little Virginia, who smelled of milk and sweetness, her happy smile belying the suffering all around her.

My desire to escape the company of the other colonists made me decide to go to Dasemunkepeuc on that fateful day. Graham, as usual, accompanied me. Alice left her baby with Eleanor and joined us, saying she was weary of her husband's talk of conspiracies. Jane Pierce was also glad to come. She had confessed to me she was afraid of Roger Bailey.

"He has called me a whore and denied the child is his," she said, pulling up her sleeves to show me the bruises on her arms.

"You must not marry him," I said. "All your days will be miserable."

"But it would make me an outcast to have no father for my baby," she said, touching her belly.

"I will be your friend," I said, "if you promise not to be such a gossip." Once she had asked me if I had a lover at the Indians' village, to which I had responded with a cold stare.

We were in the rowboat when, to my surprise, Manteo appeared on the shore.

"I do not wish you to go to Dasemunkepeuc," he said. "You may be in danger there."

Jane glanced from Manteo to me and raised her eyebrows. I knew what she was thinking and I gave her a warning look.

"Lord Manteo," I said. "At present we are in more danger from certain men here at Fort Ralegh."

"*You do not understand. Some of the Croatoan have gone over to Wanchese,*" he said to me in his tongue.

"*Surely not our friends at Dasemunkepeuc,*" I said. "*They are too few to merit Wanchese's interest.*"

Rather than argue, Manteo climbed into the boat. He picked up an oar and stood in the stern holding it like a staff. To show his displeasure, he refused to row. His back was to me. A deerskin hung down over his loins, and a leather thong held his bow and a case of arrows behind his shoulder. The muscles in his legs quivered, holding him in perfect balance.

I took a spare oar and, surprised by my own strength, helped Graham row the crowded little boat to Dasemunkepeuc. The village looked as peaceful as ever. Because of the warm day, the mats over the doors of Tameoc's house were tied back. Jane exclaimed over everything from the houses to the frames for tanning hides, for this was her first visit to the village. A bowl of grain sat beside a quern as if someone had just been grinding it. Then Mika appeared at the door. If I had looked more closely at her eyes, I might have seen a warning there. But I was watching with some dismay the direction of Graham's gaze, which had settled on Mika's uncovered breasts.

Jane also noticed and began to giggle.

"Where is everyone?" Alice said.

And then events befell in a confused and rapid sequence.

Manteo shouted a warning and drew out his bow. Graham whirled around and aimed his musket. From the bushes warriors rushed forth with sharp cries. They were bedecked with feathers and paint and carried their muskets as if they were mattocks for breaking the ground. Graham fired but had no time to reload before they were upon him. Jane, Alice, and I fell to the ground in a huddle, too frightened even to cry out.

Manteo was soon disarmed by the leader of the attackers, a smaller Indian with a beaked nose and scars on his face. I recognized him from long ago, when he strode with Manteo into the queen's banquet hall. It was the hated Wanchese. He and Manteo were arguing, speaking so rapidly I could not understand them.

"Manteo, you betrayed us!" cried Graham.

Manteo turned to him with a look of fierce denial. I did not want to believe he had led us into a trap. He had warned us, after all. *Some of the Croatoan have gone over to Wanchese.*

Then I saw the sword Tameoc had stolen—in Wanchese's

hand. Tameoc himself stood beside the Roanoke chief. I thought he had promised John White he would not become Wanchese's ally. Since then he had not only stolen the sword, but apparently the muskets now in the Roanoke warriors' hands.

"Graham, don't blame Manteo. It was Tameoc's doing," I said. "See the sword?" I suspected Tameoc had been forced to do Wanchese's bidding, for he would not have given up the fine sword of his own will.

The warriors made us rise and they bound our hands. Alice began to weep.

"My son, my dear little boy, what will he do without his mother?"

"*Let her go. She has an infant to care for,*" Manteo said.

Wanchese hesitated, then motioned for Alice to be freed.

"*Take her back. And warn the English what their fate will be if they do not leave the island,*" Wanchese ordered Manteo.

"*If I return there, they will say I gave you these captives, and they will kill me,*" Manteo said. "*If I am dead, who will persuade the rest of the Croatoan to take your side?*"

I stared at Manteo in confusion. Was he planning to deliver his own people to Wanchese? Perhaps he was simply afraid to face Bailey and Ananias with news that Wanchese had captured us. Why had he let Wanchese take us without a fight?

"*If the English kill you, then the Croatoan will turn against them, which will serve my ends,*" said Wanchese with a sneer.

"*You forget that I am Lord of Roanoke and Dasemunkepeuc. I have allies throughout Ossomocomuck,*" said Manteo calmly. "*You have need of me.*"

Wanchese hesitated.

"*Send Graham back with the woman. I exchange myself for him,*" said Manteo, holding out his hands to be bound. "*If he brings soldiers against us, you may hold me to account.*"

"What are they saying? What will become of us?" said Jane in a voice shaking with tears.

I shook my head, for I did not understand Manteo's deed. Like me, Graham was attentive to everything that passed between Manteo and Wanchese. I hoped he could make sense of it.

After a long moment, Wanchese reached his decision. He told Tameoc to take Graham and Alice to the boat. But Graham, though his hands were tied together, threw off Tameoc.

"I have sworn to protect the Lady Catherine!" he shouted. "Lord Manteo, you are the queen's deputy. Command him to release the women."

But Manteo knew he was powerless. Tameoc shoved Graham, who glanced over his shoulder at me with a look of such defeat and regret that my eyes clouded over with tears.

"Thomas, trust Manteo!" I called after him. "He must have a plan."

The Croatoan women and children now came out of the house, carrying their belongings in bundles. When Takiwa saw Jane and me, she looked away in shame. Tameoc went to her but she pushed him away. Mika's thin shoulders shook with tears.

I realized we were all Wanchese's captives.

Chapter 31

Captivity

All my dreams about living in friendship with the Indians now mocked me as childish fantasies. Nor could I have imagined, while enjoying the comforts of Whitehall and the queen's favor not fifteen months ago, the stark and perilous state in which I now found myself: captive to the serpent Wanchese in a ruined Eden.

More than myself, I pitied Jane. Her only mistake was to heed my reassurances that no harm would befall us at Dasemunkepeuc. It was my fault we had been taken captive. If I had heeded Manteo's warnings, we would not have left the fort.

Jane clung to me as we were marched through the woods. "Where are they taking us, do you suppose? How long do we have to live?"

I had no answers to Jane's questions or my own. Why had Manteo offered himself to his supposed enemy? Why didn't Wanchese kill us outright? To add to my confusion, Wanchese's behavior changed once the confrontation at Dasemunkepeuc was ended. He was not at all cruel. When we came to a clearing where several horses were tethered, he permitted the women and children to ride and left the men to walk. Later, when his men killed a deer and her fawn, we were given the fawn's tender meat, the bones themselves soft enough to eat. Clearly he meant to keep us alive for some purpose.

For two days we journeyed through thick forests and swampland where sharp-edged grasses snagged my clothes and whipped my hands and face. They were so tall they hid us from sight, but the splashing of water and the sucking sound of feet in the mire gave us away. Shrill frogs ceased their calls at our approach and resumed when we had passed, but the biting flies and mosquitos never ceased. Soon Jane and I were covered with sores and our skin was scratched and sunburned, increasing the pain. When we stopped for the night, Takiwa took out a pot of bear grease and showed us how to smear it on our skin. It smelled foul but brought some relief.

Jane and I grew less fearful for our lives, but Jane was concerned for her child. "What will become of him if he is born among Indians?" she asked. "Will they take him from me?"

"All Indians are good to children," I said, trying to reassure her. "The Croatoan woman was allowed to keep her child. Besides, we will be rescued before your time comes."

Jane was easily encouraged, which made her a good companion for distressing circumstances. She also had a curiosity that sometimes made her forget the seriousness of our plight and succumb to amazement at anything new.

After several days we came to a village surrounded by a palisade. Larger than Dasemunkepeuc, it was known as Nantioc, and Wanchese was the weroance. I could not say how far we had come since leaving Dasemunkepeuc. It seemed to me Wanchese had backtracked, perhaps to keep from being followed, and we had crossed two rivers—or had we crossed the same river in two places?

Sobaki, the woman who greeted us, was Wanchese's wife. Her dark hair was cut short in front and circled with a kind of wreath. Her cheeks and chin were marked in a curious pattern, and the skin between her breasts as well. From her ears hung strings of small pearls. I recalled in passing how Sir Walter liked to wear a pearl earring.

Sobaki escorted us into her lodging, where there were two other women, also wives of Wanchese. They spoke unguardedly, not knowing I could understand them. They took off our clothes to clean them and washed us from head to toe. I was chastened to learn they considered Jane and me to be dirty and ignorant creatures because we did not bathe our whole bodies daily as they did. They gave us deerskins to wear, and Jane and I covered ourselves as thoroughly as we could. The skins were soft and fringed at the edges.

Then Sobaki began to mark our faces with dye. I knew this was done before a celebration, so I told Jane not to be alarmed. The other wives gave much attention to Jane's golden hair, touching it in wonderment. They tied it back using thin strips of hide. Jane seemed to enjoy the attention. My dark hair was not so remarkable to them, and Sobaki merely cut off the front with the sharpened edge of a shell, giving me a fringe like hers.

Then Sobaki led us to the center of the village where the flames of a bonfire leapt to the sky. Men and women danced in a wide circle around the fire, the women's breasts and the men's buttocks visible to all. Musicians sat on the ground, playing pipes and shaking gourds filled with seeds or shells and something that swished like sand. Their steady chanting rose to a high pitch and wavered there, making me shiver. I thought if I could find Manteo and speak to him, I might learn the meaning of this ritual. Finally I spotted him among Wanchese's warriors. His hands were loosely bound before him, but he stood unbowed and unafraid. I could not approach him, for Jane and I were made to sit with Wanchese's wives.

Wanchese sat with a long tobacco pipe in his mouth under a canopy made of skins and hung with tufts of brightly colored feathers. His councilors flanked him, still and solemn, with festive markings on their bodies. Despite the strangeness of the setting, I was reminded of the queen's court. Here Wanchese was at the center, with dancers and players all performing for his pleasure. Yet how could I compare Wanchese to Elizabeth? She was a Christian monarch with no husband; Wanchese, a pagan prince with two wives. But all rulers were alike in one important regard: they had enemies. And didn't they often find it necessary to destroy those enemies in order to hold on to their power? Now I began to wonder if our capture was the cause of the celebration, which would end in our deaths.

I glanced toward Jane, but she seemed to have no such fear. Sobaki was offering her a pipe. Jane put it to her lips, took a small breath, and coughed. She handed the pipe to me, but I declined it. My head ached with confusion.

"Try it," Jane urged. "You do not want to offend them."

Indeed I did not. I recalled from reading John White's journals that you do not give a tobacco pipe to someone you mean to kill. So I took the pipe and breathed in a little. The smoke stung my throat and brought sharp tears to my eyes. But there was a flavor to it, as if sweet herbs had been added to the leaves. I took another draft, deeper this time. When I had breathed out all the smoke, I felt calmer.

The next moment two Roanoke warriors lifted Jane and me to our feet and swept us toward the whirling bodies around the fire. The pitch of the chanting rose again, and to the rattling of gourds was added the drumming of sticks on the ground. The Indian held me firmly. His hair was shorn on the sides and stood up in tufts in the center and he glistened with sweat and paint. I felt the fire's heat like a wave.

"No, no!" I said, full of distrust.

But he pulled me into the midst of the dancers, forcing me to follow them. I saw Jane holding her belly with one arm as she stumbled after the dancer in front of her. Takiwa and Mika were visible in the glow of flames, leaping lightly. Around and around we went until the drummers and the rattlers became a blur. I felt their rough music like the beating of my heart against my ribs, faster and faster. I tripped but the Indian held me firmly. Across from me Jane shuffled and stepped with the drumbeat. Her mouth was open in a grimace of fear. No, I was mistaken. To my astonishment, Jane was smiling. She clapped her hands. She was dancing!

Could not the foolish girl see—as I did now—the purpose of this ceremony? Wanchese had given us the pipe to lull and deceive us. Now he meant to tire us out, as the hunter wears down his prey so it cannot run, but be easily slain.

When the bonfire died down the dancing stopped, and Wanchese stepped out from beneath his canopy. The gourds and drums fell quiet. The singing and chanting ceased. Wanchese pointed to Jane and then to me. His eyes, black and small, bore into me in a discomforting way. He looked pleased as he opened his mouth to pronounce our fates.

"*Now,*" he said, "*you are one of us.*"

Chapter 32

I, Manteo, Try to Free Ladi-cate

I stared at my bound hands, into the fire, anywhere but Ladi-cate's eyes. They would say to me: *You did not keep me safe.* They might even say: *You betrayed us.* I could not bear for her to think I had brought them to Dasemunkepeuc to be Wanchese's victims. Though I was innocent of any betrayal, my shame was like a burden on my back. Why had I, the Lord of Roanoke and Dasemunkepeuc, let the English women fall into the hands of their worst enemy? I scorned Wanchese and yet I, Manteo the Croatoan, son of a wero-ance, had allowed myself to become his captive. Why, when I could have gone back to Fort Ralegh, led the English to rescue the women, and become a great hero?

Ladi-cate had called to Grem: *Trust Manteo.* How could she trust me now? I was one of Wanchese's party. He kept me closely guarded and was suspicious of my seeming loyalty. He did not permit me to speak to Ladi-cate or her friend. I tried to gain his trust, saying I had intended to bring more of the English to Dase-munkepeuc, but the men had been kept at the fort by their duties.

All the while I pondered some way to free the women. But my mind was as barren as a field in winter.

Whether they knew it or not, Ladi-cate and Jane-peers were more fortunate than most captives. A great sickness had passed through Nantioc, killing dozens. Mostly women and children. Without mothers, a village will soon vanish and an entire people perish. Wanchese needed healthy women to bear children so men could live on after themselves. Thus the English women were adopted and treated as equals, not slaves or servants. They took part in the daily life of the Roanoke women, going out to gather berries, nuts, and firewood, grinding meal and preparing skins. I saw Ladi-cate at these tasks, but I could never manage to speak to her.

Two weeks after the adoption ceremony, some hunters returned carrying an English woman on a sledge. She was weak and thin, her clothes torn, and her hand bent and useless. When she saw Ladi-cate, she could not stop weeping. The maid kissed the hurt woman, and this kindness stirred me. I saw she was the one Baylee had tortured and banished to the wilderness. By the goodwill of the gods, she had survived. Sobaki set about to heal her wounded hand.

It was Ladi-cate who found the means to speak to me. One day as I was passing near Wanchese's house, she boldly came up to me, putting her hand on my arm. Her touch surprised my every sense. I wanted to take her hand in turn, but caution prevented me.

"Manteo, I will speak quickly," she said. "Our captivity must end soon. Betty Vickers is desperate with grief for her lost kin. Jane Pierce is becoming too familiar with this life, she is treated so well. As for me, I have had enough of this adventure."

"Ladi-cate, I am sorry for your plight. It is my fault," I said.

She shook her head. "No, Manteo. I was wrong not to heed your warnings. Now I am trusting you to get us back to Fort Ralegh."

Behind Ladi-cate I saw Wanchese emerge from his lodge. When he spied us, a look of jealousy spread over his face. I stiffened, warning Ladi-cate. She glanced behind her, and when she looked back at me, I saw she knew the kind of danger she faced.

"I will free you somehow. Until then, stay away from Wanchese. Do not flatter or please him," I said in a low and rapid voice.

Then I said loudly for the benefit of Wanchese, "*I will not speak with you, woman.*" And though it pained me to perform any act of cruelty toward her, I pushed aside my Ladi-cate. Walked away from my Moon Maiden.

I was not clever, but I devised a plan I thought would succeed. I let a week pass after my encounter with Ladi-cate, then went to Wanchese and proposed that I go to Roanoke and offer to exchange the English women for muskets and ammunition. Wanchese knew that with good weapons he could drive away the English. Then he could take all their weapons and their women too. But I did not plan on letting this happen.

A flame of greed lit up Wanchese's eyes. Still, he was suspicious.

"*You were too slow to help me before. Why are you so eager now?*"

"*My friendship with the English is no longer strong,*" I said. This at least was true. "*More and more they mistrust me. Since you took their women and I have not returned to them, they must believe I am your ally. They will not welcome me, but they will heed me because I can return the women to them.*"

Wanchese considered my offer. He knew he needed me to

negotiate with the English. If he refused to negotiate, he had no choice but warfare against them. He would surely lose, for he lacked enough weapons.

Wanchese's eyes narrowed into slits. *"How can I be certain you will demand the weapons and not lead the the English against me?"*

"Because if I fail in this, you will not spare the Croatoan." I knew Wanchese was building an alliance to make war on the English. If necessary he would compel my mother's people to join him. I had to protect them, so I made this condition for promising to help Wanchese: that when I obtained the weapons, he would use no force against the Croatoan.

He agreed, but I knew he was lying. Nor did he trust me, for he sent six warriors to accompany me to Fort Ralegh. Once we were away from Nantioc they began to question me about the white men. I described the wonders they possessed: compasses, magnets, chiming clocks. And those they could make: bricks and tile of many colors, houses on top of one another. How they could shape wood with their machines. The warriors were in awe of me and desired to see such things themselves.

Then I praised Wanchese for his bounty and the mercy he showed the captives. This was to test their loyalty to him.

But the men began to deny his virtues and speak ill of him. *"He does not listen to the elders, who want to move inland to avoid the white men. Wanchese wants to fight the white men, and more of us will die then."*

They said Wanchese had attacked the village of Secotan and killed their weroance. Now he governed the people harshly. He made them pay for his protection with food, so they hungered while the people of Nantioc were fed. As they numbered his abuses, I saw how I could use their discontent to my advantage.

Three days of walking brought us to the river, and after two days in a canoe we came to Dasemunkepeuc, which was deserted. When we came to the fort, the soldiers surrounded us. They held the Roanoke warriors and made me enter alone. The assistants regarded me warily, as they would a wild animal in their midst. I was surprised to see Ambrose-vickers there, for I thought he had led those who stole away in the pinnace. When I told him his wife was alive, he put his head in his hands and seemed to weep. Then I presented Wanchese's offer to release the three women in exchange for muskets. I said he would not use the weapons against us, though he had made no such promise.

"Do you expect me to believe Wanchese?" Bay-lee growled. "How many muskets does he demand?"

"Twelve. Four for each of the women—"

Bay-lee laughed. "Tell Wanchese we will keep our weapons and he can keep the women. We cannot spare so many guns, and we have no need of that proud Cate Archer, the Pierce whore, or the papist."

Ambrose-vickers leapt to his feet. "I fought against the taking of the pinnace and made my way back here alone to find my wife banished for no cause. You will do whatever they demand to get her back!" He shook his fist, but Bay-lee ignored him.

"I do not trust the words of savages," Bay-lee said to me.

"You're the one who's a damned savage," Ambrose-vickers said. "Before God you ought to marry that Pierce woman, not leave her to die."

Ana-nias and the other men did not speak, only looked at their feet. Why would no one heed my words? Had all the English lost their courage? Had they no care for their women?

I returned to Wanchese's men, who were camped outside the palisade. While they slept I lay awake without any idea of how to proceed. In the blackest hour of night, I heard someone approach. It was Ambrose-vickers, bidding me come to the governor's house. Ana-nias, Grem, and five others were there. All armed. Muskets and sacks of provisions on the table.

"We are coming with you to negotiate with Wanchese," said Ana-nias. "But if he will not release our women, we are prepared to fight."

My heart leapt up and pounded at my ribs. I also was prepared to fight. I thought of Ladi-cate's plea and Wanchese's desire and grew resolute. I would cut Wanchese's throat to prevent him from making Ladi-cate one of his wives.

We left without Bay-lee's knowledge. Grem knocked out two of the guards and took their weapons. The other two soldiers joined our party. With Wanchese's men, our number was fifteen. There were ten muskets and ten powder horns between us. Twenty-two bandoliers of ammunition. To show he trusted me, Ana-nias gave me a musket.

"We will offer Wanchese not twelve, but six muskets; two at the moment of exchange and four when all of us have safely returned to the fort," he said.

I knew he did not mean to part with all six muskets.

"Wanchese will not accept those terms," I said.

"He does not set the terms," Ana-nias replied. "We have the weapons."

All the way to Nantioc, I considered whether the English were using me to lead them to Wanchese so they could destroy him. It was a burden, the knowledge that both sides were bent on battle. The English and Wanchese were like two banks of storm clouds rolling toward each other. Like two stags that lock antlers and fight until one of them is gored to death, while the doe waits to be claimed by the victor.

No man can stop the lightning and the thunder or come between the warring stags. No matter how powerful his words. There would be a battle, and to the winner would go the English women.

Chapter 33

A Daring Rescue

It was not long after our arrival in Nantioc when I realized why Jane and I had been adopted along with the Croatoan women. Because so many had been killed by smallpox and fevers, the men needed wives. Takiwa and Mika would have their choice of husbands.

Jane and Betty were also desirable to the men. The Indians favored a meek demeanor in a wife, and Betty had become passive and timid because of her ordeal. Her damaged hand was healing, and she was young enough to bear more children. Jane Pierce's belly proclaimed her fruitfulness, a trait that men in every part of the world wanted in a wife. She was treated like a princess about to bear an heir to the throne. She seemed almost contented in Nantioc. I had once read of mariners who were taken captive, and the weak-minded among them became so dependent upon their captors that they no longer sought their release. But Jane was far from weak-minded. She was practical, like Emme, and determined.

As for me, I hoped my black hair was too common to attract much interest. Or that I was deemed unsuitable because I spoke too much, translating everything necessary. Yet I had seen Wanchese regard me, if not with lust, then like someone eyeing a prize taken in battle. And Manteo's brief warning had confirmed what I suspected: Wanchese intended to make me his third wife.

"We must discourage the men from wanting to marry us," I said to Jane and Betty. "I will tell Sobaki we have husbands already."

"But we don't have husbands, and Betty is probably a widow. No one cares enough to rescue us," Jane said bitterly. "Certainly not Roger Bailey, though I am carrying his child."

"Thomas Graham is a true friend of mine," I said. "If he had known we were here, he would have come to our aid. Now Manteo has gone to bargain for our release. I trust him to free us."

Betty looked doubtful, and despair clouded her face at the talk of husbands. She could not accept that Ambrose had stolen away in the pinnace, leaving her behind.

"Please do not give any man a look of encouragement," I pleaded. "Seem sullen and unwilling."

Jane persisted. "What if we are not rescued? We will need to make a life here. I believe these people will welcome my child. And they have a midwife to deliver me safely. Our fate could be worse."

"You would be content to remain among savages?" Betty asked in disbelief.

"Some of them are fine looking, in their way, and capable hunters, like Tameoc," Jane replied. "And I do not see them mistreating their women or children."

"But they are not Christians," Betty said.

"They saved your life and brought you to Nantioc," I reminded her. "Like the good Samaritan in the parable. I think 'savage' is too harsh a word, even for our enemies. They live in an organized manner, with meaningful customs and rituals. They can be kind and generous; they know how to heal wounds and make food from the most unlikely plants and animals."

I smiled, realizing I sounded like one of John White's notebooks. Truthfully, I felt a deep affection for Mika and Takiwa and a growing appreciation even for Sobaki. I understood how Tameoc made choices in order to safeguard his kin and provide for them. And Manteo—why, every day I longed for his return. Even though we hardly spoke, his presence made me feel safer in Nantioc. But I had no desire to stay there, for I missed the familiarity of life at the fort, and though we had quarreled, I missed Eleanor and her child.

Jane was regarding me with raised eyebrows. "Cate, you must admit that Lord Manteo is a most proper man. I have seen the way you look at him when you think no one is watching. In fact, you were thinking of him just now."

I reached out to put my hand over Jane's mouth. "Hush now, that's hardly the point—"

But Jane would not be silent. "It was noble of him to give himself for Alice's freedom, but he did it to be with you. Certainly you can see this if I can."

"Now are you both talking about *marrying* savages?" said Betty slowly. Her bemused tone made us burst out in laughter.

It was no matter for comedy, however, when Wanchese began to court me with small favors: a necklace of shells, an ornament for my hair. Each of his gifts I accepted but laid aside without wearing. I was afraid he would touch me or make me lie with him. Every day I dreaded some preparation would begin for the unwelcome ceremony where I would become his wife. It was worse than serving the most fickle queen and waiting for her next demand.

Two weeks had passed since Manteo's departure, and my uneasiness was rising to a pitch when I finally approached Sobaki.

"*I have no wish to take Wanchese's affections from you,*" I said.

"*He does not care for your wishes or for mine,*" Sobaki said. "*A weroance may take whatever woman he pleases.*"

I tried another strategy. "*I am considered proud and troublesome by my own people. It may be a wayward spirit within me.*"

Sobaki understood this, but to my dismay, she brought in a conjurer. His head was shaved except for a crest from his forehead to the nape of his neck, and he had a small black bird fastened over one ear like a badge. He wore nothing but the pelt of a fox, face and all, over his loins.

"*She has an evil spirit, and Wanchese will not be pleased with her until it is cast out,*" Sobaki explained to him. "*It is a strong one, so it will take much time.*"

The conjurer began to sway and chant as if he were casting a spell. He grew more animated, and his clapping and capering put me in mind of the queen's fool Dick Tarleton. Suddenly his eyes rolled up in his head and he sank to the ground in a trance. When he came to himself again, he seemed disappointed to see me unchanged.

Sobaki, too, regarded me. I could see she did not believe I had a demon. "*We will try again another day,*" she said, smiling at me.

I felt like a prisoner granted a reprieve.

The very next day, the storm of violence broke over Nantioc like a tempest conjured out of the air.

Jane and I were sitting with Mika and Takiwa, and I was letting out the seams of Jane's dress to accommodate her growing belly. Jane was wrapped in deerskins and remarking what a tolerable and easy way it was to dress, when Ananias and Ambrose Vickers walked into the village. They were wearing armor but holding their weapons loosely at their sides. I clapped my hand to my mouth, stifling a cry of surprise. Manteo was with them, as were Wanchese's men who had gone to Fort Ralegh. At once they were surrounded by tense and uncertain Nantioc warriors.

"Betty, come quickly!" said Jane, but Ambrose had already spotted his wife. He broke away from Wanchese's men and ran to her. She dropped the water gourd she was carrying and with a loud cry fell into his arms.

Apparently startled, or thinking he was defending Betty, one of the Nantioc warriors grabbed a musket and pointed it at Ambrose. Upon seeing the gun, Betty screamed again while Ambrose sheltered her with his body.

"*Peace! We have not come to fight,*" said Manteo.

But the Indian, whether by accident or intention, fired the musket. The ball struck Ambrose's armor, spinning him out of Betty's arms. A high-pitched wailing rose from the Nantioc warriors, like a call to arms. At the same moment there was a burst of gunfire from outside the palisade. The warriors within drew their bows and fitted them with arrows. Wanchese came running, a knife in his hand. Takiwa and Mika darted away. I pulled Jane to the ground and we hid behind a heavy log. Explosions of musket fire seemed to come from all around, and a ball struck the log. Jane buried her head in my hair. Her ragged breath was hot in my ear.

English and Algonkian voices mingled in my ears with the sound of blows and cries of agony. I peered over the log to see Graham and half a dozen Englishmen firing on the Nantioc warriors. Tameoc had joined the battle, taking our side. To my amazement, the Indians were fighting each other. The ones who had gone with Manteo were now fighting against the Nantioc warriors loyal to Wanchese. Had Manteo turned his guards into his allies?

Not thirty feet away from me, Manteo and Wanchese faced each other, crouching and ready to spring. Wanchese brandished his knife, Manteo an axe. Wanchese's scarred face was twisted with rage, while Manteo's was tense and alert. Wanchese lunged; the taller Manteo jumped nimbly aside.

"*You are a traitor to your people and Kewasa will punish you,*" Wanchese said, panting. Kewasa was their malevolent god.

"*I brought the English and their weapons as I promised,*" said Manteo almost as if he were taunting his opponent.

Wanchese thrust with his knife, slashing Manteo's arm, and Manteo responded with a swing of his hatchet, the flat blade hitting Wanchese's shoulder and barely missing his neck.

His rage growing, Wanchese said, "*You made my men betray me.*"

"*No, they turned against you because you are a tyrant,*" Manteo countered. "*Throw down your weapon and let us parley. If you kill me, the English will kill you.*"

Wanchese hesitated before unleashing a series of blows so swift I could hardly follow his movements. He kicked Manteo, who whirled around but stayed on his feet. I saw he meant to fight to the death. Red stripes on Manteo's trunk and legs dripped blood into the dirt. He staggered and it seemed he would fall. Wanchese tensed his knife arm to stab again, but in that instant Manteo lifted himself up and landed his axe on Wanchese's skull with a loud crack. Together they fell to the ground, writhing and groaning. I covered my mouth to suppress a scream.

Wanchese's skull was split open and spilling blood. He lay motionless; there was so much blood he had to be dead. The battle was now over. Two Englishmen lay on the ground, arrows protruding from them. One was John Chapman. Almost a dozen Indians were dead or wounded. The six who had become Manteo's allies stood with their eyes fixed on the two bloody figures in the dust.

Manteo had not moved either. My stomach tightened. After all he had risked to bring about our rescue, to see him bleeding in the dirt! I felt tears cloud my sight. I remembered how proud he looked when John White gave him his robe of office, how firm he stood when the assistants showed prejudice and mistrust. I remembered his warnings about Dasemunkepeuc, his steady vigilance, and his promise of rescue. He had fulfilled that promise, and now he might die. I had done nothing to deserve his sacrifice.

Get up, Manteo! With my thoughts I willed him to rise. *You must not die like this.*

Graham and Ananias knelt at Manteo's side and leaned close to him. Then they nodded to each other. He was alive! They lifted him by the shoulders until he was sitting.

"Jane, go fetch water," I said. Tearing her dress that I had been mending into strips, I ran toward Manteo and crouched beside him.

His eyes fluttered open. They were unfocused. "Moon . . . Maiden," he murmured.

Perhaps I looked like the moon with my pale, round face hovering over his. Most likely he was half dreaming. I was so glad to hear him breathe and speak I put my hand to his cheek. "Thank you, Lord Manteo," I whispered.

Thank you for not dying. Thank you for coming back.

When Sobaki realized that Wanchese was past help, she came and tended to Manteo's wounds. None were deep enough to endanger him. In a week he was well enough to lead negotiations. Wanchese's supporters had either been killed or had run away, and the rest submitted to Manteo as their chief. He appointed one of the elders to govern Nantioc. To show their appreciation for these new allies, Ananias offered three muskets and various trinkets in exchange for us. He and the assistants showed a new respect to Manteo, treating him as their equal.

I spent much time pondering that confused battle, the memory of which made my heart pound. Would fighting have broken out if the warrior had not seized the musket and fired at Ambrose? But the soldiers outside were so quick to respond they must have expected a battle. Manteo had called for peace, but he had fought in earnest, taking our side without hesitation. Was it for my sake, or did he also want Wanchese dead? And who was the Moon Maiden? I longed to ask Manteo but was too overcome by my debt to him. Perhaps there would be time later, and then I would know what to say.

A few days after the battle, Jane took me aside. She still wore deerskins, since I had torn up her dress.

"I'm sorry I ruined your clothes," I said. "I shall make you a new bodice and skirt once we get home."

Jane smiled ruefully. "It is too late."

"I'll make it to fit after the babe is born," I said.

"No, Cate, that is not what I mean." She sighed. "Did you see how Ambrose Vickers and all the men looked at me? I am an object of disgust and scorn to them," she said, her lips starting to tremble. "I have made myself an outcast by this"—she pointed to her belly—"and I shall forever remain one to men like Vickers and Bailey."

"You can live with me. When we go to Chesapeake, I will have my own house, and you and I shall share it," I pleaded.

"Oh, I should be so glad!" she said. "But I fear I would not be happy, even there. For I think . . ." She looked down shyly. "I think Tameoc favors me."

I remembered Jane praising Tameoc once before. Manteo had made him one of the councilors of Nantioc. He might become a leader now that Wanchese was dead. Jane could do far worse than marry Tameoc. Still, to abandon English ways and live the rest of her life among Indians? I knew I could not do it.

"Would you stay here, Jane? Would you leave your other life altogether?"

"I might," she said.

The day came when we were to depart for Roanoke. I said my bittersweet good-byes to Mika and Takiwa, who had chosen to stay in Nantioc with their kin. When Jane embraced me, I knew she had made her decision. I clung to her as she had clung to me when we were first captured. Then she needed me; now I felt I needed her. As much as I wanted to see Eleanor again, I knew I would miss Jane even more.

Then she turned to Ananias and Ambrose Vickers and in a calm voice told them she would remain in Nantioc rather than be an outcast in Roanoke.

"Don't be foolish, Mistress Pierce. There is no sin that cannot be forgiven," Ambrose Vickers said. But his words lacked conviction.

"I repent of nothing," she said, her eyes flashing. "I simply choose to live among those who will not judge me."

She walked over and stood beside the Croatoan women. I was startled to see Mika stealing glances at Thomas Graham, an expression of sadness on her face. While Ananias and the others had averted their eyes from the women, Graham was gazing at Mika as if his Anne had never existed. My mind reeled, trying to take this in. *Graham and Mika?*

Tameoc reached out and put his hand on Jane's shoulder, and I was glad for her. But Ambrose Vickers was horrified.

"Whore!" The single word came from his mouth before Graham seized him by the collar, almost choking him.

"Judge not, lest ye be judged," he growled, a phrase Vickers surely recognized from his Bible.

Ambrose shook off Graham and strode out of Nantioc so fast Betty had to run to catch up with him.

I went up to Jane and said through my tears, "Maybe someday you can rejoin us—with Tameoc and your baby. I will always welcome you."

There were eleven in the party that returned to Roanoke Island: Betty and I; Ambrose, Ananias, Graham, and three other soldiers; Manteo and two Indians. The journey was slow due to Manteo's injuries. A week after setting out, we arrived at Roanoke Island on a day sunny with promise and loud with the buzz of late summer insects. I was giddy with relief and gratefulness. Graham helped me ashore and spun me around in a sudden dance. Ambrose and Betty knelt in prayer. But as we approached the fort, our joys dissolved. Fresh mounds of dirt in the graveyard and an ominous silence spoke of some calamity. My first thought was that the fort had been attacked and everyone was dead. Had it been the Spanish or hostile Indians?

It was neither. No, the attacker had been a mortal sickness that killed seven people. Roger Bailey and thirty-four healthy colonists had filled both shallops and sailed for Chesapeake, leaving behind those who were ill. Now there were fewer than thirty people at Fort Ralegh. One of them was the motherless child, Virginia Dare, for, to my sorrow and Ananias's inconsolable grief, Eleanor had been the latest casualty.

Chapter 34

I, Manteo, Have a Dream from Ahone

When I found the white men lost in the forests of Ossomoco-muck and went with them across the sea, learned their tongue and let them make me a lord, how could I foresee that my promises to my new friends would one day lead me to kill Wanchese? He had been my companion on the voyage to London. His people and mine were once friends. His blood and mine, two rivers flowing through Ossomocomuck to the same sea.

Yet I did not regret my deed. Wanchese had mistreated Nantioc's neighbors and did not deserve to rule them. He had made himself an enemy of the English when he could have prospered by them. He would have forced Ladi-cate to marry him, although not even a weroance should take a woman against her will. Wanchese sought war and died by his own words: *In war one must slay or be slain.*

When I thought of our fight, I was surprised at the strength I had found to defeat him. It did not feel like montoac from the gods but like something already burning within me. I had killed Wanchese to free Ladi-cate. Surely Algon would have done as much for his Moon Maiden. But when did I begin to think of Ladi-cate as mine? Was it when I first glimpsed her among the maids of Kwin-lissa-bet? When I saw her in the stream, holding the spear to protect herself? She had never fled from me but showed me respect, even when the others mistrusted me. Could she become mine not through deception or force, but by her choice? I had let Wanchese capture me, that I might free her, that she might then choose me.

Yet Ladi-cate did not appear grateful for my sacrifice. I wanted her to regard me as Jane-peers regarded Tameoc. But she hardly looked at me, nor did she attempt to speak to me. Did she consider me no better than Wanchese?

If Ladi-cate did not seem glad, the Englishmen were pleased that I had slain their enemy. They asked me to remain at the fort to aid them if Wanchese's allies attacked. I said I had to visit the peoples of Ossomocomuck to persuade them not to take revenge. To befriend the Croatoan and the English instead.

So I left Fort Ralegh. The colonists were still in some peril. No ships had come to their aid, and they had not even a pinnace to sail in. I could best serve them by seeking peace among their neighbors, so I spent the harvest months going from village to village, sometimes with Tameoc as my councilor. He spoke of the virtues of his wife, Jane-peers. Told how Ladi-cate had brought a white medicine woman to treat their sickness the winter before. Entertained them with stories in which the red-bearded soldier, Grem, became the trickster Fox. All to make them see that the English were like us in many ways.

To those who could not be persuaded to friendship, I offered this counsel: the English, being few, might soon die of hunger if left alone. Still they were suspicious, and in their mistrust I heard the echo of Wanchese's long-ago taunt: *You are one of them now, are you?* Had I betrayed the native peoples? Brought them harm? No, they had warred among themselves before the big ships came. But

I had been mistaken about the montoac of the English. I thought it would bring us power and prosperity. Instead it had stirred up only trouble, which it was my purpose now to settle.

As I returned to my mother's village for the winter, I reflected that my dreams of being a hero were like a copper trinket dimmed by foul weather. During the bitter months that followed, the lee-ward shores of Croataon froze as hard as stone. The lodges were half buried by snow. The air inside was rank and smoky. The hunters came back empty-handed, having killed nearly every deer in the forest. I considered how Ladi-cate must be suffering from cold and hunger and felt helpless to relieve her.

One night I dreamed that a white hare lost in the snowy woods stumbled into the den of a black bear, awakening it. The bear growled, angry at being disturbed, but the hare conquered its fear to ask for the bear's protection. Admiring the hare's bravery, the bear permitted it to live in the cave. In time the hare gave birth to a human child with a white face and a mane of black hair who grew up to be a weroance capable of great feats of strength. He lifted a canoe filled with many people and set it on a river that flowed into the sunset. When I woke up the bear skin I slept under had fallen to one side and I was shivering. The strange dream made me confused, as if I had a fever.

I thought I would forget the dream, but it did not leave me. It came back the next night, so lifelike I decided it must have come from Ahone, the creator. A man must not ignore such a dream but try to discern its truth. I thought about it for many hours, and after dreaming it a third night, I awoke with an understanding of Ahone's message.

He was demanding that I save Ladi-cate and her people.

Chapter 35

From the Papers of Sir Walter Ralegh

Memorandum

10 March 1589. Myrtle Grove, Youghal, Ireland. As storms blew the great Armada into the northern seas, Her Majesty now blows my feeble bark to Ireland. I am exiled because of a poem I wrote comparing her to Venus and Lord Essex to Cupid. (I thought she fancied herself in love with the boy.) Essex dared to box me on the head and I demanded a duel, the outcome of which I decline to describe.

Here at Myrtle Grove I lick my wounds and bay at the cold, unfeeling moon while Essex, the queen's lapdog, pants to be petted. None lament my absence, for everyone loves whom the queen favors and hates whom she disdains.

I find my castle at Lismore in disrepair, my agents careless, and the tenants unruly. With better management they might have yielded enough to fund a voyage to Roanoke this year. My melancholy deepens when I consider the perilous lives, many perhaps lost, of those hopeful, enterprising folk. Lady Catherine—she of the dancing gray eyes and sleek black hair—deserved better than what poor Sir Walter Ralegh has done. They all did.

Poem

If all the world and love were young
And truth in every courtier's tongue,
Then hopes of pleasure might me move,
To come to thee and claim thy love.

But flowers fade and wanton fields
To winter's harsh reckoning yield,
The fruit in hand has fall'n, forgotten;
My folly is ripe; my reason rotten.

15 August 1589. I signed 150 new tenancy agreements, including one for Thomas Harriot, who has chosen to settle in Ireland. He is planting the root he brought back from the New World, "openauk," which he calls "potato," curious to see if it will grow in this climate and whether people will consent to eat it.

If Virginia were less remote, sea travel less perilous, and Her Majesty less thrifty, I might have had better success there. While it seems likely that Ireland, however wayward her inhabitants, may be brought to a civil state with far less trouble and expense.

3 September 1589. Visited the secretary to the queen's deputy, one Edmund Spenser, at Kilcolman Castle. He is writing an epic poem in praise of the queen that will comprise twelve books. I advised him to be very careful, for if he should write a single offensive couplet out of many thousand, Elizabeth would be sure to note it. He replied that his epic poem will be an allegory, in which the meaning is partly hidden. He read me a passage in

which Belphoebe, a beautiful virgin, takes pity upon a wounded squire and heals him with cordials and tobacco. This, he said, was meant to show my ill usage and move the queen to forgive me. I urged him to offer his work to the queen without delay. Because he is a stranger to her presence, I said I would write a sonnet to commend it.

12 December 1589. Spenser presented his *Faerie Queene* to the delight of Her Majesty. She was not so pleased with his person, however, for he is a little man and almost forty years old, but she showed him respect, which is to be preferred over wanton affection.

When Spenser had finished reading from his poem, I reminded her of my sonnet comparing her to Petrarch's Laura. She smiled, which I took for encouragement and offered her a pipe, a symbol of peace. "This is the most profitable plant in all of Virginia," I said.

"It turns to smoke, from what I can see," she said after sucking on the pipe. "What value is in that?"

Oh, she was clever but I was no lackwit. "I'll wager that I can weigh the smoke and prove to you that it is not nothing."

She said she would grant me £25 if I succeeded. So I called for a scale, a sheaf of tobacco leaves, and a metal basin. I weighed the leaves, then set them aflame in the basin. When the leaves had burned and pungent smoke filled the air, I weighed the ashes.

"Subtracting the weight of the ashes from that of the leaves, the difference must be the weight of the smoke," I said, showing my smile that used to please her so.

Elizabeth folded her hands and pressed her forefingers to her lips. I could not tell whether she appreciated my wit or was displeased at losing the wager.

"I have heard of gold turning into smoke"—was she rebuking me for failing to find precious metals in Virginia?—"but you are the first to turn smoke into gold."

Then turning to Lord Burghley, she bade him give me £25.

She leaned close and spoke in my ear. "Your sonnet did please me, Sir Warter."

My heart sprang up like a young boy's. I gambled everything, saying, "I will write a whole volume of sonnets, Your Majesty, if you will but send a ship to relieve my colonists in Virginia."

Suddenly the queen frowned. "Once again you have presumed too far," she said loudly enough to draw attention to us.

I bowed so she would not see my angry humiliation, whereupon she murmured in my ear, "Attend me in my chamber at nine o'clock tonight." Then she struck me with her fan. "Away!"

14 December 1589. I will endure a thousand blows with whatever instrument she chooses, if she remains true to her word!

At the appointed hour I went to my royal mistress. Her erratic mood had gone, and she came at once to the heart of the matter.

"I do not forgive presumption, but I admire persistence," she said. "How many times now have you tried to send your ships to Virginia despite the embargo? And John White has covered my desk with his petitions." She paused. "Do you think my colonists are still alive?"

I affirmed the land contained everything needful for their well-being. I was afraid to say more, as my words so often displeased her.

"John White failed to govern them well. Surely they have now fallen into factions."

I recalled Catherine's letter concerning that very matter. "Men cannot govern themselves if they are all equals," was all I said.

"I must also know if the Spanish have located the colony," she said. "Our spies report that King Philip has sent out a fleet to look for it."

This was what I dreaded most: that Spanish mariners, informed by spies in the West Indies, had captured the fort and now controlled Virginia. Had they slain all the colonists? Or were they taken captive, and Catherine forced into the arms of a swarthy Spaniard?

The queen was peering at me. "You loved her, did you not?" she asked.

"Your . . . Majesty?" I said in some confusion.

"You know whom I mean." Her voice was not unkind. "You gave this to her."

She held up a handkerchief with her initials in the corner. It was the very one she had given me, the one I then gave to Catherine when she visited my library. Had I loved her? The real question was, did I have the courage that Catherine had, to admit my love?

I chose my words with care. "Your Majesty, I have loved—"

She held up her hand, interrupting me. "Never mind. Do not answer me. That was long ago." Then she pressed the handkerchief into my hand. "Take it and give it to her again."

She spoke as if Lady Catherine were in the next room. I looked into her eyes for signs of debility, but those bright lights, enfolded now in tiny wrinkles, showed no signs of an aged mind.

"Now you jest with me, Your Grace. Truly I deserve your reproof and even your scorn, but—"

"I do not jest." Her voice was sharp. "I give you the opportunity—nay, I command you—to right a wrong that I regret." She turned away from me. "I banished her for nothing more than loving you."

I stood motionless, amazed by this confession.

When Elizabeth glanced back at me, her eyes were moist. "Which was no great wrong, or if it was, the greatest have been guilty of it, too."

Was she admitting her love for me as well as her sorrow for

injuring Catherine? Oh, what did it even matter? Like a gift were the words that fell from her lips.

"I cannot let those brave people perish. Sir Walter, I will release your ships, and you may use them to supply my colonists."

I sank to my knees and with choice words declared her graciousness. Then the thought of my nemesis gave me pause. "Walsingham will try to stop me," I said.

The queen pressed her lips tightly together. "Walsingham is not the king! I am sovereign here, and I declare his unreasoning envy shall no longer hinder your enterprise. I will give out that I have sent you back to Ireland because you displeased me. But in fact you will sail to Virginia secretly. There you will ensure it is duly governed and return with a report. John White may accompany you. No one will know about the voyage but the three of us."

For a moment I was stunned that the queen would act without the knowledge and approval of her ministers. And yet I saw the wisdom of it. If they learned of the voyage, she could disavow any knowledge of it and claim I stole away against her wishes.

"When you return with the news that the colony thrives and the Indians have been civilized and converted to the true religion, even Walsingham will hail you as a hero."

What a tantalizing thought! "And the Lady Catherine?" I ventured to ask. "After I give her the handkerchief, what shall I do?"

I saw my mistress hesitate. Her long hands fluttered. Then they rested and she fixed me with her clear, bright stare.

"Bring her home, and she can be yours."

Chapter 36

Orphaned

In Nantioc I had dreamed of returning to the familiar comforts of Fort Ralegh. I planned to make peace with Eleanor and never again let a foolish disagreement threaten our relationship. Had we not become almost like sisters? I imagined the rejoicing that would greet our safe return, the stories we would have to tell. All those dreams evaporated like dew from the grass when we walked into the half-abandoned village where despair and the smell of death hung in the air.

Ananias was overcome by the loss of Eleanor. He hid his face and wept, his whole body shaking. Alice Chapman's keening rent the air when she learned her husband had been killed. To my own grief was added guilt, for I had failed to keep my promise to John White to watch over his daughter.

Though Ananias urged him to stay, Manteo left Fort Ralegh to rebuild alliances among the native peoples. This, he said, would benefit us. But I think it pained him to see how desperate we had become, how fallen from our first hopes. I watched him go, regretting that I had not properly thanked him for rescuing us. I was afraid he would rebuke me, for in my heart I felt our late misfortunes had all sprung from my foolish insistence on going to Dasemunkepeuc.

In his absence, I found I missed Manteo. I felt as if new dangers were imminent and I was unprotected. Betty and I were the objects of much curiosity, but I did not want to discuss my sojourn in Nantioc. I could not boast about how well we had been treated while our fellow colonists had been sick and dying, abandoned by those who fled to Chesapeake. Nor could I make them understand why Jane had decided to stay with Tameoc. Even Alice Chapman was horrified by that.

With the departure of Roger Bailey and his party to Chesapeake, we were like a body cut in half. There were only eighteen men left in the village, plus three boys barely able to grow a beard. To them fell the task of defending us all. Day and night Georgie Howe patrolled the towers like a lumbering ghost.

"They will come back someday and take Georgie with them. Did they go where my papa went? All of them into the cold ground? George is cold out here," he said over and over.

Thus as our second year on Roanoke Island began, misery settled in like a grim lodger. Not since my father's death had I felt so hopeless. The weeks spent in the Tower, the long sea crossing, even the captivity in Nantioc were like child's games compared to the hardships we would face if another winter passed without ships bringing relief. It was men that we needed most—to work and to protect the fort, then women for their companionship, and finally animals to raise for meat.

October threw its brazen cloak over the landscape; the leaves drifted from the branches like a million lost hopes scattered on the ground. Corn and pumpkins and sunflower seeds had to be picked, openauk dug from the ground. The abundance mocked us, so few in number. We stored the harvest in a cellar dug beneath the armory, precious as the few firearms that remained, since Bailey took most of them to Chesapeake. He had promised to return for the rest of the colonists, but as the months passed that promise began to look like a lie. One day I admitted to Betty I hoped they had all perished.

"Perhaps they have, and it was God's will. But take heart, for we have been preserved," she said.

"Our preservation was Manteo's doing, not God's. I think God and England both have abandoned us," I said.

But Betty's faith, despite her ordeal, was unshaken. "The Bible says not even a sparrow falls without His knowledge, yet man is more precious to Him than a sparrow."

Her complacency irked me. "Our lives were lately held rather cheap, exchanged for a single musket each," I reminded her. "The food stored in the armory and guarded day and night is more valuable than any one of us. I am worth less than a handful of empty shells." I thought sadly of Eleanor lying in the cold ground.

"But you are alive! Therefore, thank the Lord."

Betty tried to encourage me, but hope was hard to come by. November brought cold, sharp rain and two more deaths. The men were so few and so weakened by illness that many tasks went neglected. Ananias was too despondent to lead us. By December the firewood was all depleted and Ambrose Vickers sent out men to cut more. Some of the houses leaked and needed repairs. Alice and her baby came to live in the governor's house for the sake of thrift. We tried to keep one another from becoming fearful or dispirited.

There was reason to be afraid, for Indians had been spotted lurking in the underbrush nearby. In small bands of three or four, they shot arrows over the palisade, but fortunately these fell harmless to the ground. They ran away when the soldiers fired their muskets. It was Thomas Graham who realized their intention was to provoke us to waste our ammunition. So he ordered the guards not to fire unless the Indians came too near, and he had all the grass and shrubs cut down within thirty feet of the palisade, giving them nowhere to hide. We carried buckets of water from the bay and kept them beside our doors, in the event the Indians aimed burning arrows at the thatched roofs. I wished Manteo were with us, for he might be able to persuade them to stop troubling us.

One December night I was roused by the squawking of hens, and my heart pounded with the certainty that we were being attacked. I listened, dreading to hear whooping and the crackling of flames on the roof. But the intruder was only a wolf that had found a gap in the palisade and slunk into the henhouse. Graham shot the wolf and the dogs quickly devoured the carcass. But a dozen chickens were dead. And before the hole could be repaired—a difficult task, for the blacksmith had gone to Chesapeake and taken all the nails—three pigs escaped and only one could be recovered. Then rats got into the seed corn and ruined half of it. Like lifeblood seeping from a sick patient, our means of survival were trickling away.

Then in the deep of winter, on a night so cold that Alice and I slept in a single bed with her baby and Virginia between us, Indians did attack. Ananias heard them first and woke us, then ran out to raise the alarm. We hid under the bed, and I nearly smothered Virginia in my attempt to keep her from crying out. The skirmish was brief, the gunshots and screeching soon fading to silence. Running outside without regard for the cold, I learned the intruders had scaled the palisade and entered the fort undetected, where they pillaged the armory for food. Two of the guards had been asleep, leaving Georgie Howe to fight them alone. He took an arrow in the leg. By the laws of the colony, the two guards should have been charged with a crime. But there was no one to administer justice, for Ananias Dare, the last of John White's assistants, had been killed by a single arrow that pierced his throat.

Virginia Dare, the first English child born in this New World only sixteen months ago, was now an orphan. She could barely say "Mama" when her mother died, and now "Papa" was gone, too. Soon she would remember neither of them. I knew, for the memories of my father were already growing faint, and those of my mother were even dimmer.

The child, as if sensing her loss, toddled over to Alice and plucked at her bodice.

Alice shook her head sadly. "You have been weaned, little one. I have no more milk for you."

"Come here, Virginia," I said, and held open my arms.

With a chubby fist thrust into her mouth, the trusting child came to me and put her head in my lap. I parted her tangled curls with my fingers. I had promised John White I would care for Eleanor, and I had failed. I would not fail his grandchild. My chest hurt with love for little Virginia and fear for her uncertain future.

"You will be mine now," I said. "You must call me 'Mama Cate.'" With those words, my melancholy began to fade and a fierce determination took its place. My life might be cheap, but this child was worth more than all the food and weapons and copper and pearls in the New World. Come what may, I would put her life before anything.

And that meant that I, too, must be a survivor.

Chapter 37

Leaving the Island

I began to view Roanoke Island as a prison surrounded not by high walls but by impassable waters. We had no means to leave the island even if we knew how to find Chesapeake, even if travel in the winter were not so beset with risk. It would be spring before a ship could reach us or one of the shallops return from Chesapeake. There were days when I was convinced that neither would ever come.

Snow blanketed the village, muffling all sound and confining us to our houses. To keep my mind occupied, I began writing again, using the empty pages from John White's journals. I wrote about the brave journey of Ananias and Eleanor Dare, so one day Virginia could read about her parents and be proud of them. I described my captivity in Nantioc and my relationships with the Croatoan women. Most likely my account would never be published. Most likely I would never build my own house in Chesapeake, deal in dried tobacco, or introduce Indian designs to Londoners. I could scarcely have said what I did hope for, as the future seemed as bleak and featureless as the open sea.

And the past? It was as lost to me as were my own parents. The queen's court was a setting that belonged to someone else's story, not mine. I doubted Emme would even recognize me if I should reappear there. And Sir Walter, his letters and poems, his touch, the handkerchief—all were like pieces of a dream that scattered as soon as I awoke. What color were his eyes? What had civet smelled like? Or the lavender and rosewater that ladies perfumed themselves with? The queen—had she forgiven me? Had Sir Walter forgotten me? The present had a way of declining those questions, saying instead, *Here is the place where you now must live.*

We were still in the cold grip of winter when Manteo returned to Fort Ralegh. He had come by sledge and canoe, bringing six men with him, a brace of waterfowl, and a creel of fish. I felt hope stir in me, not only because of the food, but also to see Manteo again. It was like the promise of spring when winter has begun to seem eternal.

I gathered the women to cook the fowl and fish and to bake cakes out of flour and ground walnuts. We carried the food to the armory, where the remnant of our colony and the natives feasted together. While the English sat at trestle tables and used trenchers and spoons, the Indians seated themselves on the ground and ate with their fingers. Manteo hesitated, sat at the table, and began to eat with his fingers. It made me smile to see how he had chosen a middle path.

Georgie Howe sat with the Indians, imitating their manner of eating. Fortunately, he did not connect these men with the death of his father. But some of the colonists were uneasy in the Indians' presence. They stared at the faces marked with paint and ritual scars; the hair, long on one side and shorn on the other; and the motley mantles sewn from animal skins. But everyone ate the food Manteo had brought, for we were hungry.

Because we had no governor or assistants, Ambrose Vickers made himself our spokesman. But he was blunt and unused to diplomacy. When the meal was done, he stood up with his arms akimbo and addressed Manteo loudly.

"We must know why you have come. What do you want from us now?"

I feared Manteo and his party would take offense at Ambrose's rough manner. Manteo did not reply at once but regarded all our company with a look of dismay, even sadness.

"We have no men or weapons to spare," continued Ambrose. He looked at Graham, who shook his head in confirmation.

I beckoned Ambrose from the table and whispered to him. "Let us be careful not to displease him after all he has done for us. First, express our gratitude for the food."

Ambrose threw up his hands. "I know we ought to thank him, but I'll be damned if I know how. I'm a woodworker, not an orator."

"Then will you allow me to speak on our behalf?"

Ambrose glanced again at Graham, who nodded once. Griffen Jones, the Welsh farmer, frowned, then shrugged his consent. Though he was of mean status, his opinion was valued by the men.

"Speak, then," Ambrose said grudgingly. "It may not be proper, you being a woman, but it's necessary."

Recalling how John White had treated his Indian visitors, I had Graham place two chairs before the fire. I sat in one and offered Manteo the other. Two of his men flanked him, and Ambrose and Jones stood beside my chair.

"Lord Manteo, we greet you as a faithful ally and welcome you to Fort Ralegh," I said in English, then added in Algonkian, *"Do not take offense, for none was intended. Ambrose Vickers is grateful to have his wife back, and I also thank you for my deliverance and for this food."*

Spoken in a rush, those words left me short of breath. I folded my hands in my lap. The armchair was too big for me and I felt like a child playing at being a queen. The color rose to my cheeks, whether from the nearness of the fire or the excitement of my role I could not say.

"I am pleased to be among you again," Manteo said.

I could feel his eyes on me. To parley with him, I would have to meet his gaze as a man would. So I looked into his face, which was familiar to me but, after several months, somehow new and remarkable. His nose was straight, his mouth and the bones of his cheeks wide. The tawny hue of his skin pleased me. He was handsome, though not in the manner of Englishmen. His eyes were so dark they were almost black. To my surprise I was not afraid to look into them. No, I even wanted to see behind them, to see within Manteo himself.

I tried to rein in my wandering thoughts and organize some fitting words to speak. What would Elizabeth say to one of her foreign princes to discern his purpose and gain his trust?

First, because I longed to know her fate, I asked after Jane Pierce, and Manteo said she had given birth to a son, whom Tameoc treated as his own. The news made me glad. I could not see how the others reacted, but I spoke on behalf of their better natures.

"We are pleased and hope for greater fellowship between our people," I said. "Nantioc remains at peace, then?"

Manteo nodded. "With Tameoc's help I have made an alliance between the people of Nantioc and the Croatoan. Those who followed Wanchese have scattered," he said, spreading his hands for emphasis.

While murmurs of relief ran through the small assembly, Manteo lowered his voice. *"Tell me what has happened here."*

I realized our appearance must be startling. We were thin, hollow-eyed with hunger, and our clothes hung in rags. Vainly I hoped I did not look quite so miserable as the others.

"Our circumstances are worse than when you left us last summer," I said. *"Our food stores were plundered. Ananias Dare has been slain by Indians. And due to sickness there are but two dozen of us remaining."*

"And you, Ladi-cate. Have you suffered too?" The gentle tone of his voice caught me by surprise.

"Not as much as I deserved," I said, glancing away.

"Your ordeal was not your fault," he said.

I knew he meant my ordeal of captivity. For months I had wished for an opportunity to show my gratitude to Manteo. Now it had come. *"I thank you that I did not become Wanchese's wife,"* I said. The remembrance of that day returned to me: Manteo lying motionless on the ground, covered with blood, then finally stirring to life. My curiosity had to be satisfied, and I asked, *"Did you kill him for my sake only? And why did you call me 'Moon Maiden'?"*

Manteo looked down. Perhaps he did not like to be reminded of that day. Then he blushed, if that is possible for one with such tawny skin.

"Ladi-cate, there is a legend of the hunter Algon—"

Jones interrupted. "Enough of this formal parley. Cate, ask him in plain English if he knows who attacked us and killed Ananias."

I had risen halfway from my chair, sensing that Manteo was about to disclose a deep truth I wanted to hear. But at Jones's words I sat down again. Could they hear the catch in my voice as I asked Manteo what he knew about these enemies?

"They are allies of Wanchese who will not accept me as their weroance." He paused, then spoke to all of us. "When spring comes they will return. There are enough of them to take this fort."

I heard the sharp intake of breath and a muttered oath from Ambrose.

"We must strengthen the palisade without delay," said Graham. "And train every able-bodied person to handle a musket."

"My people can help you," Manteo said.

"Can you teach the men to use bows and arrows? The women, too?" Ambrose paced back and forth. "We will trade anything for weapons."

"You misunderstand," Manteo said.

Ambrose and Graham ignored him, caught up in their planning. "*How then can your people help us?*" I asked Manteo.

He leaned toward me, his dark eyes wide and intense.

"*You must come and live with me. With us.*"

My heart was pounding. The edges of my sight grew blurred, until Manteo's face was all I could see. The air in the armory was heavy with heat from the fire and thick with the smells of roasted fish and game and the bear grease from the Indians' bodies. What did Manteo mean?

"*You, Moon Maiden, and the others. You would all be safer,*" he was saying.

Feeling dazed, I said, "*How can we leave here? This has become our home, despite our troubles here.*" I realized he had called me "Moon Maiden" again.

"*I must not ignore a message from the god Ahone. Ladi-cate, your destiny as a people lies with us. You must persuade the others.*"

Astonished and confused though I was, I did not for a moment consider Manteo deceitful or his mind unsound. I trusted him. Indeed, there was no one in all of Virginia I trusted more. His gaze was direct and intent upon me. His words fell on my ears like rays of moonlight on a field at midnight. I felt reckless with new hope. Our English God and His deputy, Elizabeth, had seemingly forgotten us, but Manteo and his god had not. Sir Walter's ships could not make it across the ocean to relieve us, but Manteo had managed to reach us in waist-deep snow to offer us the means to survive.

When Ambrose and Jones had silenced the hubbub, I stood up so I could be seen and heard by all and relayed Manteo's offer. A clamor of voices, mocking laughter, and cries of "Live among savages? Never!" greeted my words.

Then Betty spoke up in a loud, clear voice. "I have lived among them and they are God's creatures, just as we are."

"Silence!" roared Ambrose, pressing his hands against his head. But the uproar continued, with voices insisting a supply ship would come, Bailey would return for us, or we could find our own way to Chesapeake.

Manteo sat with his hands on his knees, staring straight ahead. His men looked tense as the colonists argued. He stood up and everyone fell quiet.

"My people will accept you as brothers and sisters, our equals," he said.

"That would be to debase ourselves," muttered Ambrose.

This made my temper rise. "I am already kin to many Roanoke, for I was adopted by them," I said. "How does that debase me?"

"Nay, rather to live among Indians would be a betrayal of our country and our race," said Jones, looking troubled.

Graham pounded his fist on the table. "Our countrymen have betrayed us! The very ones with whom we shared the voyage and the labor of building this colony. Our best revenge is to stay alive however we can."

Alice Chapman spoke in a trembling voice. "I have lost my husband. Am I now to lose all my household goods, even my clothes, and dress in animal skins like Eve after the Fall?"

Alice's plea awakened my sympathy. I had once imagined Virginia to be a paradise and hoped for riches, not the poverty and misery in which we now found ourselves. Moved to speak, I demanded that the others listen.

"This New World is nothing like what we expected. We cannot control the misfortunes that have occurred here," I began. "Perhaps it is time for us to abandon our belief that we are superior in every regard, that we were meant to rule and not to submit." My eyes were glistening with tears, and I could see nothing clearly save the truth I was trying to express. "Maybe nothing is more fitting than for us, newcomers in this land, to live in common with its native inhabitants. By fellowship we may end the strife between us, so all may prosper and none seek to destroy another. One day we may even restore the Eden we sought in coming here."

I had never spoken out at such length, yet no one interrupted me. I paused to gather the threads of my thoughts to a conclusion. "So let us accept Manteo's hospitality. Let us all go and remain together. It will not be the end of our troubles. It will be difficult for some of us to adapt. But it is our best hope."

Our best hope. I blinked away tears until I could make out little Virginia sitting on one of the tables. I knew what Eleanor would choose, if only for the sake of her daughter. When she saw me looking at her, Virginia clambered down and toddled over to me. She gurgled with laughter as if it were a game to walk with no one holding her strings. I picked her up and said, "I have made my decision. We will go to Croatoan and make our future there."

I closed my eyes and buried my face in Virginia's hair. I heard the voices around me. Of course no one was surprised that Cate Archer would choose to live with the savages.

I felt a hand on my shoulder and heard Alice say, "My baby and I have no one but you and Virginia. Take us with you."

Then Georgie's aunt pushed back her stool from the foot of the table. "We will come, too," she announced. "I won't let the Indians kill Georgie like they did his father."

Ambrose exploded, stamping his feet. "I won't have any of it! I will stay here and live and die an Englishman."

"Then you'll do it alone," said Betty sharply. "I nearly perished at the hand of an Englishman, but the Indians who were our enemies saved me. I would rather live among them than die among Christians, I swear to Jesus."

Ambrose gasped as his wife stepped to my side and held on to my arm for dear life.

"Look at those shrews," came a man's scornful voice. "What's wrong with you men, letting your wives rule you?"

"The women are right and you know it," said Graham. "Face the truth. There is no relief on the way. We are too few to defend ourselves. I'm for casting our lot with Manteo. Let's take what we need and leave here."

Then Jones, the farmer, expressed his own doubts. "We can't remake this island in the image of England. The soil is nothing but sand. I consent to leave also."

In the end even Ambrose Vickers relented, for he had lost his wife once and could not bear to lose her again.

In the month between our decision and our departure, I had occasion to reflect on Manteo's offer and to wonder about the wisdom of it. How could he be sure his people would welcome us? Would we not strain their own scarce resources? And could our planters expect any better success with the soil on Croatoan, an island similar to Roanoke, though larger? Was Manteo not concerned that our enemies might choose to attack us at Croatoan, thus endangering his people? Finally, I wondered if it was wise for us to abandon the fort. Though it had always struck me as insubstantial, it was better than nothing at all.

To prepare for our departure, I packed the contents of John White's household in two trunks, choosing only the most useful and valuable items. I buried White's papers in a locked trunk because I knew how much he valued them, but I put aside Harriot's book of Algonkian and my own papers. Meanwhile the men pulled down several of the houses and stacked up the planks and hardware to take to Croatoan along with their tools. They gathered all the remaining weapons and armor and dismantled two guns from the fort. Ambrose finished building a shallop. As soon as the snow melted Manteo sent three twenty-foot canoes, and we filled these and the shallop with all our useful goods. On the second of March, in the year of our Lord 1589, we trod for the last time the path leading from the fort to the sandy shore with the solemnity of a congregation leaving a church after a funeral.

The canoes were poised for departure when I remembered another promise made before John White left us. He had said to Ananias: *If you should leave this island, carve on a tree or doorpost the name of your destination.* I jumped from the shallop, getting wet all the way to my waist, and called to Ambrose to bring one of his carving tools. I found a tree near the shore that would be visible to anyone landing and explained why he must carve "Croatoan" into the trunk.

"But John White is not returning," he said, frowning.

"Please, just do it. I'm fulfilling a promise."

Ambrose had finished the *C*, and beneath it an *R*, and then an *O* when Graham came down the path from the fort.

"What are you doing, man?" he asked Ambrose. "Look, the canoes are pulling away. Come, Cate."

"But John White wanted us to leave a message," I protested. "If we don't, how will anyone know—"

"Three letters are enough," said Ambrose abruptly, wiping off his tool. I watched him board the shallop and thought with dismay that nothing John White wanted had come to pass.

Graham took my chin and gently turned my face to his.

"It's no use, Cate," he said. His eyes were soft with pity. "He is never coming. You must forget Ralegh, and I, Anne."

Chapter 38

I, Manteo, Dance with the Moon Maiden

And so, to fulfill Ahone's will, I brought the twelve men, seven women, and six children to dwell on Croatoan. My mother welcomed them with due ceremony. Most of my people had never seen a person without black hair and tawny skin. I had to explain the strangers' appearance and their way of dressing.

"They are from a land beyond where the sun rises," I said, pointing toward the sea once, twice, and a third time to indicate a great distance. *"Therefore their skin and eyes are pale, and they must cover themselves so the sun will not harm them."*

That summer the Englishmen's bodies grew brown from the sun when their shirts turned to rags and fell from their backs. The women began to wear soft hides, and their arms and legs also darkened.

"They are of our land now, and hence their skin becomes more like ours," I said to explain the change.

"But their hair does not darken, nor their eyes," objected the suspicious ones.

I related the dream I had received from Ahone. *"As the black bear gave refuge to the hare, the strong must aid the weak."* If we fulfilled this duty, I said, Ahone would make our offspring great heroes. Because I was the son of Weyawinga, they believed I spoke truth. Thus their suspicion gave way to trust, and I began to hope when the English returned, as they must one day, they would know the goodwill of the Croatoan.

The English, too, were suspicious when they first arrived in my village. They would not yield their armaments until we agreed two of their number and two of ours would guard them. They built four small houses from timber and dwelt six to a house. In that first planting season they worked their own fields. Then Ladi-cate and the medicine woman moved into one of our unused houses. They declared it warm and comfortable. With the two children they went about the village in a friendly manner. I was proud to see Ladi-cate speaking with my kin and showing them respect. The English and Croatoan children played together without regard for their differences. Over time they led their elders to trust one another, as a clever weroance brings about an alliance between unlike peoples.

Grem was the first to take a Croatoan wife. When Tameoc visited with Jane-peers and his kinswomen, Mika and the soldier were full of joy to see each other. The joining ceremony took place during the season of ripening. Grem wore trousers, a jerkin made from hides, and feathers in his hair.

I was glad of the marriage, for it would make the English and the Croatoan closer allies. Tameoc called Grem his brother. Our priests chanted their prayers and Ambrose-vickers read from his Bible. There were squash and wild turkeys roasted over the fires. Pies such as I had tasted in London. One of the soldiers played a tune on a pipe and Mika and Grem danced. Then all the English men and women. The steps were simple, with no leaping and crying out as is our custom.

I watched Ladi-cate. Her hands touching as she smiled at Mika and Grem. Her skin, her eyes, and even her teeth shining as if the moon glowed within her. More than anything in the world, I desired to hold her hands and touch her lips. To dance with her as Grem danced with Mika. But how did one begin this English custom? I stood by gazing at her helplessly.

Then Ladi-cate's eyes met mine. She understood what I wanted. She came up to me and reached for my hand. Drew me toward the other dancers. Stepped and skipped and clapped her hands. I did the same. She put one of my hands on her waist and held the other, teaching me how to move with her. She released my hands, retreated, and bowed. Then returned to me. Laughed, a sound like the song of a thrush. We said not a word to each other. There was no need. A shiver passed through me whenever I touched her. Like the shock of plunging into a river on a hot day, only a thousand times more pleasurable. When the dance was over I dared to touch the back of her head, wanting only to keep her near. Would she draw back? She remained as still as a bird in my hand. Her long hair brushed my forearm. The gods made me bold. I put my free hand to my lips, then reached out and touched her lips. She pressed them against my fingers. Her gray eyes did not leave my face.

Algon never had such joy with his Moon Maiden as I did with my Ladi-cate that night. Then I released her, for I knew in my heart she would not run, but stay near me.

Chapter 39

From the Papers of Sir Walter Ralegh

25 January 1590

My dear brother Carew,

Her Majesty has at last granted my wish and I am to sail for Virginia! But here is the irony of my good fortune: I must pretend misfortune. The world will believe I am hiding in Ireland, out of favor with Her Majesty yet again. Conceal my true whereabouts as you would a stolen treasure. For you know the envious (and now ailing) Walsingham strives to block my every enterprise.

I expect to report the colonists thriving, the savages converted, and Virginia producing copper, pearls, and all manner of riches. That will silence every critic.

Bid me good luck in this endeavor and destroy the evidence of this letter.

Yours, W.R.

7 February 1590

To William Fitzwilliam, Lord Deputy of Ireland

Having roused Her Majesty's wrath yet again, I am retiring to a remote place until my offenses are forgiven or forgotten. In my absence I hereby authorize my cousin, Sir George Carew, to sign leases in my name and continue the renovation of Lismore Castle. Do not attempt to communicate with me, as I desire not to be found.

W.R.

10 February 1590

To John White, Esq.

I am at last in a position to respond to your many petitions regarding the relief of the Virginia colonists.

Her Majesty has graciously released three of my ships for the voyage. The Hopewell *at 150 tons will carry ordnance, equipment, and colonists, with the* Little John *and* John Evangelist *as escorts. The Caribbean waters are thick with Spanish pirates this year, so the risk is great. Capts. Christopher Newport and Abraham Cooke have been persuaded by the promise of gain to undertake the voyage. Such is the state of my financial affairs that privateering must be the means to provision the colony.*

Present yourself at Plymouth in four weeks' time where you shall learn more.

Yours, Sir W. Ralegh

Narrative of a Voyage to Virginia.

Departed Plymouth on the 20th of March, 1590. Fair and auspicious winds SSE. John White and I aboard the *Hopewell* with Captain Abraham Cooke.

Just before sailing, Cooke announced he would carry no colonists, saying they would be endangered in the event of a sea battle. His refusal angered White, for several of the passengers were kin to those already in Virginia and had sold all their goods to join them. I settled the matter by putting them aboard the *Moonlight* captained by my loyal friend Edward Spicer. Our ships will rendezvous near Hispaniola in July and thence to Roanoke Island.

White had his second shock when he saw me in ordinary gentlemen's clothing and heard the reason for my disguise. (I have had to bring Cooke into my confidence as well, but no others.) I do miss my pearl earring, which I am wont to dally with when I am thinking.

I anticipate a merry adventure once I overcome the customary seasickness.

I have not been disappointed. On the 5th of April, in the Canary Islands, we chased a flyboat and took her along with a cargo of wine, cinnamon, and other goods. Then we passed on to Dominica, where the savages rowed their canoes out to our ships and we traded with them. At the isle of St. John we took on water, then captured a 10-ton frigate laden with hides and ginger.

At the isle of Mona, on the 9th of May, one of the seamen ran away to the Spaniards, to whom he no doubt revealed our destination and its location. Hoping to root out the conspirators, we burned the Spaniards' houses and chased them, but they hid from us in caves where we could not reach them without danger to ourselves. I don't know if we killed the treacherous seaman.

On the 25th of May the *Hopewell* and *John Evangelist* came to Cape Tiburon, where we expected to meet the Santo Domingo fleet laden with riches for Spain. We rescued two Spanish castaways from a shore scattered with the bones of others who had perished there. Though we pressed them they had no knowledge of the fleet. The *John Evangelist* sighted a frigate and easily took her; she carries hides, ginger, copper pans, and cassava.

On the 2nd of July we made contact with the *Moonlight* and her escort ship. With the prizes taken, our fleet of ships now totals eight. The same day we sighted fourteen ships of the Santo Domingo fleet and gave chase, losing them in the darkness. In the morning, finding them near again, the *Hopewell* poured shot in the starboard side of the rearmost ship until its captain raised the flag of surrender. Newport, in the *Little John*, continued to chase the Spanish fleet.

With Cooke I boarded our prize, the 300-ton *El Buen Jesus* of Seville. Spent two days rummaging through her cargo and fitting her to sail with us. Sweet is the pride of such a conquest. How England is magnified when her enemy is brought low!

Returned to the *Hopewell* and John White's demands that we sail at once for Roanoke. I reminded him our share of the profits and pirated goods would provide the means to relieve the colonists. I urged him not to anger Capt. Cooke, in whom I discerned a reluctance to abandon this lucrative business, despite his agreement to take us to Virginia.

Close upon our success with the *El Buen Jesus*, came misfortune as Capt. Newport lost 24 men and his own right arm in a desperate battle. The ship he captured was so damaged that it sank before it was unladen, taking with it thirteen casks of silver. Thus defeated, injured, and with a scant force of seamen, Newport and the *Little John* returned to England.

For six days we drifted, becalmed, the sun unbearably hot. The Spanish castaways pestered us to such an extreme that we left them on Cuba. A week later we sighted the cape of Florida to our west, and on the 30th of July bore out to sea to catch the swifter current for Virginia.

Now my mind is alive with anticipation of a prize soon to be my own. What good to me is a galleon stuffed with plunder? Let it sink to the bottom of the sea! The treasure I seek cannot be bought, sold, or bargained for.

Poem

To seek new worlds of gold, for glory
And for praise I once aspired;
But now my care is all love's story
Her favor, the wealth that I desire.
And so I prove that love, though severed far,
Means more to me than a thousand ships of war.

I touch my ear, where now hangs a silver ring taken from a Spaniard. In my pocket is the handkerchief the queen gave me. I will give them to her and say, "Catherine, I have come at last."

But will I still know her? Will she remember me?

From the 1st of August the weather turned foul, with rain, thunder, and waterspouts breaking over the ship. We kept to sea because of the risk of being wrecked upon the shoals.

On the 16th the *Hopewell*, *Moonlight*, and *El Buen Jesus* anchored near Hatorask, and on the 17th the captains, John White, and I set out in the longboats. Then, a tragedy! The NE wind, blowing in gales, gathered at the inlet, buffeting Capt. Spicer's boat ahead of us. As the steersman struggled to hold his course, a mighty wave overturned the boat and cast her sailors into the perilous waters. Four of the men swam to safety but the other seven, including the brave Capt. Spicer, perished.

The loss brought White to tears, for Spicer had been his loyal companion through many setbacks. Also, five of those who perished had kin at Roanoke, whom they intended to join.

After witnessing the deadly mishap, the seamen in Cooke's boat were of one mind: not to go any farther but to return to the ship. White and I cajoled, even threatened them, and Cooke, though shaken, stood by us. Thus we prevented a small mutiny, recovered Spicer's boat and the surviving men, and proceeded to the island.

As darkness had fallen, we dropped a grapnel to anchor us near the shore. Cooke sounded a trumpet and we sang English songs loudly but heard no reply. We spent a long, dismal night in our boats, haunted by the loss of our shipmates and pondering what had befallen the colonists that they did not respond to our noise. It was profoundly unsettling to be within hailing distance of Virginia's shores and yet to feel she was as remote and unpeopled as the farthest antipodes of the earth. I did not sleep a wink all the night.

At daybreak on the 18th we finally came ashore. Struggling to walk in the soft mounds of sand, we found a disused and overgrown path leading to the ruins of an earthen fort. The palisade around it was broken down in many places. Some of the houses had been taken apart and nothing remained but the foundations. Iron bars, leaden crocks, and other heavy things had been tossed about and were half buried by weeds. John White found his trunks broken into and all his maps and papers rotted, the covers torn from his books and ruined by rain. His armor was also rusted.

"How could they do this to me?" he lamented. "I befriended them, and they destroyed everything I valued!"

I had never heard him speak against the savages before. But I suspect his anger was also for his countrymen.

"They cannot all be dead," he went on. (I knew he meant his family.) "Where did everyone go?"

Seeing no sign of a slaughter, I wondered aloud if they had

removed to Chesapeake as planned. Then White seemed to recall something.

"We must look for a sign that will reveal their destination," he said and we divided into parties for that purpose. Soon I spotted a tree carved with the letters C, R, and O. When John White came and beheld this, he grew bright with hope.

"They must have gone to Croatoan," he said. "With Manteo, certainly. And they were in no distress, for if they had been, Ananias would have made the mark of a cross."

Capt. Cooke offered his opinion. "He did not finish the letters. Perhaps they were being attacked and he had no time."

White sighed and leaned against the tree. He looked old and weak.

"We have our clue and now must follow the thread," I said bravely, to keep up his courage. "It leads us to Croatoan, to search for them there."

But I, too, was beginning to fear a calamity had taken place and neither of us would find those we had come to seek.

Chapter 40

A Decision Is Made

It had been almost a year since Graham and Mika's wedding. Since then we had lived, for the most part, peaceably among the Croatoan. There was one crisis during the winter, when a hunting party of Indians and Englishmen had gone to the mainland. Five of our men, discontented by the lack of marriageable women, had gone away on their own, stealing all the game. The theft of the meat left the Croatoan feeling betrayed, with some calling for us to be expelled from their village. Eventually Manteo succeeded in calming them.

This incident had damaged Graham's reputation among his new brothers, and he released his humiliation upon us. "Do you not understand what is at stake here?" he demanded. "What would become of us if the Croatoan turned against us?"

We were twelve men, seven women, and six children remaining. No one defended the thieves. Like Graham, we were ashamed of them.

"Anyone who is not satisfied must leave now," he said. "If you stay only to wreck our relationship with Weyawinga's people, no mercy will be shown you."

No one left. No one even stirred as if to leave. By an unspoken agreement, we had cast our lot with the Indians.

Jane and Tameoc now lived on Croatoan Island and she and Mika and I were the closest of friends. Alice was learning the Indians' healing arts and could identify every edible and medicinal plant on the island. Takiwa had taken a husband and Betty was expecting another baby. Ambrose had built a lathe out of a sapling and rope and spent hours turning out stools and tables and other useful implements. Jones tilled his field and benefitted from the advice of Takiwa's husband, his neighbor. For the first time in three years, rainfall had been plentiful and we could expect an abundant harvest.

I had my own house in the village. On the outside it resembled a loaf of bread and on the inside, with its poles bent overhead, an arbor. On the walls hung storage baskets I had made myself. I could raise the mats to allow fresh air to flow through, and the bed I shared with Virginia was more soft and warm than any mattress I had ever slept on. Alice and her little son were also part of my household. We cooked our meals outdoors on a common hearth lined with bricks.

Weyawinga had appointed Graham and Jones to her council, and they and Manteo often asked my advice on matters that concerned the general welfare. From time to time I would catch Manteo regarding me with a look of satisfaction that puzzled me. Whenever I was near him, I remembered what it had been like to dance with him and my face would become flushed. I thought of his fingers touching my lips and my insides seemed to melt like wax.

"It is love," said Jane Pierce, noting my confusion. "I recognize all the signs."

I knew that Manteo, as the son of a weroance, was like a prince and would no doubt marry a princess from another village to secure an alliance. He was too great for me, just as Sir Walter had been. I denied to Jane that it was love I felt. It was only a kind of weakness that came over me from time to time.

"I respect Manteo. I do not wish to be married to him, for I have decided no man will rule me." Eleanor and I used to laugh when I said this.

"I would not expect you, of all people, to be ashamed of loving an Indian," Jane replied, seeming offended.

But shame was not the matter. It was a deeper fear. What I knew of love was that it liked to fill me with longing, then leave me empty.

The day the English ships appeared was one that otherwise followed the peaceful pattern of our new lives. Jane and I were tearing apart *pemminaw* grass to make a thread as fine as flax, while Jane and Tameoc's baby slept in a basket. Georgie Howe kicked a ball to entertain Virginia, who was now three years old. I was glad she was growing into such a sturdy child. Even without her parents she was happy. Around midday Tameoc, who had gone out earlier to dig for oysters, ran into the village shouting for Manteo and waving his hands. I heard the words *"great canoe."*

Jane's hand went to her throat. "No, it cannot be," she whispered.

Leaving Virginia with Georgie, I followed Manteo and the others to the top of a sandy knoll. As we stared at the sea, three vessels took on distinct shapes, resembling the tiny ships that dotted the maps in Sir Walter's library.

Why did the men not act? I wondered if we should start a brush fire, so the smoke would rise and signal the ships. I glanced at Tameoc, whose mouth was set in a grim line. Of course he did not want the ships to come and take Jane away.

Graham finally broke the silence. "The biggest ship looks like a Spanish galleon. And the two smaller ones are English merchant vessels, I think."

"The English ships have taken the Spanish one!" Jones said in a tone of triumph. "Let us signal them."

"No!" I said. "What if the galleon has captured the others and now sails for Roanoke Island?" The arrival of the Spanish had been one of our greatest fears while we lived at Fort Ralegh. We were fortunate to have left there.

"I cannot make out their flags without a glass," said Graham, squinting. "But they are bound northward, not for this shore."

"We could sail the shallop up the sound and intercept the ships at Hatorask," said Jones.

"And make ourselves known to them?" said Graham. "That is hardly wise. Manteo, what do you think?"

With a solemn, almost troubled look Manteo gazed out to sea, where the ships seemed all but motionless. Then he said, "It is a matter for the council to discuss."

Meeting without delay, Weyawinga and her advisers decided to spy on the ships and report if they were bound for Roanoke Island. Graham and Tameoc set out with eight men, paddling their canoe so swiftly it resembled a seabird skimming the water.

When we left Roanoke Island, rescue had seemed impossible. Now with the appearance of the ships everything had changed. Three days of intense speculation followed while we awaited the canoe's return. Hope alternated with uncertainty. Were the English or the Spanish in command of the ships? And if the latter, would they occupy the deserted fort or continue onward?

Ambrose Vickers was convinced we were in danger. "The Spanish will force the English captains to take them to Roanoke

Island, and they'll know at once we came here." He looked accus-
ingly at me, for I was the one who had made him carve the letters in
the tree. "For our safety we ought to go to the mainland and hide."

The soldiers were of the opinion that we could fight the Spanish
with the help of the Croatoan.

"And what if they are English ships come to our aid?" Alice
Chapman asked. "Would we leave here and go with them? Cate,
will you take Virginia back to England to live with her grandfa-
ther?"

I did not want to face that terrible choice. "Let us wait until we
know more," I said.

That night Mika came to my house and told me stories about
Algon the hunter, the great Ahone, and Rabbit the trickster. She
had a round belly; before the harvest time she would bear a child.
Graham, if given the chance, would not go back to England, I
knew. He had laid his love for Anne to rest and found a new one.

"*Do not go away, my friend*," Mika said. "*I dreamed of a canoe
swallowed by the waves. You must not be on it. I want you to stay here.*"

When the men returned, Graham reported that the ships all flew
the royal standard of Elizabeth and were sailing for Roanoke.
Their purpose could only be to find us.

Jones shook his head. "After three years? I can scarcely
believe it."

"Think of the stores of food! The new cloth!" said Alice, smiling.

"The armaments and tools and hardware," said Ambrose, his
fear gone.

Jones wondered aloud what we had all been thinking, "Could
it be John White at last?" Hopes, so long submerged, rose to the
surface and broke like waves over us.

Betty's eyes shone. "Perhaps my cousin and his family have

come at last. I wrote to them three years ago. Oh, to think of new people joining us!"

The excitement began to distress Georgie, who rocked back and forth saying, "Is Papa coming back? Is my papa on the ship?"

Graham, when he finally spoke, was harsh. "Do you think any of our countrymen would choose to live as we do now? Would they wear hides and moccasins, delve in the dirt and hunt with arrows, sleep on animal pelts, and eat roots?"

He swept his arm in a wide arc encompassing our entire settlement within the Croatoan village. It was even more rustic than Roanoke had been. But it was now home.

Ambrose stroked his chin gravely. "I think they will judge our failures, for we have not built a civil society or brought the true religion to the natives."

"Worse than that," said Graham. "We have abandoned our posts at Fort Ralegh. They'll say we've committed treason—killed the assistants so we could rule ourselves. We'll be taken back to England and hanged," he concluded darkly.

"That is impossible!" Jones said. "We are innocent."

"No one will hang me," said Georgie's aunt. "Even so, I am too old to cross the seas again."

I had finally sorted out my own thoughts. "Even if we could return to England without penalty," I said, "how would we live there? Did you not invest all of your livelihood in this enterprise? Do you want to go back empty-handed? Most of us have no kin left, for they came here with us."

I saw the sadness in their eyes as they thought about those who were lost, and the disappointment at their own failure to become rich. My words began to flow as if from a well within me.

"We have nothing to take back, but everything if we stay here. We have one another and new kin among the Croatoan. Have we wanted for food or feared for our lives since we came here? Or given anyone cause to hate us?"

"But what if the ships have brought enough supplies and settlers for an entire village?" said one of the soldiers. "We could rebuild at Roanoke or go to Chesapeake and join Bailey."

"The soil at Roanoke is too thin. With more people to feed, we would only be hungry again," said Jones.

"At Chesapeake we face unknown dangers," I said. "Even if Roger Bailey is by some chance still alive, nothing on earth could induce me to put myself under his governance."

"I agree. That tyrant has betrayed us more than once," said Ambrose bitterly.

"Weyawinga is a benevolent weroance, like our own Elizabeth," said Graham. "Here we have a voice at her councils; we are partners in government. That will never happen in England. Why, even women are permitted to speak and give advice."

"Indeed, who can keep them quiet?" grumbled Ambrose, drawing laughter.

"I did not favor coming to Croatoan Island, but now I deem it best to stay," admitted Jones with a sigh. "For I doubt that the ships' arrival, though we have long desired it, bodes well for us."

Slowly the tide was turning. One by one we came to see that our best chance of a secure and happy future lay with the Croatoan. Manteo and Weyawinga were brought in to hear our consensus. Weyawinga looked pleased.

"If the English newcomers use force against us, will your warriors join us in battle?" Graham asked.

"*Yes,*" Weyawinga said. "*The white men shall not set their feet on this island if they offer harm to even one person here.*"

I was suddenly alarmed. I thought the question had been whether we desired to depart with the English. Now it was how far we would go to avoid being taken away by them. Of course our decision had consequences—possibly dangerous ones. But had we just determined to take up arms against the queen's envoy?

Whether such an act of rebellion succeeded or failed, it would end forever any possibility of our returning to England.

Chapter 41

From the Papers of Sir Walter Ralegh

Narrative of a Voyage to Virginia.

On the 19th of August, 1590, the *Hopewell* bore SW from Hatorask, keeping to the deepest waters between the mainland and the outer islands.

Capt. Cooke dropped anchor NW of the isle of Croatoan, deeming it unsafe to navigate the unfamiliar sound at night. The next morning, by some misfortune, a cable broke at the capstan and the anchor was lost. The ship nearly ran against the rocks before the spare anchor—our last—found its purchase. The shaken Cooke wanted to abandon our plan to land on Croatoan. Was it not enough, he said, to know the colonists had gone there? But White and I demanded he carry on with the landing.

Do I wish we had heeded Cooke and never set foot upon Croatoan Island? Alas, my pen rushes ahead with my thoughts when it is obliged to relate events in their turn.

Coming within sight of the northern tip of the isle we began to search for a landing place and signs of habitation. It was a long, low island covered in brush and pine trees, with grassy shallows extending far into the sound. Thousands of birds occupied the sandbars, their cries and the flapping of their wings loud enough to raise a dead man.

As the ship's boats were being lowered into the water, White and I had a disagreement. I preferred to go ashore with thirty men in the event the colonists were being held against their will and we would have to fight for their release. White argued that taking so many men would cause the natives to mistake our purpose.

"And what is our purpose now?" I asked, no longer certain since finding the fort deserted.

"Simply . . . to find them," he answered. (Truly, he was unable to think beyond the reunion he had so long anticipated.) And to that end he wanted only the two of us to go ashore, saying, "In the eyes of the Indians we bring disease and death. A large party will only antagonize them."

I thought the Indians might easily capture two men, but I did not want to seem fearful. So while we labored at the oars of the landing boat, I hoped Manteo would be the one to welcome us, for he would recognize John White. I was still disguised in my pirate's garb.

Three well-formed warriors met us on the shore and led us to a village that bore only a passing resemblance to the ones I had seen in drawings. Alongside the savage huts stood motley houses made of timber and wattle, with reed mats over the windows and doorways. Amidst them I saw a brick oven and a frame piled with fish over a smoking pit. These were tended by a native woman whose naked breasts drew my startled eyes. I confess I noticed little else about her. I did observe one of the savages wearing a waist-belt that had once been part of a doublet and others carrying English knives. It was as if the pieces of an Indian settlement and an English town had been thrown together by the hand of some careless god.

Though it was evidently in need of a civilizing hand, I felt no sense of mastery upon entering this village that was part of Virginia and hence mine to govern. I began to wish I had arrived with greater ceremony and in finer clothing. It also made me uneasy not to see my countrymen, despite evidence of their presence. Would Lady Catherine show herself? Having been disappointed at Roanoke Island, I was almost afraid to hope. And to be truthful, my immediate concern was statecraft, not love.

"We must demand to see Ananias and the other assistants before we offer any gifts," I said to White. We had with us pipes made from fine wood and ivory.

He gave me a sharp look. "Let me be the one to speak to them," he said. I know he thought me proud and precipitous, while I thought him soft and timid. But I let him take the lead because of his experience.

Finally we spotted Manteo approaching us. Three years had brought him to the full height and strength of manhood, giving him broad shoulders and an assured stance. He and White greeted each other warmly, and Manteo led us to a canopy woven of reeds and hung with feathers and furs. There, in an English armchair with a high, carved back, sat a woman neither young nor old, festooned with strands of beads and copper and glistening shells. This was their queen! Covering her breasts was a bib fashioned from pieces of gold braid, velvet, and glass beads. Pearls hung at her ears and a woven diadem surrounded her head. She, like the surroundings, was a mixture of elements strange to me and yet familiar. Overcome by an unexpected sense of reverence, I knelt to this chief as I would have to my own mistress Elizabeth.

John White parleyed with her, then relayed their conversation to me. "Weyawinga says we bring strong blood to the Croatoan . . . The gods are pleased with Manteo for bringing good fortune . . . When two fields of maize are planted beside each other, they will produce new stalks with stronger and sweeter kernels."

I was not interested in hearing Manteo praised or an allegory about plants. I told White to ask the queen where our countrymen were.

Just then three men appeared, dressed in trousers pieced together from animal skins. Their bare chests were browned, though not so tawny as Manteo's skin, and their hair fell below their shoulders. But their faces revealed them to be Englishmen, especially the one half covered with a red beard. I stared at them in astonishment.

John White leapt to his feet. "Ambrose Vickers? Griffen Jones and . . . Thomas Graham?" His voice rose with emotion as he greeted the men. I had not recognized the bearded fellow as Lady Anne's unfortunate lover. And Vickers, was he not the malcontent White had described?

The men were restrained in their welcome of John White, which made me indignant. Why were they not more pleased to see us? Perhaps they were compelled to remain on Croatoan Island and thus not free to express their joy.

Judging it time for me to abandon my disguise, I announced myself as Sir Walter Ralegh, governor of Virginia, and greeted all parties on Her Majesty's behalf. Their response was as puzzling as everything else on this island. Manteo made no gesture of submission such as a lord should make to the queen's envoy. Had he grown proud and forgotten his place? As for my countrymen, they regarded me with doubt and even suspicion—perhaps because of my rough clothing.

"I know you, Sir Walter," said Graham, nonplussed by my

declaration. "Tell us, why did you wait so long before coming? And what is your purpose here now?" He spoke as if he were the one in authority.

Was all degree and dignity here rubbed out? I would ask the questions, not he! I demanded to speak to the assistants and Graham answered that none remained. How many of the colonists were left? Only twenty-six, the rest having died, disappeared, fled with the pinnace, or gone to Chesapeake and not returned.

Upon hearing that his daughter and son-in-law had perished, White began to weep and was incapable of speech.

I could not believe nearly a hundred colonists had been lost and wondered aloud if Vickers and the others had conspired against them. "Did you not, Master Vickers, often disagree with Governor White and encourage the others to flout his authority?" I asked. "Was there a conspiracy to expel him from your midst?"

Vickers raised his hand and made a fist, thought the better of it, and said, "My judgment was poor, Sir Walter, but I have made amends by more suffering than you can imagine."

"That does not undo your insubordination," I replied. "Sedition is treason."

"Arrest me then," he challenged, knowing I would not risk drawing my pistol in this assembly. Again I wished John White and I had not come alone. I would never have ventured into the savage parts of Ireland so defenseless.

"We were the faithful ones. We were the ones betrayed by Roger Bailey," said Graham angrily. "Had Manteo not offered this refuge, we would be dead from starvation or slain by our enemies."

Was Graham lying? Finding the truth, I realized, would be as difficult as trying to walk on shifting sand. I demanded of their queen, "Bring out the others where I may see them and test what you say."

Manteo translated, the queen gave a sign, and twelve men and boys stepped forward from the crowd that had gathered. They were also dressed like natives, a few wearing shirts or loose trousers made of cheap homespun.

I asked them, "Are you captives here? Speak, I charge you."

Each one testified he had come to Croatoan freely.

"Then you are free to leave, one and all. We will sail to Chesapeake and find those who settled there. While you failed to hold Roanoke Island, perhaps *they* have fulfilled my instruction and founded the city of Ralegh," I said, not sparing my tone of rebuke. "We will weigh your claims against theirs and see justice done."

Graham stepped forward from the others. "No, Sir Walter, we will not leave. We are content here."

Beholding these motley men and boys, half English and half savage, fury surged in me like the wave that had capsized Edward Spicer's boat.

"Do you defy every man sent to govern you? Are you loyal Englishmen, or have you become savages in your inward selves, too?"

"Sir Walter, peace," said John White wearily. "Understand that this land leaves no man unchanged. It is not England and it never will be."

"England has abandoned us, while the Croatoan have welcomed us," said Graham. "I have taken a wife here, who is about to bear me a son, God willing."

I stared at him, ashamed on his behalf, but I reasoned it would take a holy man indeed to resist a half-clothed woman.

"Where are the women—if any of them remain?" I asked. Graham said they had hidden themselves for safety, along with the children.

"Do they dress like savages, too?" I asked, distaste battling with desire at the thought of my Catherine wearing skins, her long hair falling over her shoulders. I had dreamed such a scene once, so lifelike that it roused me from sleep. Was it possible such a dream might now be realized?

"Are there any small children?" asked John White.

"Your granddaughter is well," said Vickers. "She is being raised by Lady Cate."

"Lady Catherine Archer?" I heard my voice rise with hope.

"She is Cate now," said Graham coldly. "She is much changed."

"I would know her anywhere. Tell me where she waits."

But Graham would not reply. I glanced around, hoping to spy where she was hiding. My gaze fell on Manteo, who stood with all his muscles tense, like a lynx about to leap.

Then I knew with a bitter certainty the reason why Catherine hid herself from me. It was a blow I had not foreseen, yet one I deserved.

"Has she found a husband then?" I asked, trying to sound careless.

"No." Manteo's simple denial was sharp with warning.

Yet my hopes soared again. Catherine had no one to bind her to this place. She had kept herself free and waited for me.

"Then I will find her," I said.

Chapter 42

Cate's Choice

When it was clear the Englishmen would come ashore, Weyawinga sent the women and children into the woods about a mile from the village. No palisade or fort could provide better cover than the groves of trees and thick bushes, and there we hid. Some of us were armed, should it become necessary to protect the others. I carried a bow and arrows, which Manteo had taught me to use, although I did not relish using them to shoot a man. Alice had a pistol and the Croatoan women had knives.

Betty would not carry a weapon. "I trust God to defend me," she said.

Mika kept the children calm by singing quietly to them. Her belly was visibly round, and I wondered whether her babe would resemble her or Graham. Takiwa, unafraid, had stayed in the village. We waited for hours, expecting to hear the crack of musket fire and war whoops, but the only sounds were the wind in the trees, small creatures in the underbrush, and birdsong. Then a breathless Takiwa came running and said a single boat had landed and its two passengers were talking with Weyawinga.

I was relieved there would be no bloodshed, but somewhat bewildered. *"Who are the two men?"* I asked her.

"One, Manteo says, is the English governor."

"It must be John White!" I said. *"And who is the other?"* I asked Takiwa.

She shrugged. *"He is not clothed like a man of any importance."*

"There is no danger, so let's go back," said Alice. "I want to hear the news from England—how the queen fares, whether there has been war with Spain, what the ladies are wearing now." Her eyes shone with excitement.

I, too, was full of questions. Was Emme still in the queen's favor? Was she married yet? And Frances, had she been rewarded for her spying? Did the queen, who once said she would be like my mother, ever speak of me? John White could not satisfy me on these matters, but surely he could answer one question that still tugged at my vanity: *Had Sir Walter forgotten me?*

"Yes, we must welcome John White," I said, taking Virginia's hand.

Betty and Alice and her boy rose to follow me, but Joan Mannering held back.

"Nay, I am ashamed to be seen by an outsider," she said. "At my age, to be dressed in this manner?"

"Our breasts are covered, and our loins, with cloth and skins. Eve wore far less," said Betty.

"Yes, and Eve had reason to be ashamed," said Joan, unpersuaded. She chose to stay with the Croatoan women until Weyawinga summoned them back.

As we neared the village I began to have misgivings.

"Alice, Betty, wait!" I pleaded. "What if John White has come to take Virginia away with him? I can't let her go."

"He has no doubt learned of Eleanor's death. After coming all this way, he deserves to see that his granddaughter lives," said Betty gently. "You cannot deny him that."

She was right. And so with hesitant steps I led Virginia to the outskirts of the village, where we waited to be certain it was safe to enter. I saw John White sitting on a stool near Weyawinga's canopy, looking old and defeated. His companion was acting like someone of importance, though he was rudely clothed. He remonstrated with Graham and the others, demanding something they would not give him. As he looked back and forth, his long hair flew from side to side. His face was bearded and he wore a silver earring. Indeed, he resembled nothing so much as the pirates I had seen on the wharves in London and Portsmouth. Presently he dashed from the scene, and I ventured forth, carrying John White's granddaughter.

When he saw me, Manteo looked alarmed. He glanced over his shoulder at the departing figure and moved closer as if to protect me. I wondered if there were some danger I could not see, even as I felt the familiar pleasure of his nearness.

John White looked up at me with his eyebrows raised. I was startled by his appeareance. The last three years had whitened his hair and stolen much flesh from his bones. Eleanor would have rushed to feed him.

"Good day, Governor White, and welcome," I said.

"Lady Catherine. I, too, would know you anywhere," he replied.

Those were strange words of greeting, I thought. Was his mind broken from grief? I turned the child in my arms so he could see her.

"Is it Virginia Dare? My Virginia?" he whispered. Tears glistened in his eyes.

No, she is mine. My dear one. But I nodded and set the child on his lap for him to hold. *If he takes Virginia away, I must go too, for I promised Eleanor I would take care of her.*

White held his granddaughter as if she were made of glass and kissed her head. "Ah, Virginia. You've never known any world but this one for which you are named."

The child began to wriggle and fret. Did she sense he meant to take her away? She held out her arms to me. "You hold me, Mama Cate."

"In a minute, dear heart," I said, holding myself back with difficulty. "This is your grandpapa, who has not seen you since you were born." My voice caught as I remembered how afraid I had been of Eleanor dying in childbirth. That was before our troubles began in earnest: before disease and starvation; before the cruel hanging, Betty Vickers's banishment, and my own captivity; before Ananias was killed by Indians and Eleanor by a fever; before our exodus from Fort Ralegh more than a year ago. How much this hardy child and I had survived together!

"I am sorry about Eleanor," I said, old guilt pressing against my ribs.

White sighed heavily. "I tried many times to return. I wanted nothing more than to grow old in this New World with my family." He tilted Virginia's head so he could see her face. "Her eyes are like her mother's."

Then he stood up and handed me the child. Virginia wrapped her hands around my neck and her feet around my waist, holding on like an opossum clinging to a branch.

"Now it is enough for me to know my daughter's daughter will live out her life here," he said. "If you choose to remain, she must stay with you."

"Thank you!" My breath rushed out and I embraced him, the

child between us. I felt I had been given a gift more valuable than any trinket from the queen, any nickname or words of praise, a treasure worth more than a hundred baskets of pearls.

But then John White made my complete little world quake and quiver.

"Leave the child with me for a moment, and go that way." He pointed to the seaward side of the island. "Sir Walter searches for you."

At first I could not comprehend his words. The pirate I had seen with John White bore no resemblance to Ralegh. I wondered if the governor had fallen in with brigands and was now engaged in their deceptions. But why would he lure me to follow one of them? Did he intend in my absence to steal Virginia and row back to the ship? That made no sense. But why should I leave the child and run after an unknown sea-rover, putting myself in danger?

"Sir Walter Ralegh, you mean? Is this some jest?"

"Trust me, Lady Catherine," he said. He smiled at me with the same honest eyes I remembered. He was not lying to me.

I set Virginia down and in a daze walked out of the village and over the sandy hills leading to the seaward shore. Perhaps Sir Walter had not come into the village with John White and the pirate, but had set out to look for me. Had he come at last to govern Virginia himself?

At the top of a sandy cliff I paused and surveyed the empty strand below. The wind gusted, pushing me backward. Out to sea, slanted curtains of rain hung from distant clouds. Beyond the curve of the horizon lay England, only weeks away by ship, but years away in my memory. I tried to remember Sir Walter's face, but his features blurred in my mind. I could not be certain of the color of his eyes or the sound of his voice. What had he said to me in the library while he secretly put the handkerchief in my sleeve? Or the time we met in his garden? I could not remember. Nor could I recall a single line from all the letters and poems he had written to me. They were lost from my mind, as they had been stolen from my chest and used to betray me. The particulars of my past, once so sharp, had grown as hazy as the line where the gray blue sea met the gray blue sky.

When I closed my eyes what filled my mind were the faces of the people I saw every day. What filled my ears were the shrill cries of seabirds, the burbling of frogs, Virginia's laughter, and the drone of insects on a summer night. I smelled woodsmoke and bear grease, tasted roasted maize and salty air on my tongue. These were the particulars of my new life. What pleasures they provided— the wind on my bare arms, the warm furs I slept on, the medley of voices speaking English and Algonkian, Manteo's dark eyes on me! A longing for everything filled me. Or was it the fullness itself I felt, and gratitude for it?

I, whispered a prayer to whatever gods or spirits surrounded me. "Please don't let me lose what I have or be lost myself."

I sensed rather than heard someone nearby. I opened my eyes and turned, expecting to see Sir Walter standing there. But it was not the finely dressed courtier who had thrown his cloak in the mire for the queen to step on. Nor was it the pirate I had seen with John White. No, it was Manteo, watching me from a distance. I knew the stories of Algon and had come to understand that Manteo thought of me as a Moon Maiden he had brought to live with his own people. He felt responsible for me and so he followed me, remaining half a dozen swift strides from my side. I found his presence reassuring. It meant I had nothing to fear.

I scrambled down the sandy cliff, grasping tufts of grass and shrubs to keep from falling, until I stood on the tide-soaked sand. The gulls cried out to each other, and brown pelicans dipped into the sea and came up with fish flapping in their throats. I waited for Sir Walter to find me.

It was not long before I caught sight of the pirate, who began running toward me. My first thought was to flee, but remembering Manteo's nearness I stood fast. As the pirate drew nearer, I saw by his curly brown hair, his sharp nose, and his long, well-shaped legs that it was none other than Sir Walter. If I had wanted to run I could not, for my feet seemed rooted to the shifting ground. He slowed his steps. He was breathing hard. When he was about twenty paces away I held up my hand for him to stop.

"Lady Catherine!" he said. "I knew you at once. Do you not know me?"

I nodded without speaking. A flush spread over my face and I felt my heartbeat quicken.

"Have you nothing to say?"

I had dreamed about this moment a hundred times. Now I could not remember a single word I had planned to say.

"Words are worth so little," I said, lifting my hand and letting it fall again. "I would be sparing with them." I thought of all the poems and letters that had passed between us and were now lost and forgotten. What could be said that held any meaning for long?

Sir Walter's gaze traveled from my head to my feet.

"Dark as an Ethiop you are, though more lovely by far," he said as if he were beginning a poem. "All my senses are offended—yet stirred—by this transformation in you."

"I am the one offended," I said.

"I don't mean you, but the others," he hastened to explain.

"What of *your* transformation?" I asked. "Have you turned pirate?"

He laughed. "I am unchanged. This disguise merely permits me to travel in secret. I am always Sir Walter Ralegh, and you"—he made a gallant gesture with his arm, as if laying down a cloak in the wet sand—"you are always my Lady Catherine."

There was a time when I would have rejoiced to hear Sir Walter speak to me so. But to be flattered and called Lady Catherine while I stood barefoot, garbed in deerskins, and so much altered by my experiences did not please me.

"You do not know me. I am Cate now."

He made another attempt. "Well, resume your usual clothing and manner and you will be Lady Catherine again."

"This *is* my usual clothing, and it pleases me," I said.

Sir Walter stared at me as if I lacked the capacity of reason. "This cannot be happening," he said. "I expected my colonists to bring the tenets of civil society and true religion to the savages. I expected to find the natives living like us, not . . . what I have seen." Words failed him and he tugged at his beard, becoming distraught. "Manteo—who was made a lord and baptized—has returned to his savage life, and every one of you has regressed to a primitive state. How did this come about?"

"It is a long story with many chapters," I said. "I wrote much of it down, for I once hoped it would be published."

For a moment his eyes gleamed, then he shook his head. "It cannot be the story Her Majesty expects to hear or one that will bring me fame."

"Why did you come here then, if you could not bear the truth?" I said. "If fame is all you seek?"

"I came for you, Catherine!" he cried out, extending his hands toward me. "The queen realizes she wronged you. I also am at fault for your plight and full of regret."

Those, too, were words I had longed to hear. But what meaning did they hold here in Virginia? "Does Elizabeth forgive me?" I asked. "Is she sorry she banished me?"

Sir Walter beckoned. "Come, and you will hear it from her own lips."

I wondered, was the queen aboard his ship? Had she come with Sir Walter to see the New World, to find me? "I don't understand," I whispered. "What do these regrets mean now?"

He replied with patient earnest, "Lady Catherine, I have come to make amends. I am taking you back to England with me. Her Majesty has promised you can be mine at last."

Mine at last! Desire for Sir Walter, long buried and almost forgotten, rose up in me again. It had been part of me for so many years, how could it ever go away? And what was to be done with it now? I turned my head to let the wind blow my hair out of my eyes. My thoughts, my hair, everything was tangled.

A breaking wave rushed onto the shore and over my feet, then receded, pulling the sand from beneath me. I lost my balance and stumbled backward. Sir Walter stepped toward me. It was like a dance where the partners do not touch. At court Sir Walter and I had never danced. So much had been forbidden that would now be permitted. But could either of us truly live or love freely while we served England's queen? My words and deeds would still be overseen and possibly censured. Again I thought of the letters stolen from my chest, like a heart from a body. Though I had forgotten what was in them, I now recalled clearly what had been missing.

"Sir Walter, you never once said to me 'I love you.'"

His eyes widened. Light brown they were; I had forgotten. They flickered away from mine for an instant, then returned. "But of course I do! Even as you are now, despite everything," he protested. "Haven't I come for you at last?"

I felt my eyes fill up with tears. They rolled down my cheeks and into the corners of my mouth. They were salty like the enormous, endless sea.

Through the blur I saw Sir Walter take something from his pocket. It was a handkerchief edged with lace, once white but now worn and stained. At once I recognized that token of such conflicted sentiment.

"Let me wipe your tears, my dear," he said.

I stood perfectly still while he came to within an arm's length of me. His face was dark and lined from the sun. In place of his usual pearl, he wore a wide silver ring in one ear. The faint but familiar scent of civet tickled my nose. He reached out with the handkerchief and wiped my left cheek, then my right. With his thumb he wiped another tear from my chin. The fingers seemed those of a well-meaning stranger, and their touch did not stir me. I turned my head aside.

"Now live with me and be my love," he said softly.

These words were still no pledge of love. I heard a sweetly phrased demand that would tempt many a maid. But it did not move me. If Sir Walter had declared "I love you" on his knees and produced a priest to marry us, it would not have made a difference now. For I had made my decision, not on the spur of that moment, but over the course of many long months.

Taking a deep breath, I looked into his eyes. "I will not come and live with you, Sir Walter, for I do not love you."

He froze. On his face was a look of pure astonishment, as if a deer or a bird had suddenly spoken to him. Slowly he withdrew his hand and dropped the handkerchief. It fell to the sand and neither of us stooped to pick it up.

"And so, farewell," I said with a faint smile, beginning to walk backward and away from him. The sand was wet but firm beneath my feet.

"But I love you, Lady Catherine!"

At last he had said it. Spoken out of sorrow, it was a forgiveable lie.

I shook my head, still backing away. "No, Sir Walter, you do not love me. You love your queen." I had to shout to raise my small voice over the crying of gulls and the crash of waves. "You love favor, wealth, and glory. May they be yours! You love success."

"And you—," he cried, something between a protest and a question.

"And I?" My next words spilled out without a moment's forethought. "I love Manteo!"

I clapped my hands over my mouth, then threw my arms open. "I love you, Manteo!" I cried again, laughing to hear those words dancing in the air. *This* was the truth I sought. I turned and began to run just out of reach of the waves, until I came to the base of the sandy cliff.

Manteo had always taken the hero's way, regardless of its dangers. Had he not crossed the sea four times? Borne the hatred and distrust of colonists and Indians alike, yet sought to reconcile them because he promised friendship to the English? Sir Walter had let others chance their lives and fortunes for his colony, while Manteo let himself be taken captive and risked his life to free us. And when we were perishing for lack of the aid Sir Walter promised, Manteo offered refuge. The pieces fell together in my mind like a broken pot mended. I saw how many of Manteo's actions were motivated by his regard for me. I realized his demeanor toward me signified a love not accustomed to poetic phrases and outward passion. I decided I would be Manteo's, if he would have me. But I would not be like the Moon Maiden, hungering for a lost homeland. Not a minute longer.

The roaring sea and far-off England lay behind me. I had a

new home now. It was not paradise, but it was more interesting by far. I thought about our first mother, Eve, sent from Eden for eating an apple, her eyes opened to suffering but also knowing hope. Beyond Croatoan lay an unknown continent, wide as an ocean itself and surely full of unimaginable wonders. The sun crossed it every day in its journey from east to west. How much of it might I see in the rest of my life?

I climbed the cliff, unhindered by the sands shifting beneath my feet, fairly leaping with sudden strength. Before I reached the top, he was there with his hand outstretched. *Manteo!* The wind blew his hair back from his forehead, and his whole face, even his black eyes, were lit up by a smile. I grasped his hand with both of mine, and he pulled me to him. We tumbled backward onto the sand and lay beside each other.

"I love you, too, Ladi-cate," he said.

I touched my fingers to his lips as I had longed to do since the night we danced together. They were smooth and warm and still parted in a smile. Gently Manteo kissed my fingers, then nudged them aside and with his hands tangled in my hair, brought me close and pressed his lips to mine. *Mine at last.* All my insides stirred and shivered, and I felt I would faint with happiness. Manteo tasted like salt, like tears, like the sea, like the very air that sustained my life.

In him I was lost; in him I found myself.

Epilogue

From the Papers of Sir Walter Ralegh

The Conclusion of the Narrative of a Voyage to Virginia

Returning to the Croatoan village, I informed John White I had found the Lady Catherine in a primitive state, not amenable to reason. We departed from the island that evening.

How appalling it was to see my countrymen living like savages! How humiliating to be refused and rebuked by one who has so forgotten her own nature that she fancies herself in love with Manteo. For his part, White bore his griefs like one of the ancients, satisfied merely to know the fate of his colonists, shameful though it was.

When we returned to the ship, I told the captain we had found no Englishmen on the island and no sign of their recent habitation. I decided we would give the same report to the queen, reasoning that because the colonists would not return to England, they should be considered as lost.

"They do not wish to be found. That is not the same as being lost," White said. He maintained Her Majesty would want to know the fate of her colonists; that was the reason she permitted the voyage.

"How, then, will I explain why they were not brought to justice for abandoning Fort Ralegh?" I asked. "She will hold me accountable and send me back to hang them all. No, I will give no one cause to seek them. I am done with this Virginia enterprise."

Finally White agreed that to save ourselves and his colonists further trouble, we would say we found no English settlers on the island. Moreover, due to the loss of the anchor, we could not risk a further search of the mainland or sail for Chesapeake.

Alas, Lady Catherine is right: I love success and hate my failures. It is bad enough there is no city of Ralegh to boast of. I will not have Her Majesty discover that her subjects have chosen to live like heathens under a foreign queen. No one must ever know that she whom I sought as my reward has rejected me for a tawny-skinned Indian. This would make me the laughingstock of all England.

If I had gone to Virginia at the very outset and ruled the colonists myself, would my city now be flourishing? Or would my decisions have brought more suffering and a worse fate for everyone?

If I had said "I love you" to Lady Catherine even once, would she have consented to be mine?

Vain are all regrets, for they change not the truth: I have lost what I most desired to possess.

Hopewell. The very name of this ship mocks me.

On the 24th of August we made our rendezvous with the *Moonlight* and *El Buen Jesus* by the inlet south of Croatoan Island. Thereafter the weather turned foul, forcing us to alter course for the Azores. On the 19th of September we came upon several of the queen's ships and private men-of-war. Capt. Cooke lingered, hoping to waylay the Spanish fleet. I had no heart for prize taking, so I was not dismayed when we missed the fleet. Cooke resumed course for

England, and without further misadventure we came safely to Plymouth harbor on the 24th of October.

I have had enough of the sea, and I forswear love. For now. My papers from this voyage, the evidence of my failure, must be destroyed. Shall I throw them into the sea or burn them and commit the ashes of my ambition to the cold ground?

Alas, I am brought low, but not quite to despair. For there are willing maids galore, and new rumors of gold in far Guiana. And there is always England, and my queen, and poetry.

Poem

Sir W. R. to himself:

Away my thoughts; give no more rein to mem'ry;
Be silent, voice of woe and sorrow's sound!
Complaints cure not, and tears do but allay
Griefs for a time, which after more abound.

Cate's gone, she is lost, she is found, she is ever fair!
Sorrow draws naught, where love draws not too.
Woe's cries sound nothing in her closed ear.
Do then by leaving, what loving cannot do.

Behold her standing on that distant strand
My thoughts, and nobler mercy take your part;
Sorrow, complaints, griefs—thee I reprimand:
Mar not what true love seeks: her content heart.

The fate of the 117 men, women, and children who landed on Roanoke Island in 1587 is perhaps the greatest unsolved mystery in American history. Before Plymouth, before Jamestown, was Roanoke Island, now known as the "Lost Colony." It takes up a few paragraphs in history books, but stays in the imagination long after school lets out. Stories about the struggle to survive in a hostile and unfamiliar wilderness deeply appeal to us, a nation of immigrants and pioneers. Witness the popularity of shows like *Lost* and *Survivor.* The Roanoke colony was our first reality show. But it was *real.* And no one knows what happened to its inhabitants.

Cate of the Lost Colony is fiction intertwined with history. With a few exceptions I follow the historical record, as far as it goes. No records survive from the colony itself. The voyages of 1584, 1585, 1587, and 1590 are extensively chronicled, and there is even a list of those who made the voyage in 1587. All my characters who go to Virginia are given the names of actual colonists, but their backgrounds are wholly invented. My protagonist is an exception, for Elizabeth never had a maid named Catherine Archer, nor did any of the colonists bear that name.

If you like your history to come alive, visit Roanoke Island, which is now part of North Carolina. There you can see a performance of an outdoor pageant, *The Lost Colony*, written by Paul Green in 1937. It sacrifices historical nuance for high drama but is still fun. Go to Festival Park and see the replica of the sixteenth-century ship and the settlement site. There I met Dr. Jack Jones, in the role of Darby the Irish seaman, and Lindsay Kitchen, who answered all my questions and gave me new ones to pursue. Sarah Downing and Tama Creef of the Outer Banks History Center pulled books off their shelves I couldn't find anywhere else. Alicia McGraw of the National Park Service, whom I found with Oberg's book in her hands, was a fount of information about Fort Raleigh. And closer to home, Clare Simmons helped me get titles and forms of address right. Archaeologist Paul Gardner shared his knowledge of native culture and helped me to think about the practical details of life on Roanoke Island. A visit to Jamestown is also a must, for its Powhatan village, the museum, and especially the ships; the *Susan Constant* is the same size as the *Lion* that bore my Catherine to Roanoke Island. No wonder everyone was seasick!

In doing research I relied primarily on David Beers Quinn's comprehensive *Set Fair for Roanoke*. An excellent, and shorter, narrative is the one by David Stick. Lee Miller's *Roanoke: Solving the Mystery of the Lost Colony* is nonfiction but reads like fiction, with first-person narration and (unattributed) quotations woven in. In it I found the suggestion that Sir Francis Walsingham tried to sabotage Ralegh's colony.

The Library of America edition of the writings of John Smith, soldier and Jamestown founder, is a valuable resource. It contains Barlowe's *Discourse of the First Voyage* (1584) and all the existing writings of Ralph Lane, John White, and Thomas Harriot regarding the Roanoke voyages, reproductions of John White's drawings, and William Strachey's account of the Virginia Indians (1612).

These were my main sources for the customs of Virginia's native inhabitants. Accurate or not, the writings do represent how the English saw the Indians. The terms "Indian" and "savage" (though they might offend modern readers) were the ones used at the time. "Savage" meant wild and uncivilized. The English saw the natives as human and capable of being civilized (as *they* understood civilization, of course). Manteo, as he learned English and became a lord, was proof of that. Harriot and White were surprisingly without prejudice in their observations of the natives and their customs. Most of those who came to the New World were not so objective.

Nothing is known about the particular customs of Manteo's people, the inhabitants of Croatoan (known as Hatteras Island today). They did have a female chief who was Manteo's mother. They probably spoke an Algonkian language like the Powhatan and other tribes of tidewater Virginia and northern New England, and possessed similar religious beliefs. Knowing no other way to craft a character so remote from my own experience, I have adapted Algonkian legends in order to convey how Manteo might have understood himself and his world before and after the English came into it. An immense help in this regard was Michael Leroy Oberg's book. He analyzes the colonization effort from the Native American perspective, showing how the English failed to understand the native's society and upset its balance. His title, *The Head in Edward Nugent's Hand*, refers to the killing of Wingina and its consequences.

Now, about my treatment of Sir Walter Ralegh. I have opted to spell his name "Ralegh" rather than the more familiar "Raleigh," because the first was more common in his time. (Spoiler alert! Skip the rest of this paragraph if you haven't read the book yet.) Despite his association with the Virginia colony and its most famous export, tobacco, Ralegh never went there. At least not officially. No biographers are specific about what Ralegh was up to from March to October of 1590 (the time of John White's final voyage). They assume he was in London serving the queen. There is only one extant letter from this period with Ralegh's signature: a recommendation for an unemployed vicar, written in a clerk's hand. I am pretending it was signed by a deputy to conceal that Ralegh had secretly left the country. It is not impossible that Ralegh sailed to Roanoke Island with John White, but there is no historical evidence to support my fiction. This is the one occasion where I stretched the truth for the sake of a good story.

I do take considerable license with Ralegh's poetry, selecting verses that seem to illuminate his fortunes in love and politics, then editing and rewriting them for a modern reader. (His poetry is known for its obscurity.) His poetic works were not published until years later, but like most poets of his time, he shared his poems among friends. So consider the poetic fragments here to be his works in progress, or early drafts. The letters and papers of Ralegh are fictitious but based on historical sources.

What happened to Ralegh after the failure of his Roanoke colony? In 1592 he seduced and married one of Queen Elizabeth's ladies, Elizabeth Throckmorton. The queen threw them both in the Tower for a time, and he was banished for five years. During that time he sailed to South America, pursuing a dream of gold, and published *The Discoverie of Guiana*. In 1602 he made another effort to locate the colonists; some said that this was an effort to keep his Virginia patent from expiring by claiming English planters still lived there. Queen Elizabeth died in 1603, and under King James Ralegh was imprisoned on suspicion of treason, where he wrote *The History of the World*, only getting as far as 168 BC. He made a voyage to Guiana in hopes of finding gold, but it was unsuccessful, and in 1618 he was finally executed on the old treason charges.

The 1590 voyage was not the end of attempts to locate the Roanoke colonists. The Jamestown settlers tried to find them. On an expedition inland in 1607, one of their leaders, George Percy, reported: "We saw a Savage Boy about the age of ten yeeres, which had a head of haire of a perfect yellow and a reasonable white skinne." John Smith spoke to two Indian chiefs who described men clothed like Smith who lived in English-style houses. There was also a report the colonists were slain by Powhatan, but a few survived. Powhatan, the chief of an alliance of tribes in the Chesapeake region, also claimed that he killed them. The explorations by Smith's men turned up no one, and they concluded by 1612 that all of Ralegh's colonists were dead. There was no proof either way. In 1660 a Welshman reported preaching to light-colored Indians along the Neuse River. In 1709 John Lawson surveyed the Carolinas and encountered Hatteras Indians who told him that "several of their Ancestors were white People, and could talk in a Book, as we do; the Truth of which is confirm'd by gray Eyes being found frequently amongst these Indians." After this point legends take over, including an elaborate hoax involving stones with Eleanor Dare's initials, reflecting an intense desire to know the fate of America's first-born English child, Virginia Dare. Today the Lumbee Indians of Robeson County, North Carolina, the descendants of the Hatteras Indians who migrated from Croatoan Island, also claim to be descendants of the "lost" colonists. This is likely, but impossible to prove. There were other lost Englishmen—the three left behind by Lane and Drake in 1586 and the fifteen left by Grenville—who may have survived and intermingled with the natives also.

John White, by the way, gave up his search for the colonists after the voyage of 1590, declaring himself contented. From Ireland he wrote to his friend Richard Hakluyt that he was "committing the relief of my discomfortable company the planters in Virginia to the merciful help of the Almighty, whom I most humbly beseech to help and comfort them, according to his most holy will and their good desire." He certainly sounds as if he believed the colonists were still alive.

In the 1605 comedy *Eastward Ho,* which predates the sightings by the Jamestown settlers, Captain Seagull says of Virginia: "A whole country of English is there, man, bred of those that were left there in '87; they have married with the Indians, and make 'em bring forth as beautiful faces as any we have in England."

Seagull is joking with another character, but he has hit upon a truth that lies at the heart of the Roanoke mystery. No one can migrate to a new land without being changed by it and leaving a mark on it. Sometimes this happens by violence, and sometimes it happens quietly and no one writes about it. Probably there were colonists still alive in 1590, and in 1605, and even forty years after that. They had children with beautiful faces who gave birth to more children with beautiful faces, and on and on. In that way, they are still among us.

For Further Reading and Research

Algonquians of the East Coast. By the editors of Time-Life Books. Alexandria, Virginia, 1995.

Harriot, Thomas. *A Briefe and True Report of the New Found Land of Virginia.* Originally published in 1588. New York: Dover Publications, 1972.

Lacey, Robert. *Sir Walter Ralegh.* New York: Atheneum, 1974.

Leland, Charles G. *Algonquin Legends.* New York: Dover Books, 1992. Rpt. Of *Algonquin Legends of New England.* Boston, 1884.

Miller, Lee. *Roanoke: Solving the Mystery of the Lost Colony.* New York: Arcade Publishing, 2000.

Milton, Giles. *Big Chief Elizabeth: The Adventures and Fate of the First English Colonists in America.* New York: Farrar, Strauss & Giroux, 2000.

Oberg, Michael Leroy. *The Head in Edward Nugent's Hand: Roanoke's Forgotten Indians.* Philadelphia: University of Pennsylvania Press, 2008.

Quinn, David Beers. *Set Fair for Roanoke: Voyages and Colonies, 1584–1606.* Chapel Hill: University of North Carolina Press, 1984.

Ralegh, Sir Walter. *The Poems of Sir Walter Ralegh.* Agnes M. C. Latham, ed. London: Constable and Co., Ltd., 1929.